THE FURTHER EDUCATION OF MIKE CARTER

Richard Ayres

*Dedicated to all those with whom I have worked
over my 30 years in Further Education.*

PART ONE - EIGHT DAYS IN JANUARY 2001

Monday daytime

The alarm clock jangled her awake. She groaned and turned over, her bobbed blonde hair tousled on the pillow. A smooth-skinned, firm-fleshed leg protruded from the duvet. She nudged her companion, snoring softly beside her.

'Mike! Get up.'

Her bedmate continued to snore. She shook him roughly.

'Mike! Wake up. Vacation's over. You've got a nine o'clock lecture.'

He grunted, then sat up suddenly, pulling the duvet from her.

'Oh, Christ,' he moaned. His sallow face, framed by a beard and collar-length greying hair, was creased and his eyes were bleary with sleep.

She jerked back the duvet. He sat upright for a moment, then heaved himself from the bed and stumbled towards the bathroom. She turned over on her stomach, hoping to return to oblivion, but she knew she wouldn't. His protracted morning routine would irritate her into complete wakefulness.

She heard the bathroom door open and yes, as ever, he left it open. She pictured his actions, etched as they were into her brain from the days when they used to share their morning ablutions. He'd be examining himself in the mirror, his blue eyes squinting without his spectacles. His latest obsession was his teeth: they were still white, amazingly so for a committed smoker, but uneven. He'd asked her several times recently whether he ought to get them capped. Her eventual sharp retort had been to ask where the hell he was going to get the money for that on a lecturer's salary, given that he had no savings.

She heard him defecate, noisily. Now would come the washing of hands and face, yes – God, why did he have to splutter as though he were drowning? Teeth now: he allowed the electric brush to buzz, echoing, for a full two minutes. Shower turned on: she pictured the careful soaping of his private parts. Shower off, aggressive rubbing with the bath towel. There was a pause: would he return to the bedroom to do his exercises? No, he was too late for that this morning. He'd be applying his patchouli oil, admiring his torso as he did so. A few moments later he pattered down the stairs: now he'd be making a cup of tea; he'd carry it into the living room to drink it. A few minutes peace: she relaxed.

Her gradual descent into semi-consciousness was halted by the sound of clattering from downstairs and an exasperated 'Shit!' A few moments silence: now he was climbing the stairs – oh God, here comes the dressing routine.

He entered, turned on the bedside light, advanced on the chest of drawers, all of which shuddered as he opened them. She sat up in the bed.

'What have you broken?'

'Nothing,' he grunted, not looking at her. Recently he seemed to avoid looking at her nakedness.

'Do you have to have the light on?' she said.

'Can't find clothes in the dark.'

Fiona abandoned any thought of sleep and remained sitting up, watching him. He dropped his bathrobe on the floor and examined himself again in the bedroom mirror. Broad shoulders, firm pectorals and an almost flat stomach bore witness to his assiduous workouts: however, she thought with a touch of malice, no amount of exercising could remove the slight creeping of the skin across his chest, the more visible in winter when he was unable to indulge in his carefully timed sunbathing sessions. He pulled on his undershirt and pants, then advanced on the wardrobe for his jeans. They were slim-fit blue Levis. He was constantly complaining about how difficult they were to get in these days of relaxed styling: Fiona had to suppress a smile as she watched him grappling with them, trying to persuade the small roll of loose flesh over the belt to disappear. She was aware that winter held one consolation for him – roll-neck sweaters could be worn outside the jeans. Summer's close-fitting white tee-shirts, which he liked to tuck in, were beginning to pose a problem.

He pulled on his suede boots and struggled into his brown leather jacket before turning to her.

'I'm off then, Fi. What are you doing today?'

'Meeting Belinda and Charlotte at ten, then I'm having my hair done, then I'm calling on mummy for afternoon tea.'

7

'Another productive day, then.'

'Oh piss off, Mike.' She lay back down on her stomach and pulled the pillow over her head to muffle the squeaking of the bedroom door and his deliberate clumping down the stairs. The front door slammed.

It was no use lying there. She swung out of bed, pulled on a towelling robe and went downstairs. Nothing untoward in the kitchen. She went through into the living room. It was small, despite occupying the entire frontage of the terrace house, and was made smaller by the floor-to-ceiling bookshelves that lined three of the walls. It was like living in a bloody library. When she'd first moved in with him she'd suggested that it would look better if the books could be re-arranged according to their height and colour, but he'd had looked aghast and launched into a lecture about the Dewey classification system.

She looked round the room and saw what had caused the clatter and the oath. On the floor behind the arm of the shabby sofa last night's ash and roaches were scattered over the threadbare carpet, soaking up the tea that had evidently been spilled at the same time. Under her breath, Fiona employed to the full all the foul language that she had learned during her four-year residence with her partner.

***

Mike Carter's colleague, Rhodri Evans, was not burdened by a nine o'clock lecture that day, and after a leisurely breakfast of fried eggs, bacon and strong black coffee (which, he maintained, was the most effective cure for a hangover) followed by the briefest of washes at his kitchen sink, he ambled to work thinking that one advantage of his newly-single status was the absence of hassle from a female about the state of his kitchen and bathroom.

Arriving at the College he went straight to the staff lounge, nodded at the knot of tweed-jacketed Engineering lecturers who sat gawping at their copies of *The Sun*, and collected his internal post from his pigeonhole. He glanced at a memorandum from the Principal, then looked at it more closely, then read it thoroughly.

'Bloody hell!' he muttered to himself, then thrust the document in the back pocket of his jeans. He lit a cigarette with ostentatious deliberation, this generating ironic cheers from the Engineers. 'Stuff you' he mouthed. He settled in an easy chair to start *The Guardian* crossword, but couldn't concentrate on it: Carter's likely reaction to the memorandum would be entertaining to say the least. At eleven o'clock, he folded his paper and walked down the corridor to the student refectory: Carter as a matter of principle never frequented the staff lounge.

He was sitting alone at a refectory table, seemingly invisible to the teenage students milling around him.

'Now then Carter: survived your first lecture of 2001, have you? Got the buggers eating out of your hand, entranced by your erudition and whatever arcane crap you historians deal in?'

Carter scowled. 'I tried the Holocaust this morning, but as far as that lot is concerned it might as well have been Caesar's invasion of Gaul.'

Rhodri sat down. They were an oddly matched pair, Carter's casual but neat and carefully manicured appearance contrasting with his companion's distinct seediness. Rhodri, thin and wiry, wore a pair of faded frayed jeans, a tattered woollen sweater that failed to hide the worn collar of his shirt, and rimless glasses, which did little for his pale blue eyes. His sparse greying ginger hair straggled down over his lined forehead; his beard was overdue a trim.

'It's the same with me,' said Rhodri. 'Last term I tried enthusing my GCSE Lit group for *Romeo and Juliet* by references to Jets and Sharks, but their faces were blank. It was only later I remembered that none of the little buggers was born when *West Side Story* was around. Not that I ever saw the thing.'

'Dunno why you're complaining,' said Carter. 'You can always get the little sods engaged by references to sex; *you* can find sex in any work of literature that's ever been published, Evans. We poor bloody historians have to ferret around, day in day out to try and find something that the kiddies can relate to and I can tell you –'

'Hang on, man.' Rhodri interrupted what had become in recent years a familiar Carter rant delivered in an accent that became affectedly mock-cockney as he warmed to his theme. 'You

10

need to have a look at this latest memo from Ski-slopes (this a reference to the ample bosom of the recently appointed Principal). Looks like the purge has started.'

***

Fiona sat in the hair salon, head festooned with foils, *Hello* magazine in her lap, awaiting the further attentions of Gordon and hoping that his cheerful banter would lift her out of the mood of mild discontent that had been with her since waking. It was partly the unending January gloom, but coffee with Charlotte and Belinda had not been a success. They had insisted on meeting at the Riverside Balcony, which was too far from the house to walk to comfortably, requiring her to get the MG from its lock-up garage two streets away and then spend an age searching for a parking space on Riverside.

Charlotte and Belinda had greeted her with their usual air kisses, saying that it was super to see her again and asking perfunctorily how Mike was, before launching into a shrill competitive dialogue about how well their children were doing at their preparatory and private schools. Fiona had sat and watched her old friends, one in quilted jacket and cord jeans, the other in a Barbour and denims, both in cashmere roll-neck sweaters and with tanning-studio complexions, and wondered why she continued with these coffee meetings. Since she had left Simon she was rarely invited to their homes, and then only in the absence of their

11

respective husbands. Charlotte and Belinda had at first been intrigued by the sexual spell that Mike had cast over her ('He's obviously doing you a lot of good darling, even though he's so much older'), but their husbands loathed everything that Mike represented, a result partly of their long-standing friendship with Simon forged at their minor public school and cemented at the golf club, partly because of their own secret lusts for Fiona who, after leaving Simon, had added the hint of availability to her other charms.

Gordon glided over to her to resume his ministrations accompanied by his usual giggles and coy remarks that included a query as to how sexy Mike was faring. Gordon had been a hairdressing student at the College back in the 70s and had been taught Liberal Studies by Mike in the days before a 'rigid orthodoxy' (a favourite saying of Mike's) had been imposed on further education. Fiona had become familiar with the term when she had first joined his 'A' level History evening class as a means of seeking relief from the stifling and repetitive social round that she had been sucked into by playing hostess for Simon's business associates. Simon had first been baffled, asking why the hell she needed to spend evenings with that bunch of losers: annoyed when she began writing essays instead of joining him in front of the TV: finally enraged when she began, at dinner parties, to challenge mildly the more outrageous right-wing assertions of his colleagues.

She found herself unable to flirt with Gordon as he continued to flutter and chatter round her, being still deep in the introspection that had dogged her all day. She was now faced with the prospect, long promised, of an afternoon with her mother in the shabby Georgian house in Wenford where she had been brought up. She blanched at the thought of her mother's long monologues which increasingly dwelt on her daughter's childhood and adolescence with pointed references to all the nice friends she used to have who would still love to see her if only she would call on them, because let's face it darling they can hardly call on you in that poky little house even if *that man* were out at work.

After four years her mother could still not bring herself to utter Mike's name: her distress at Fiona's desertion of Simon was compounded when she found that Mike was only a teacher. Fiona recalled with a shudder the occasion when she had dragged a reluctant Mike to Wenford to take tea: the initial ice seemed to be starting to thaw (her mother mollified by Mike's charm, received pronunciation and newly purchased close-fitting cord trousers) when, with obvious malice aforethought he had pulled from his pocket tobacco, skins and home-grown dope, and proceeded to roll up. To her mother's incomprehension was added blind panic when, after taking a couple of drags he had handed the spliff to her. Feigning not to notice her mother's anguish he had become increasingly mellow and began to lapse into his estuary English laced with the usual profanities. Her mother had eventually recovered and responded with her passable impression of Lady Bracknell, at which point the afternoon had degenerated to pure farce, Mike being dragged to the MG by Fiona, protesting that he was beginning to enjoy himself and that her mother was quite a game old biddy.

With a start she realised that Gordon was glissading behind her waving a mirror and that the time had come for the usual farewell exchange of thanks, compliments and risqué jokes. Out in the street, fortified by her newly-burnished bob, she came to an instant decision, pulled her phone from her bag, and keyed in her mother's number.

***

Geoff and Stu had been in the pub since twelve o'clock. Both were free of the constraints of a teaching timetable, having left the College in the early 80s. Geoff Baines, who had taught Geography, had accepted with relief the offer that his father-in-law had made for him to manage one of his thriving newsagents shops. He found he was a natural entrepreneur, and he widened the shop's clientele by diversifying into videos, magazines, soft drinks and soft porn. His former colleagues had engaged in gentle ribbing at his new career, but nevertheless were frequent customers at the shop, and throughout the twenty years since leaving the college he was always a welcome presence at their drinking sessions. Despite his managerial status Geoff stayed with the style of his youth – his long curly hair and Zapata moustache still jet black; his dress casual, his figure slight but with the hint of a belly.

14

Stu Markham had never had any love for his subject – Economics – or for imparting it, and had been forced into the job on graduating by the need to provide for his wife Lisa. He had loathed the pedagogic process and the bureaucracy that accompanied it. But he'd enjoyed counselling young students, so had joined the Local Authority as a social work assistant and acquired a qualification by part time study. But he was now finding that his second career was no more to his taste than his first. And he hated the fact that he was now grey-haired, lined and running to fat.

It had become a weekly ritual for Geoff and Stu to meet with Rhodri and Mike every Monday lunchtime in the *Waggoner*. This was a hangover from their early days as lecturers when it was a cosy local with several small rooms and an accommodating landlord: it had then been called the *Seven Bells* but with its change of name had undergone the metamorphosis that had afflicted most of the inns in the town. It now catered for tourists, so it at least had the advantage of being empty on a January afternoon. They were on their second pint of Flowers when Rhodri entered.

'Ey up,' Geoff greeted him as he sat down with his pint. 'How's the first day back then?'

Rhodri took a long pull at his glass, sighed appreciatively and pulled out his cigarettes.

'Same as ever man, not complaining. It's a way of earning a living. I know it doesn't compare with making vast profits from selling porn, nor with sectioning loonies, and the kids are mostly semi-literate, but there's the odd one who seems to be able to relate to what I'm saying.'

'Seems to be able to relate to your ability to sexualise the entire 'A' level Literature syllabus, you mean,' Stu sneered.

'Of course you never indulged in anything remotely libidinous during your time at the college, did you Stu?' retorted Rhodri. 'Don't I remember – '

'Is Mike coming today?' interjected Geoff. A contented man, unconcerned about Rhodri's jibe about pornography, he had come to dislike the spats that characterised exchanges between his two companions, and took every opportunity to try and head them off.

'Said he was.' Rhodri took a deep drag at his cigarette. Stu, with all the zeal of the recent convert, ostentatiously flapped his hand at the exhalation. 'I think our Carter might treat you to a rant today: we were greeted on our first morning by a consummate work of literature from Ski-slopes. He's not happy.'

'What's it all about then?' Geoff asked.

Rhodri half-pulled the Principal's memorandum from his pocket, then hesitated and reinserted it. 'I'll wait and give Carter the pleasure of telling you' He emptied his pint glass in a few effortless swallows. 'Who's for another?'

They did not have long to wait for Carter to enter. Stu came straight to the point.

'What's this about a memo from the Principal then? Let's have it man; unlike you lot I've got appointments to keep. Oh Christ, not you as well-' this as Carter lit a cigarette even before he'd taken a bite from his sandwich.

Carter extracted the Principal's memorandum from his duffle bag and waved it in front of his companions.

'Would you believe this crap? Would you believe this from someone who purports to lead an educational establishment? We've had some shit dumped on us in recent years but this is fascism, and illiterate fascism at that. You thought things were bad when you left,' (this to Geoff) 'but I tell you mate, this is the start of a Nazi regime, and –'

Geoff, aware of Carter's predilection for extended historical analogy and conscious of Stu's increasing restlessness, interrupted: 'Oh just read it, Mike, we haven't got all day.'

Carter held the memorandum at arms length, cleared his throat and adopted the Thatcheresque muted harshness of the Principal's voice to read –

To All College Staff
January 7 2001

When I addressed you all in September in my first week in post, I indicated that, at that point in time, I was conscious of the need to make changes but that I would take a term to further investigate the workings of the college and to consult with my senior colleagues before taking action.

There will have to be changes to our product and our systems of delivery if the

College is to grow its business and to compete successfully in a harsh market. Some advances have been made under my predecessor, but we are not at a stage where we can relax. At the end of the day, we must move forward: standing still is not an option. I will therefore be consulting further with senior colleagues and will put forward proposals to the Academic Board for fundamental changes not only to product and delivery and marketing systems but also to our internal management structure.

There are however some things that require immediate change, and which are not a matter for consultation. The image of our institution is of paramount importance. We must be and must be seen to be proactive and to respond to the way society is developing. We are not living in the 1960s: the environment of the 21st century requires us to behave in a professional and businesslike manner: all staff are ambassadors for the business, and we cannot afford for our customers to be alienated by unprofessional behaviour, attitudes or appearance.

From next week therefore, I require all staff to abide by the following reasonable regulations.
• During hours of work and on College business, all members of staff are expected to dress smartly as befits professionals. For

males this means collar and tie: a sports jacket is acceptable in the classroom, but a suit is required when outside on College business or when meeting clients (and that includes parents) in formal situations. For females a comparable degree of smartness is required: if trousers are to be worn, they must be tailored. Under no circumstances must jeans, either denim or corduroy, or other casual wear, be worn.

• Under no circumstances should staff frequent public houses during the lunch period. Those staff entertaining or being entertained by clients in licensed premises should refrain from alcohol. Staff dining in the training restaurant should similarly abstain.

• Social contact with students under the age of 19 is strictly forbidden, during vacations as well as in term time.

• In the classroom the syllabus should be rigidly adhered to. Staff should never use profane or foul language in this environment, nor discuss sexual or political matters with students except where this is a requirement of the syllabus.

• Smoking is not permitted on any part of the campus. The smoking-room facility is withdrawn with immediate effect.

Should any member of staff feel that, for whatever reason, they are unable to comply with the above, they are invited to make an appointment to see me before next Monday.

Marcia Martel
Principal and Chief Executive

Carter dropped the document onto the table top with an 'I rest my case' flourish.

Stu grinned, rose from his seat and with a 'Reckon you've met your Waterloo now, Carter', hurried from the pub.

Geoff picked up the memo and read it through again. 'Bloody hell' he remarked when he had done, 'What are you buggers going to do?'

Carter finally gave attention to his sandwich and beer, and between bites and swallows pronounced that it was time to make a stand, that she couldn't get away with it, that the Union would have to get involved, in any case he was going to make his own personal protest to the bitch and what did he, Evans, think?

'I think Ski-slopes should be arraigned before OFSTED charged with the rape of the English language,' Rhodri said mildly. 'Don't get so bloody wound up, Carter: if you ignore these things they tend to go away'

'But this is one step beyond,' insisted Carter. 'It isn't just aimed at us, it affects the whole bloody college. There are smokers in every Programme Area, aren't there? And I bet half the caterers are in the bar in the Training Restaurant right now. And the luvvies in the Drama Area: they're always in the pub with their students. I reckon we could get together a cross-college alliance of libertarians, and I reckon the Academic Board might have something to say about this attempt to dictate what we can and can't do in the classroom.' He paused to take a gulp at his beer.

'For God's sake Carter.' said Rhodri. 'Can you really see those buggers in the vocational programme areas making common cause with us? Most of them will be only too pleased to see us being hammered. Face it man, most of the staff are frightened conformists if they're not out-and-out bastards.'

'What about the smokers? There are enough of us to make common cause.'

'Do what at lot of them do already, those who can't face that freezing smoking shed they forced us into: have a drag in the boiler room where the caretakers have their coffee. It's warm there, and I can't see Ski-slopes braving that place. Circumvent, Carter, don't confront.'

'What are you going to do about the dress edict then, you scruffy bastard? You're still wearing the same sweater and jeans you did 20 years ago.'

'Wait and see what happens. If she forces the issue, I'll go and see her and win her over with reason and charm – I might even meet her halfway and buy a new pair of jeans. The individual approach, Carter, that's what get results, see? Haven't the lessons of recent history taught you the futility of the collectivist approach?'

Carter launched into a lecture on how freedoms were won by collective action by trades unions in the late 19th and early 20th century and how the

Thatcher years were a minor hiccup on the long road leading to full industrial democracy and...

As Carter continued his harangue Geoff felt momentarily the sharp wrench of dislike which lurked within him ever since the day when the bastard had... he pulled himself up with a start, shuffled in his chair to dispel the unwelcome images that had materialised in his mind's eye; stood, and said that he couldn't sit here all day, he had a business to run.

After his departure Carter and Rhodri continued discussing the various approaches that might be adopted to thwart the Principal's directive, before engaging in more animated exchange concerning the relative attractiveness of two recently appointed young lecturers in the Humanities programme area. Eventually Carter, who had a lecture at 2.00pm, reluctantly departed, leaving Rhodri, not required for a further hour, to order another pint and settle back in his chair. After a moment's thought he smiled to himself, pulled the Principal's memorandum, now decidedly tattered, from his back pocket, groped under his sweater for a red ball-pen that he kept in the breast pocket of his shirt, and began to annotate the document, his smile growing broader as he warmed to the task.

***

After a five-minute conversation Fiona had managed to pacify her mother with promises that she would instead see her for lunch the following day. Her relief was instantly tempered by the realisation that she couldn't remember whether Mike had a two- or three-o'clock lecture. Her mood darkened further when she realised she had left her car on Riverside, and she dithered undecidedly for several minutes before realising that she'd be unlikely to find a parking space near the pub, eventually setting off to walk through the town.

She was a striking figure as she loped on her long legs through the street, which at this time of year was mainly the preserve of local shoppers, though the odd hardy Japanese visitor stood peering forlornly into the bric-a-brac stores. Elderly men muffled against the damp and carrying plastic bags eyed her wistfully, thinking of days gone by. She called in at Chapman's, the newsagents, for a packet of cigarettes. She felt she owed the place some loyalty; it was one of the few outlets remaining in the town still locally owned, and was managed by Geoff.

Reaching the *Waggoner*, she pushed open the door and peered around. At this time on a winter afternoon it was almost empty, but she was greeted by 'Fiona!' from Rhodri, sitting alone at a table next to the artificial log fire.

'Has Mike been and gone?'

'Yes, he's got a two o'clock,' replied Rhodri, 'but you can stay and have a drink with me. What do you want?'

Fiona hesitated. 'What the hell; okay I'll have a fruit juice; no -' as Rhodri started to rise - 'I'll get it.'

She walked to the bar and stood waiting to be served. She was aware that Rhodri was indulging in his usual ogle at her backside, but she had some time ago realised that he was, if not harmless, then manageable: at times he could be charming, and always showed an interest in what she had to say. She grinned at the memory of their first meeting: Carter had introduced her to him one evening in the *Woodman* after her evening class; he had been drunk to the point of incoherence and his first slurred words to her had been 'Hello Fiona, show us your tits'. Her mother's daughter, she had been outraged, and it had taken several weeks of Carter's persuasion before she could bring herself to meet him for a second time. On that occasion he had been sober, polite, and though still inclined to stare fixedly at her breasts, has engaged her in a lengthy conversation comparing their respective upbringings in which he had shown no trace of the mockery indulged in by some of Mike's colleagues. Over the years she had become quite fond of him.

She carried her orange juice back to the table and sat down. 'I can never remember Mike's timetable,' she complained. 'No doubt you're here for the afternoon?'

'No, I've a lecture at three.'

'What a hard life you lot lead.'

'Come on, Fi – tomorrow I have lectures all day, no break *and* a bloody evening class; you try *that* for a week or two and see if it's easy. Anyway, what's got into you bach? You're not

24

your usual sweetness and light; Carter not paying you enough attention isn't he?'

Fiona was won over by the mildness of his reproach. 'Sorry Rhod, I've had a bad morning. Since you ask, I *am* worried about Mike: all over the vacation he's been withdrawn and moody. Do you have any idea what might be bugging him?'

'Probably another midlife crisis' Rhodri said sagely 'He's been having them for nigh on twenty years now. The holiday probably gave him too much time to stare in the mirror and brood over his physical deterioration.'

'Look who's talking! You're not exactly God's gift to women, are you?'

'No, but at least I don't ooze vanity from every pore.' He smiled. 'Anyway, since this morning he's got a lot more to worry about than his looks,'

'Why? What's happened?'

Rhodri gave her a resume of the contents of the Principal's memorandum.

Fiona moaned. 'Oh my God. Mike won't be worth living with. Once he gets a cause to fight for he's bloody insufferable. I might just as well not be there.'

'Well in that case do you fancy coming round to my place this evening for a cuddle?'

'In your dreams, Rhod. You never give up do you?'

'I can't afford to, bach. Ugly bastards like me have to rely on the force of our personalities. If I never ask, I never get.'

Fiona looked at him appraisingly. 'You don't do yourself any favours, Rhod; you could make so much more of yourself. Get your hair cut short for a start: balding men look terrible with long wisps blowing about. And why not get a decent pair of glasses? And what's wrong with a new shirt and a fleece perhaps? You could make yourself look quite presentable. In any case it looks like you might have to.'

'Oh, I might have to compromise a bit on the dress aspect,' acknowledged Rhodri 'but then I've got another six years to go before retirement, and I need my pension. Now Carter, he's quite likely to make some grand futile gesture like resigning on a matter of principle: how old is he, 58? If I were he I'd just keep a low profile for his last two years.' He took a swallow of his beer and eyed her. 'You have amazingly pert breasts for your age, Fiona.'

Despite herself Fiona burst into her husky guffaw. 'Well at least you know how to make a girl feel appreciated, you randy old bastard. Talking of bastards, I suppose Stu Markham was in here with Geoff earlier?'

'Yes. Why?'

'Well, I know he doesn't like *me*, but last night, in the *Woodman*, he was really objectionable to Mike; kept on making innuendos. Mike looked pretty uncomfortable. Has he got something on him? Come on Rhod, you've known them all for ages: you can tell me can't you? It's no use me asking Mike. He never talks about his past.'

'Bloody hell Fi, most of the time I can't remember what happened yesterday. No, don't worry about Stu, he's an embittered man; thinks the world's against him, hates his job, stuck with a neurotic woman, envious of anyone. He's got nothing against you personally, except your accent and your upbringing and the fact that you're sexy but unavailable. I can't think what he's got specifically against Mike. Fancy another? I've got another ten minutes.'

'No thanks, I've got things to do before Mike gets back.'

'Going to the *Woodman* tonight?'

'It depends on Mike's mood: I don't think I can face listening to him sounding off to all and sundry in the pub. Bye Rhod.'

She rose and marched out purposefully.

Rhodri thought for a moment, drained his glass, and lurched rather unsteadily into the street, fortified for his encounter with his GCSE students, and with a growing sense of pleasurable anticipation of the week that lay ahead.

Monday Evening

Derek Surman, lecturer in Politics and chair of the college NATFHE branch, was being harangued by Mike Carter, despite it being after six o'clock. Carter, having failed to obtain Derek's support for the idea of a union protest against the edicts in the Principal's memorandum, had launched into an attack on the union executive, accusing it of kowtowing to management. At this point Derek lost his temper and challenged Carter to stand for office on the executive instead of ranting on the sidelines, and an evidently chastened Carter was then silent for a moment before apologising.

'I didn't mean to hassle you, Derek, he said. 'It's just that this memo from Ski-slopes represents everything that's gone wrong with FE. It's not about education any more, it's all to do with training a compliant workforce. What is it with bloody Principals these days? Sparrow was bad enough, but Ski-slopes is beyond.'

'What do you expect, Mike? Martell's never stood in front of a class in her life.'

'You've gotta be joking! How d'you know that?'

Derek tapped the side of his nose. 'From my contacts in the NATFHE branch at her last college where she was Vice Principal. Apparently she was recruited direct from private industry. Never had any experience in education at all.'

'Jesus!'

'That's the way things are going now, Mike. College corporations are looking for managers with experience in running a business. Not only does Martell have a degree in Business Studies, but her experience was in project management in finance companies. That was enough to get her the job – oh, and the fact that apparently she had a reputation for ruthlessness.'

'Christ, and now we're landed with her. No wonder she wants us all to dress like fuckin' business executives. Everything in her memo points to her wanting to screw us into the ground. Bloody hell, Derek, I can remember when working in this place was *fun*.'

Derek sighed. 'I don't think work's meant to be fun any more, Mike. Look, I'm with you on a lot of what you say, but I'm not going to expend energy on fighting a battle we can't win. I'd prefer to wait, because I've an idea we might have an even bigger battle on our hands in the near future.'

'What sort of battle?' Carter was instantly alert. 'Do you know something that we don't? Has Ski-slopes said something to you?'

'Good God no. It's just that she's a newly appointed Principal, and what do all newly appointed Principals do?'

'Get the Corporation Chair to give them an instant salary increase, usually.'

'Well, yes, perhaps, but didn't you read the first part of her memo? The bit about changes to the management structure? She's like all new Principals; first thing they do is re-organise. It does their ego a power of good to implement something that's instantly attributable to their vision. I'm sure Martell's no exception. She's had a term to get her feet under the table and squeeze the balls of the SMT, so I forecast that we'll have her restructuring proposals before this term's out. That's what I'm saving my energy for, Mike, that and deciding on our pay claim.'

'OK Derek, sorry I sounded off. But I'm still probably going to go and see Ski-slopes about her memo – she did invite staff to do that, so what have I got to lose?'

'A hell of a lot if you go in all guns blazing. Try a reasoned approach Mike, and try to avoid swearing. Look, she's not the brightest of buttons; why not discomfort her with a show of the famous Carter erudition? Oh, and for God's sake keep your eyes off her tits.'

Carter grinned. 'I'm not a tit man, Derek; that's more Evans's bag'. He shouldered his duffle-bag and with a 'Seeya Derek' strolled out into the corridor.

Derek sighed with relief and sat back in his chair. The desk in front of him was littered with lecture notes, memoranda, minutes of branch meetings, newsletters from NATFHE head office, and the shopping list provided for him that morning by Jenny which he'd not had a chance to act on. The strip-lighting cast a yellowish murk over the cramped workroom. Bookshelves and filing cabinets were arranged in an attempt to give a modicum of privacy to those required to work there, and this, Derek was aware, was by no means the worst workroom in the college. He remembered how the former Principal, Sparrow, seeking to ingratiate himself with the staff, had said that he regarded all lecturers as fellow-managers, managers of the learning process. This statement prompted an acerbic comment from Mike Carter to the effect that he assumed therefore that as a manager and a graduate he could look forward to enjoying the same sort of working conditions as his peers in industry, and when would his private office, telephone, secretary and company car be forthcoming?

You had to hand it to Carter, mused Derek: he wasn't one to suffer fools gladly even if the fool happened to be his superior in the hierarchy. He was a talented teacher with an enviable record of student examination success to his credit, but any chances of promotion had been sacrificed by his unwillingness to make compromises with those who held the power, not to mention his dubious lifestyle. Who was it, Derek couldn't remember, who had said that one could get away with unorthodox opinions, and possibly with unconventional appearance or behaviour, but not with all three at the same time?

Derek stuffed his briefcase with his lecture notes, half-heartedly added a sheaf of union correspondence, pulled on his shabby anorak and shuffled to the door comforting himself with the thought of his dinner and a glass of wine. He was half way home when he remembered that he'd not done the shopping.

***

Marcia swung her BMW into the long drive of her house on the Tedrington Road. The garage doors opened obligingly allowing her to glide in effortlessly and turn off the lights and engine before they silently swung shut.

She entered the kitchen through the connecting door, dropped her briefcase on the new oak table and walked through to the large lounge; a flick of one switch flooded the space with a subdued glow. Even after five months in the place she still felt a surge of pleasure at its opulence. The house had certainly won the approval of those of her former colleagues in industry with whom she had retained an admittedly slightly competitive friendship; she had, however, yet to invite any of her senior managers from the college to share an evening with her. She was finding it difficult to gauge how FE college staff operated socially, and as a single woman she felt at a slight disadvantage given that all but one of her senior colleagues were fully equipped with spouses or partners.

She strode into the bedroom and pulled a tee shirt and jogger bottoms from the chest of drawers. She caught sight of herself in the full-length mirror on the fitted wardrobe door, and mindful of the flattering light of the bedroom allowed herself a few moment's self-appraisal. A tall, strikingly handsome woman of 45 gazed back at her: glossy black hair drawn back in a roll, large wide-set dark eyes under thick brows, a sensual mouth, creamy complexion. A severe dark suit and white shirt complemented her generous figure, and high-heeled shoes drew attention to her best feature, long shapely legs still good enough to permit a hemline at four inches above the knee. This had been her style since her entry to management in the 1980s: this look, combined with her forceful personality had served her well and she saw no need to change the image she presented to the world despite the sub-fusc mode of dress that seemed to characterise women in the world of education.

She kicked off her shoes, peeled off her tights, and removed her suit, which she hung carefully in the wardrobe before putting on the tee shirt and jogger bottoms. She unpinned her hair, allowing it to cascade round her shoulders, a sight unknown to her professional colleagues and to which only three lovers had been privy, the last some five years ago.

'A drink, a drink,' she muttered to herself as she re-entered the lounge and headed straight for a cabinet from which she extracted a bottle of gin, and poured herself a generous portion to which she added slimline tonic from the mini-fridge incorporated in the cabinet. She collapsed heavily onto the white leather chesterfield, took a long pull at her drink, and began to take stock of the afternoon's Senior Management Team meeting.

She had inherited her Senior Management Team from her predecessor Sparrow, and he in turn had inherited two of its four members. She felt an affinity only with the newer couple who, like her, had been drawn from outside the ranks of education. They at least seemed to have some measure of the requirements of the new FE, and understood her assertive management style. That afternoon she had given the SMT a brief verbal outline of her thoughts on the reorganisation of the college, involving sweeping changes to its academic and middle-management structure.

'I want to get rid of the Programme Areas,' she'd said, 'thirteen units are far too unwieldy and over-managed. I have in mind all the disciplines being reorganised into Faculties, say about five. The Heads of Faculties would report directly me. It will mean that administrative duties can be delegated further down the hierarchy, and free you lot up to concentrate on your corporate management roles. We can then really get a grip on expenditure control. Most important, we can save money on salaries with the redundancy of some of the Programme Leaders.'

She'd asked for initial comments. As expected, the New Men (Lucas Harper, Director of Finance, and Paul Tasker, the IT and Quality Manager), were supportive. Of the Old Guard, Edgar Hickman, Human Resources Director, expressed worries about the effect on industrial relations. She'd slapped him down by saying that as far as she was concerned the threat of redundancies concentrated the mind wonderfully when it came to any thoughts of industrial action. Charles Jay, Curriculum Director, had said in his irritatingly pompous way that he never gave instant reactions to proposals until he had time to digest them and that of course the Principal was going to flesh out these somewhat sketchy proposals in a paper?

Disguising her annoyance, Marcia had confirmed that a paper would be produced. She added that she assumed that colleagues would recognise that any final decision would rest with her as Chief Executive, subject of course to the approval of the Corporation.

She had been about to close the meeting when Charles Jay had the temerity to raise the matter of her memorandum.

'Marcia, if I might just make the observation that it might perhaps have been wise to have consulted us before the distribution of your memorandum to the staff,' he'd begun. 'Whilst concurring absolutely with the sentiments expressed therein, I –'

'Glad to hear it,' Marcia had interjected. 'I naturally assumed that you would all be in agreement, and therefore thought it unnecessary to waste your time in raising the matter with you.'

'Nevertheless Marcia,' Jay had persisted, running his hand over his bald head, 'perhaps some adjustments might profitably have been made to the style – '

'No, Charles,' Marcia had said firmly, 'I stated precisely what I meant in the memorandum. I see no point in beating about the bush over matters concerning staff professionalism. There's no point in wasting my time and yours in trying to arrive at some long-winded form of words just because that's the way some of the so-called academics in this college expect me to write. The message is clear. End of discussion.'

She took another swallow of her gin and tonic, rose and walked to the kitchen where she prepared her light supper from the items purchased that morning by her daily cleaning lady and occasional shopper. She ate sparingly, having that day entertained the chairman of the Corporation to lunch in the college training restaurant, and on finishing immediately loaded crockery and cutlery into the dishwasher before returning to the lounge. She retrieved a file from her briefcase and took it to the chesterfield where she sat and, pen in hand, began to consider the draft of her plan for restructuring.

She was aware that any plan would have to go through the formality of discussion by the Academic Board, and that the plan would have to take the guise of a proposal couched in the discursive style beloved of academics, so that the Board would be given the impression that it was being consulted. She found such an approach irksome in the extreme. Of course, she'd first have to subject her paper to scrutiny by the SMT, and she could imagine the look of malicious enjoyment on Charles Jay's face as he unctuously suggested some 'minor adjustments to syntax, Principal'.

An idea came to her. Why not get Lucas Harper to draft the document? He could be trusted to deliver what she wanted in financial terms. He could chair a meeting of the SMT to fine-tune the document and draw Jay's fire before the final draft got to her. Yes, an excellent idea!

She poured a glass of wine to celebrate. But looking round the room, she felt a slight flicker of loneliness. She still missed the company of the colleagues she'd had when in private industry. She'd had a succession of relationships with business associates, but was careful never to commit herself to a permanent liaison: while enjoying sex she saw it as just another appetite that needed to be satisfied, and rapidly terminated any relationship that seemed to threaten her independence or her career advancement. But although she'd climbed rapidly up the management ladder, she had, in the early 1990s, come up against the glass ceiling that still existed in the private sector.

She'd begun to cast around for other avenues of advancement, and discovered there were opportunities available in Colleges of Further Education. They were about to cast off the shackles of Local Authority control and become self-managing Corporations, and apparently required senior staff with financial and general management expertise. They also seemed to be recruiting many women to these posts. Although it meant an initial reduction in salary, she obtained the position of Vice Principal at a large college in the West Midlands. When the post of Principal at a smaller college in Streetbridge had been advertised in January 2000, she had seized her chance and applied, having by that time acquired sufficient familiarity with FE jargon and buzzwords to lace her application with the sort of language beloved of appointments committees.

She was finding that the staff in the college, which was a rather parochial institution, needed shaking up. God, what a crowd they were. Few of the lecturers in vocational Programme Areas had the faintest idea of what it took to be an entrepreneur. Then there were the drama and creative arts lecturers - a load of prima donnas who seemed unable to comply with the simplest administrative requirements asked of them. Worst of all were the self-proclaimed intellectuals of the Humanities programme area, particularly the rump of those left over from the 1970s who gloried in their bohemian dress and life-style. The one thing that all the staff seemed to have in common was a sullen discontent with their conditions of service and salaries. She had lost count of the number of times she'd been told that they earned less than schoolteachers, and that this stemmed from the incorporation of colleges in 1993 since when national wage agreements had been largely ignored by college managers.

She saw her memorandum concerning dress and behaviour as the opening shot in her campaign to revitalise the institution: not only would it flush out the worst of the malcontents, but it was an ideal mechanism for divide-and-rule given the mistrust that evidently existed between the ageing hippie backwoodsmen and the younger elements in all Programme Areas. The latter at least seemed to adhere to more conventional dress and attitudes.

Having reviewed her game plan to her own satisfaction, and mellowed by the wine, she decided to reward herself with a rare evening devoted to her own solitary vices. She crossed the room and rummaged in a cabinet under the wide-screen television and retrieved a pack of cigarettes. She turned on TV, lit her cigarette, stretched herself out on the chesterfield and abandoned herself to the pleasures of soaps, quiz shows and police dramas.

***

'Ey up love, howya doin?' Geoff called out to Julie as he walked into the kitchen. Julie, blonde, pretty, but running to fat, turned from her cooking to greet him with a kiss.

'Had a good day darlin? Have you seen dad today?'

'Aye, he called in the shop about three o'clock. I think he's finally reconciled to the girlie magazines; at least he was when I showed him last week's takings. I think he's slowing up a bit though, Jules; he doesn't seem quite so on the ball about the business as he used to. He even mentioned turning the whole lot over to me.'

'Well, he's 70 next year; if he hangs on much longer you'll be thinking about retirement yourself, you poor old bugger.' She ruffled his hair affectionately. 'Dinner won't be ready for about an hour 'cos Jimmy's coming round to join us. Fancy a cup of tea?'

'Yes, I'll make it, love. Is Jim bringing his latest squeeze?' He busied himself with the kettle and mugs. 'Dunno where he gets his success with the girls from, certainly not from me.'

Julie eyed him speculatively. 'Whenever you make comments like that I know for a fact you've been talking to Mike Carter. Am I right?'

Geoff grinned sheepishly. 'Aye, it was our Monday club meeting in *The Waggoner*. The usual crowd. But it ain't women that Mike's got on his mind at the moment, I can tell you.'

He perched on a stool next to his wife as she continued preparing the meal, and told her about the memorandum and Mike's reaction to it.

'He gets himself into a right state about things these days,' was Julie's comment. 'Not the Mr Cool that he used to be, is he?'

Geoff grinned. 'Stu thinks he deserves his comeuppance, but then Stu's never had much time for him since...' He tailed off.

'Yeah, but Stu got his own back, didn't he?'

'Don't want to go there, Jules,' Geoff's face clouded, and he took a swig of his tea.

'Oh Geoff, all that was a long time ago. Why do you still get so upset about it?'

Geoff was silent for a few minutes. 'Sorry love,' he said eventually. 'It wasn't what happened with Stu that bugs me. It was bloody Mike. You know I like Mike: well, he's good company when he's in the right mood, but when I think of the sneaky way he... well, it still pisses me off.'

Julie left her meal preparation and moved over to sit by him. She put her arm round him. 'That was ages ago. We've had a good marriage; we've got a great son; you're doing well in the business: things are ok aren't they?'

'Course they are Jules,' Geoff stroked her back. 'It's been great and it still is. No, I don't think of those times at all; just occasionally Mike's arrogance gets to me, that's all.'

He kissed her: she responded enthusiastically, and he looked at her quizzically.

'No, we can't let the meal get cold,' she said.

***

Stu had had a tedious afternoon in the Social Services department, and his relief at the approach of five o'clock had been tempered as usual by his apprehension about what might be waiting for him when he arrived home. On entering the small semi-detached he was immediately aware that this had been one of Lisa's bad days. The remains of breakfast were still scattered over the kitchen table, together with an empty wine bottle and a half empty packet of chocolate biscuits. Gritting his teeth, he'd entered the small living room to find his wife slumped in the armchair in front of the television, wine glass in hand, magazines strewn over the floor. She'd not acknowledged his entry. He'd looked at her with distaste: she was becoming a slattern.

He decided to try and engage her in conversation on a neutral topic.

'I met the lads at lunchtime.'

'Well isn't that nice for you,' she sneered. 'While I'm stuck here alone all day you take yourself off to the pub for a liquid lunch.'

'You don't seem to have done too badly for liquids yourself,' he retorted, 'and my drinking session lasted precisely one hour. Anyway, never mind that, I've got a bit of news for you.' He proceeded to tell her about Marcia Martell's memorandum and the reaction of Mike and Rhodri to it, ending with 'I think this might finally put an end to Carter's life of Riley; it's about time the bastard started acting his bloody age.'

Lisa slammed down her glass. 'You sod,' she spat out. 'Just because you've fucked up your career you can't bear it if anyone else is good at his job and is popular with his mates. You were always jealous of Mike, weren't you? Just 'cos he was a better teacher than you and -'

'Oh piss off,' Stu shouted, 'You've still got the hots for him haven't you? You stupid cow, do you think he'd look twice at you now, you raddled old lush?'

He made to rise and go to the kitchen for a drink, but Lisa leapt to her feet and barred his way.

'Fuck you,' she screamed at him, 'You'll never let me forget it will you? The one time someone talks to me and shows a bit of affection -'

'Affection?' Stu yelled, 'Affection? Since when do you think Carter's been motivated by affection? Anyway, it was *you* came on to *him* that evening: God, it was pathetic watching you. And if you're now gonna start going on about me, just don't. What the hell did you expect me to do in that situation?'

Lisa suddenly screamed, a high-pitched keening wail, and lunged at him with her empty wine glass.

He grabbed the glass, pinioned her arms to her sides and pushed her roughly back into the chair. 'For Christ's sake woman, can we for once, just for once, have something approaching a civilised evening? Ever thought about cooking a supper? Ever thought about asking me what sort of day I've had?'

Lisa began sobbing; great, gut-wrenching sobs. Stu stood over her for a minute, shook his head as though to clear it and said 'I'll go and get some fish and chips. Do you want some?'

There was no response. He returned to the kitchen, pulled on his coat and began to walk into town.

***

After leaving Rhodri in the pub, Fiona had been faced with a long walk through town to retrieve her car. Despite this, her mood was lighter than it had been all day, and she reluctantly admitted to herself that this was probably a result of Rhodri's compliments. Rhod was a lecherous old bastard, but it was a fillip to receive some attention, something that Mike seemed unable or unwilling to provide over recent months.

Back in the house, she had set about tidying up, knowing that to keep busy was the best antidote to relapsing into introspection. It had not, however, prevented her from wondering how best to cope with the inevitable tirade from Mike about the Principal's memorandum. In the past few months there had been a change in Mike: growing periods

43

of silence had begun to alternate with outbursts of anger, not directed at her, but at the college, the world, and 21st century in general. He'd always been famed for his rants, but these used to be delivered with an underlying self-deprecating humour. This was one of the things that had most attracted her to him when she'd joined his evening class. The change in his persona was puzzling.

He had not arrived home at his usual Monday time of five-thirty, so she had begun to prepare a curry safe in the knowledge that not only was it his favourite dish, but it could be kept hot until his arrival, with only the rice then to prepare.

An hour later, still in the kitchen, she heard his key in the lock.

'Hi,' she called, 'dinner can be ready in ten minutes: do you want it now or do you fancy a beer first?'

Silence. She went to the living room door. He was slumped in the battered armchair, still in his leather jacket, duffel bag on the floor beside him.

'Mike, I said do you want -'

'I heard what you said. I'll have a beer please, I fancy a joint before eating.'

'Oh, isn't it a bit early to -'

'No it's *not* too early. If ever I needed a joint it's now. You wouldn't believe what's gone down today. That bloody bitch -'

'Mike, I know what's happened, I went to the pub at lunchtime hoping to see you. Rhod was still there. He told me about the Principal's memo. Didn't he say he'd seen me?'

'Oh. Yeah, he did say something about it. Didn't pay much attention. I've been talking to Derek. The bloody Union's not gonna challenge her. Christ, I'm gonna have to go and see her myself; she can't get away with -'

'I'll get you your beer. You have your joint and try and relax a bit while I do the rice; we'll talk about it while we eat.'

'Okay,' he said eventually, 'that sounds good. Thanks.' He reached for his pouch and began rolling up.

Over the meal, taken in the kitchen, Carter, mellowed by the dope, gave Fiona a relatively restrained account of his meeting with Derek. Fiona nodded and 'yessed' or 'noed' in the appropriate places, wondering when he would launch into a tutorial on the merits of the various courses of action open to him. It wasn't until the meal was finished and they settled with coffee and cigarettes in the living room that he began the seminar.

When he'd finished explaining the different approaches he could adopt, he asked Fiona for her opinion.

She took a drag at her cigarette, a swallow of coffee, and a deep breath. 'Well, you have another option. Compromise. Go along with- '

'Compromise? No way! Once we let her- '

'Hang on,' Fiona raised her voice. 'You asked for my opinion, let me finish. Is this how you conduct your tutorials with students?'

Carter was momentarily silent, then, 'Sorry. Go on.'

'Look,' Fiona lowered her voice again. 'Why don't you forget the politics of the thing and just concentrate on the things that directly affect you? You've only got two years before you retire; surely you can put up with a bit of hassle before you go? No, hang on,' as Carter made to interrupt again, 'you never drink with the young students now, do you? Face it Mike, you're a granddad figure to most of them. And you're always complaining that your subject doesn't lend itself to digressions about sex'n'drugs'n'rock'n'roll, so why continue making the effort? The kids probably think you're a pathetic old man when you do it... no, let me finish! And you're on a loser about smoking – hardly any workplaces allow it now.'

'How do you know?' grunted Carter. 'When was the last time you worked?'

'Cheap, Mike; I do read the newspapers - '

'You've got the bloody time to.'

'Oh piss off: do you want me to discuss this or not?'

'Okay, okay. Go on.'

'I'm sure there are places you could find if you're desperate for a fag. And the dress thing; couldn't you try and reach a compromise with her there? Point out that your leather jacket's smart, say you'll put a tie on in formal occasions like parents' evenings; see if she'll agree to cords instead of jeans. Point out that a lot of the staff who wear suits are scruffier than you are.'

'I'll never, never put on a tie,' Mike insisted.

46

'All right. But can't you see what I'm getting at? Oh I know it goes against all your precious principles, but can't you just grit your teeth for two years? If you're so determined to tell Martell what you think of her, why not do it the day you retire?'

Carter fell silent. After lighting another cigarette he said, morosely, 'I'm still going to go and see her. Don't know how I'll play it yet; depends on what sort of support I can rustle up. And I haven't given up on that.'

Fiona was relieved that the squall appeared to have blown itself out. She enquired whether he was going to the pub this evening: he surprised her again by saying no, he fancied staying in, listening to music and maybe having a few more spliffs.

She finished her cigarette. 'I'm going to have a bath, then,' she said, 'and then go to bed. See you later.'

He raised his hand in vague acknowledgement.

She was in a light sleep, and was only vaguely aware of him sliding into bed beside her. He began to caress her back and buttocks, something that never failed to arouse her. Even before she was properly awake she turned to face him, kissing him and then pulling his head down to her breasts. Within seconds she was ready, eager. Carter however, though eager, was distinctly unready, and remained so despite all that Fiona could do.

'Oh Mike,' she sighed, 'What's wrong? Is it me?'

Carter turned on his back. 'Fuck no. Just stoned that's all.'

'God, why do you take so much of that stuff?' Her irritation was seasoned with frustration.

'Oh, don't bloody start, woman.'

She turned away from him, pulling the duvet tightly round her. He lay for a few minutes before leaping out of bed and fumbling around for his clothes.

'What are you doing?'

'Getting up. Might just as well start marking those fucking essays.'

He clumped down the stairs. Fiona fumbled in the bedside cabinet for her sleeping pills.

***

Opening his front door earlier that evening, the first thing Rhodri saw was a letter on the mat: the face of the envelope was covered with familiar large, looped script, and he grinned with pleasure. He entered the dusty living room, swept a pile of books and papers off the sagging settee, sat down and opened the letter. Megan wrote very infrequently, and the mail was their only method of contact as Rhodri had neither mobile phone for texting nor access to the Internet for emails, and they had agreed not to impinge on each other's lives by unsolicited phone calls. It was a long letter, and he skim-read it to ensure that all was well, which it was, so he put it aside to savour at leisure later in the evening.

Re-entering the kitchen he retrieved a pizza from his carrier bag and put it in the oven to heat up. He thought back over the events of the day. He could have scripted in advance Carter's reaction to the Principal's memorandum, and the reaction of Derek Surman to Carter's harangue, the beginning of which he had witnessed before he had left to purchase his supper. He also thought about his meeting with Fiona. He'd grown fond of her, and respected her for her admittedly untutored intelligence, and for her indifference to the norms of the peer group into which she had been thrust after moving in with Carter. He admired her as a free spirit; she didn't give a fuck for achievement or status, she laughed at pretension. He had noted over recent months Carter's growing tendency to show impatience with her.

The pizza was ready. He poured a beer, rescued a knife and fork from the sink, and sat at the kitchen table to eat. The process took less than ten minutes. When he had finished he put the dirty plate and cutlery in the sink and poured another beer, lit a cigarette and picked up Megan's letter.

She wrote in her usual breezy style, an entertaining catalogue of events in her work and social life, interspersed with expressions of concern for Rhodri's welfare. He read the letter twice before noticing that the final page had a PS written on its reverse side, saying that she'd just decided to take a few days off and that she'd come and visit him on Wednesday night on her way to London, if that was ok by him; if not, to phone her on Tuesday evening.

Excitement at the prospect of her visit was tempered by the realisation that he had only two evenings to bring a semblance of order to the house. He jumped up to begin the daunting task of clearing up the living room.

He found an old duster in one of the kitchen drawers and began waving it ineffectually in the general direction of hard surfaces, only then to remember the requirement first to beat the cushions of the settee. Under one of the cushions he found a black thong, which he'd removed from Tracey's loins only a few weeks ago. Rhodri was not one to dwell on the past, and he had no regrets about the consequences of his easy-come, easy-go attitude to life. Holding the thong, however, he was aware that as he got older, easy-coming was ever less frequent, and easy-going tended to occur ever more quickly after the coming. His young partners quickly tired of the novelty of a mature man's tastes and sought the comfort like, of, you know, fun with me mates like. As a teacher of English he had at first been fascinated by the changes in the argot of his nubile lovers, but youthful speech-patterns were now beginning to irritate him, and one of the reasons for Tracey's recent departure had been his scornful response when, after initiating her into the darker hinterlands of lust she had expressed her appreciation with 'That was *well* bad.'

He threw the thong into the cardboard box that served as a waste-paper basket, replaced the cushions, and hoovered the floor. Deciding that upstairs could safely be left for the following day, he lit another cigarette, pulled a batch of essays from his carrier bag and began to read them. Marking essays was not an onerous task for

Rhodri: A-Level English students seemed blessed with rather more intelligence and sensitivity than their peers, such that he could sometimes justifiably ignore their often woeful syntax and rejoice in the fact that some of that generation were as appreciative as he of the delights of literature.

After an hour he'd finished the essays, and automatically moved to the kitchen to put on his anorak ready for the walk to the pub. While he was searching his jeans for cash he found the Principal's memorandum, and paused. Did he really want to spend the remainder of his evening in the pub listening to Carter sounding off? Wouldn't it be more relaxing just to pass the time in pleasurable anticipation of Megan's visit while smoking a joint and listening to music?

His mind was made up after the first question. He took off his anorak, put his tobacco, grass and skins on the arm of the settee, selected Elgar's Cello Concerto from the CD pile on the table. He then rolled a spliff, making the usual mess of it: he could never achieve the sort of tightly-packed perfect cylinder that Carter insisted on. After a few drags Du Pre's cello entered his head, slowed by the dope so that he could fix on it while simultaneously retaining in his memory the soaring accompaniment of the violins, then bringing them together in a glorious harmony seemingly of his own devising, a composition that was effortless yet so all consuming that it drove from his mind all thoughts of the college, Carter and Fiona. Megan was still present, though: it seemed as though it were her playing. He fell asleep on the settee.

Tuesday daytime

'Sorry I didn't make it to the pub last night,' said Rhodri.

'Didn't go either,' Carter grunted.

Rhodri dumped his books and notes on his desk and sat down, whistling quietly under his breath. He smiled and gave a cheerful hello to Elizabeth Selby, the recently appointed languages lecturer, sitting frowning over her lecture notes. Young, auburn haired with monkeyish features that verged on the attractive, she regarded him suspiciously. Rhodri usually either ignored her totally or made slightly suggestive remarks about her appearance.

'Good morning Rhodri,' she said eventually.

He smiled at her again. 'I'm sure you don't need to spend so much time worrying about your lecture notes, bach; the kiddies say you're a bloody good French teacher, so why don't you just go with the flow? Spontaneity is the thing to inspire students, not slavish adherence to a plan.'

Elizabeth looked taken aback. It was the first time Rhodri had ventured an opinion on the learning process in her presence. It took her a few moments to respond.

'Perhaps when I have your years of experience I might be able to do that, but at the moment I like to feel fully prepared.'

Rhodri contented himself with a 'Suit yourself, Liz,' and turned to Carter.

'So you decided to have an evening at home with the lovely Fiona?'

'Had a lot of marking to do.' Carter didn't look up but continued staring at a piece of paper on which he had been writing lists of names. 'Still had those fucking essays that the kids did before Christmas. Managed to get 'em shifted though. Anyway, what are you looking so bloody pleased about?'

Rhodri briefly considered telling him of Megan's impending arrival, but decided, given his evident moroseness that the subject would be better left.

'What's that you've got there?'

'I'm listing the likely pros, antis and undecideds.'

'Pro what? What are you on about man?'

'Ski-slopes's memo of course. Trying to work out if there are enough of us antis in the Programme Area to persuade Adrian to raise it at the Programme Leaders meeting.'

Rhodri groaned. 'For God's sake man, you're becoming obsessed.'

'If this place's gonna be worth living in we've got to stop her. I reckon there's a majority here to persuade Adrian to give it a go.'

'Go on then,' Rhodri said resignedly. 'Tell me what you've come up with.'

'Definites for action – me, you, Barbara, Graham. Probables – Derek, Heidi, Adrian himself. Those against – Elizabeth, Kelvin. Undecided – Arthur.'

'Undecided about what?' asked Arthur Giddings, who'd just entered the room.

'The Principal's memo, Arthur.'

Arthur, teacher of Spanish, head of languages and one year from retirement, launched into a long discourse, carefully weighing the pros and cons of the Principal's case, the gist of which was that while he agreed with her assertions regarding dress, drink, bad language and sexual references, he had some concerns about academic freedom in relation to what could and could not be said in the classroom, and that as to any action that Mike was proposing, well it depended on the nature of the action and that...

'What did you expect, Mike?' Rhodri muttered.

Arthur was notorious for the rambling monologues with which he sought to justify his indecisiveness. His old-womanishness had driven successive colleagues in his section to rapid applications for other jobs, with the result that the junior language teachers were always youthful, Elizabeth Selby and Heidi Stride being cases in point. Heidi, who taught German, was a petite brunette with an impish face and an inviting figure. It was Elizabeth and Heidi who had been the subject of Carter's and Rhodri's comparative study in the lunchtime pub session the previous day.

'OK Arthur, hope to discuss it more at break,' Carter halted the flow, 'Gotta go and teach.'

He rose and hurried to catch up with Rhodri who was already at the door. Arthur's presence in the workroom was the one incentive for them to be early for their lectures. Arthur in full flight had been known to empty the room in the space of a minute, save for Barbara Deakin, lecturer in Economics, who felt sorry for him, and young

Kelvin Mainwaring, lecturer in Geography, who had not the confidence to show discourtesy to his elders.

'I'll suss out how the others feel at break,' said Carter as they walked along the corridor. 'At least come and give me your support, you bastard.'

'You mean I'm expected to take the break in the workroom? Wouldn't I be better going to the staff lounge? Liz and Heidi have coffee there – I could work on them there.'

'They're a lost cause. Anyway you only go there to ogle 'em and chat 'em up.'

'Now that *would* be a lost cause, man. Heidi thinks I'm an old man and Liz is a professional virgin.'

They reached Mike's classroom door and parted.

***

Jennifer Bailey, fat and acned, sat in the classroom, early for her lecture as usual.

'Hi, young Jenny,' Carter greeted her.

'Good morning, Mr Carter,' she replied. Despite the insistence of most of the Humanities lecturers that they be called by their forenames, Jennifer could not bring herself to do it. She was not enjoying the college. Her parents had insisted that she join the GCSE course to try and improve the woeful grades she'd obtained at her private school, but, shy and withdrawn, she missed the regimentation and security that her school had provided.

She watched as Mr Carter walked round the room checking that the wall displays of charts, maps and timelines were all in symmetry and safely adhering to the surfaces. She wondered why he bothered to maintain them, given that she'd never once seen any of her peers refer to them. He then checked that the OHP was working and laid out the transparencies to be used in his lecture. Jenny, a born observer, had noted that he was obviously uncomfortable with the OHP and often forgot to use it, instead relying on the spoken word backed up when necessary by the odd phrase written on the whiteboard. This usually resulted in an outbreak of inattention, resulting in Mr Carter ranting about why it was that these days the attention span of teenagers was so limited as to require frequent changes between aural and visual stimuli.

The door opened and her fellow students made their mass entry, chattering, shouting, belching, yawning and scrambling for desks at the back. Most ignored Mr Carter's repeated 'Hi'. Jennifer thought they were all coarse and rude, and distained the way they dressed, the boys with their baggy jeans and hoods, the girls with their skimpy revealing tops and bare midriffs, tight low-slung denims revealing their thongs. In dress and attitude they exhibited all the street-cred that she lacked. Jennifer felt sorry for Mr Carter. He tried so hard to be one of the gang, to the extent of using bad language and talking about sex, but the response of her peers bordered on contempt. From her desk at the front she sometimes noticed a fleeting look of despair on his face.

The noise diminished to a level that allowed Mr Carter to speak.

'Okay, cats and chicks,' (a groan greeted this salutation) 'it's back to the General Strike of 1926,' (more groans), 'and I don't like it any more than you but it's on the fuckin' syllabus and that's what you're here for, so let's make it painless for each other, shall we?'

***

The 2nd year A-Level Literature students sitting in a rough semi-circle around Rhodri were enjoying themselves. Unusually for a nine-o'clock lecture he was in a particularly sunny mood, and the discussion on *Middlemarch* had digressed to an exploration of Victorian repressed sexuality, enlivened by his racy anecdotes. His language could sometimes be earthy and, in this as in previous years, had initially caused offence to those of a sheltered upbringing. One day he'd noticed the distress of some of the more sensitive young ladies, whereupon he'd stopped his discourse and asked them to consider whether he'd ever used such language gratuitously. In fact when discussing literature he never did; by the time the students had reached the second year they had become accustomed to his advocacy of the use of Anglo-Saxon in the right context.

He ended the discussion and said, 'Well, let's see what you've gleaned from all that. Have a think, and note down why you think *Middlemarch* could be called an erotic novel, giving examples of passages from the text. You won't get an exam question like that. I'm just seeking to establish that you've understood what I've been talking about. And it might give you a bit of fun. Get on with it then.'

The students bent to their task; Rhodri pulled his chair back behind his desk, extracted *The Guardian* from his bag and began the crossword. A silence settled over the room, which was characterised by the total absence of any aids to learning on the walls and by a general air of untidiness. Over the years successive cohorts of college cleaners had observed that somehow Mr Evans's room always seemed grubbier and dustier than any other and what did he get up to in there, they wondered?

With ten minutes left before the end of the class he put away his paper and asked if anyone had any thoughts that they wished to share. After a silence one of the boys volunteered that he was unable to find anything sexy in the novel, to which Rhodri responded that eroticism had nothing to do with explicit sex, though he appreciated that this was something that his, the lad's, generation might find hard to understand. Did any of the ladies, he asked, have any thoughts about the nature of the relationship between Dorothea and Casaubon, and whether the former's distress on her honeymoon was solely the result of the latter's intellectual aridity? One of the more perceptive girls wondered whether perhaps non-consummation of the marriage might be the reason, and, ignoring an aside from one of the wags saying that Casaubon wasn't able to get it up, he responded that this was indeed a possible interpretation. Challenged by one of the boys, he was then sidetracked into a discussion as to why reference to impotence could not be made explicit in a 19th century novel, leaving no time for an exploration of the 38th chapter of the book which he considered to be one of the most erotically charged passages in English literature.

The session over, he made his way back to the work-room. When he entered he found Carter haranguing Adrian Haver and Derek Surman. Barbara Deakin was listening, smiling wryly.

'Adrian, I'm sure the best chance of getting the cow to see reason is if you and some of the other Programme Leaders get together and point out all the hassle it's going to cause her. Bloody Derek here isn't prepared to get the union involved.'

'Mike's right,' said Derek. 'She's far more likely to take notice of middle managers on an issue like this. If NATFHE take it up it'll be a red rag to a bull.'

'Is she a bull or cow?' interjected Barbara. 'Are you going to grab her by the balls or squeeze her tits?'

Adrian winced. He had learned to cope with that sort of language when employed by Carter or Evans, but couldn't come to terms with it when used by a woman. It was the more distressing because Barbara seemed to relish her use of the words, emphasising them in her languorous, low-pitched drawl, whereas Carter and Evans swore as a matter of course, unthinkingly. Carter sometimes entered a room and greeted everyone cheerfully with a 'Fuckin' 'allo!' Adrian had taken up his post in the belief that he would be concentrating on developing his Area's provision and on marketing it to the local schools: he had been unprepared for the eclectic nature of his staff, and all his energies seemed to be expended in encouraging them to pull together as a team. He was torn between admiration for the examination success achieved by the likes of Carter, Evans and Barbara, and distress at the unprofessional way in which they conducted themselves, while on the other hand the solid sobriety of staff such as Derek Surman and Graham Sidelski seemed to come with uninspired teaching and undistinguished exam results.

Carter had sniggered at Barbara's crack and said that he assumed she was all for Adrian making a stand, to which she responded, 'Too right, mate.'

'There you are then,' he said, 'Barbara, me, Derek, Rhodri here of course, all in favour; and I'm sure Graham and Heidi will be. That's six of us, a clear majority already. How about it then, Adrian?'

Adrian rubbed his hand round his jaw. 'Well, possibly. But under this regime Programme Leaders' meetings aren't a forum for discussion. We sit there to receive our orders. We have to give notice of any other business at the start of the meeting, and more often than not it's ruled out of order. And in any case I'd like to hear exactly what your other colleagues feel. What about Arthur and the girls?'

'Girls!' Barbara exploded, 'Bloody hell, Adrian!'

Adrian blushed. 'Sorry, sorry, Barbara; I was referring to Elizabeth and Heidi, they seem so young...'

'Not like old biddies such as me, then.'

Adrian was saved from further apologies by the entry of Graham Sidelski, and turned to him gratefully. 'Graham, this question of the Principal's memo: Mike thinks that I –'

'I can guess what Mike thinks you should do, and I agree.' Graham was never one to waste words in work-room discussions, unlike in his Sociology lectures where he held forth at length and at ever-increasing speed as he warmed to his themes, to the despair of his students who in any case understood only one word in three. But although deeply serious, he had an intellectual empathy with any manifestation of nonconformity.

Seated hunched over at his desk in the corner throughout these exchanges, Kelvin Mainwaring listened with growing agitation, hoping that he would not be asked to express an opinion. Twenty-two years old and looking sixteen, fresh from his PGCE year and grappling unhappily with the teaching of geography, his crippling shyness had prevented him from establishing any social contact with any of his colleagues. He found Mike Carter particularly intimidating, but was hardly less comfortable in the company of Elizabeth and Heidi, who, although of his generation, possessed a mature self-confidence that reduced him to abject silence. On this occasion, however, he decided he would prefer to face their cool appraisal rather than be subject to interrogation from Mike, and quietly slipped out of the room when Mike resumed his offensive on Adrian.

***

In the staff common room, Heidi and Elizabeth had managed to secure their usual chairs, situated as far as it was possible to be from the corner where the Engineers gathered, and protected from their leering glances by a knot of Secretarial lecturers twittering around the coffee machine. After only a month in post Elizabeth had decided that the occasional unwelcome attentions from Engineers and Caterers were preferable to Arthur's fussiness and Mike's foul-mouthed rantings, and had elected to take her break in the company of vocational lecturers, some of whom, especially the staff from Business Studies were prepared to engage in sensible if not sparkling conversation about the pedagogic process. Heidi, less concerned about leering Engineers but equally keen to escape from Albert, had decided to keep her company. Today their conversation was following an increasingly familiar topic – how to cope with Albert, prompted by a meeting with him that both had been subjected to the previous day.

'I'm sure he's, like, a good teacher,' said Heidi, 'but why does he have to make such a fuss about everything?'

Elizabeth grimaced at the staff-room coffee. 'He's set in his ways, as my grandmother would say. Mind you, he does have a lot to contend with compared to the others – two full time staff, as well as all the part-timers.'

'But *we're* no trouble, are we?'

'Ah, but we're young, and female, with minds of our own: quite formidable to someone of his generation.'

'But he's no older than Mike, and not much older than Rhod, and *they* don't seem to find us formidable, do they?' Heidi crossed her legs, an action which brought an appreciative whistle from one of the Engineers.

Elizabeth raised her eyes heavenwards. 'There's your answer: Albert's a gentleman, for all his faults. Carter and Evans are aging roués. Despite their intellectual pretensions they're on a par with the rude mechanicals over there, though they'd be horrified to know we thought so.'

Heidi resisted the temptation to prolong the sidelong glance she had given to one of the younger Engineering lecturers and contented herself with re-crossing her legs. 'Oh, not all the Engineers are rude; some of them are very polite in fact.'

Elizabeth's eyes lifted again slightly. 'No, Heidi, my reference was Shakespearian.'

'Oh, I don't know much about Eng Lit; gave it up after GCSEs, didn't I? Anyway, I think uncle

Albert's an old woman; he had a go at me yesterday about the way I mark students' work. He was, like – "You need to give attention to your spelling when you make comments", I was, like – "But the students wouldn't notice the odd word spelt wrong", then he went on about using adverbs, so I was…'

Elizabeth let Heidi prattle on, and in the interests of feminine solidarity forbore to challenge either her criticism of Arthur or her means of interlocution. Blessed with an Independent School and Oxford education, she was depressed by the evidence of a spiralling decline in educational standards resulting from the semi-literacy of many of her contemporaries in the profession. At least Carter and Evans, when not in foul-mouthed mode, were able to construct a grammatical sentence. Heidi, it appeared, had secured her degree from Luton University by dint of her good fortune in having a multi-lingual upbringing: her mother was German.

Heidi suddenly interrupted her own monologue with a shout of 'Hey, Kelv! Over here!'

Kelvin was standing uncertainly in the doorway, peering around for somewhere to sit. Relief flooded his worried features when he saw Heidi and Elizabeth, and he hurried towards them, stumbling slightly as he passed the gaggle of Secretarial lecturers, to whom he proffered profuse apologies for being in their way.

'Hello' he said, fiddling with his ear.

'Here, drag over that chair and join us,' said Heidi.

'Right, yes, ok.' He pulled the chair towards them and sat down.

'Aren't you going to have a coffee?' asked Heidi.

'Oh, yes.' He sprang to his feet and made his way to the machine.

'That young man brings out maternal instincts in me,' said Elizabeth. 'The poor lad's given a tough time by his students, if the noise from his classroom is anything to go by. You'd think that Derek would give him a bit more support; he's his mentor, after all.'

'You're talking like you're twice his age,' said Heidi.

'Sometimes I feel that I am.'

Kelvin hurried back to them, plastic cup in hand.

'What brings you in here then?' asked Heidi. 'Don't think I've ever seen you here before.'

Kelvin sat down, spilling some coffee in the process. He dabbed ineffectually at his shirt. 'Oh, Mike Carter's having a go at Adrian, trying to persuade him to tackle the Principal about her memo. He was counting up all those who agreed with him, and I didn't want to get involved.'

'Very wise,' said Elizabeth. 'Michael Carter has his own agenda: steer clear of him.'

'What do you two think about the memo?'

'We fully support everything she is saying,' said Elizabeth, 'It's just a pity that she had to express herself in such appalling English. Carter, Evans and their like are a disgrace to the profession.'

66

'They're good teachers, though,' Heidi volunteered. 'Their results are good and the students seem to like them. And Rhod can sometimes be quite kind.'

'Those two,' Elizabeth said firmly, 'are living on their past glories, or what they perceive to be their glories. They're yesterday's men. And the most pathetic thing about them is that they still think they're God's gift to women – as if any self-respecting young woman would find them in the least attractive.'

'Oh, I dunno,' said Heidi. 'For a wrinkly, Mike Carter's quite fit.'

Seeing Elizabeth's expression, she changed the subject hurriedly. 'Hey, you two, like how about we all go for a drink one evening? I've started calling in at the *Eagle* –it's quite a cool crowd that gets in there; no teachers.'

'I'm sorry, you know I don't care for pubs,' said Elizabeth, 'and in any case I have far too much preparation to do.'

'Looks like me and you then, Kelv,' said Heidi.

Kelvin spilled the remnants of his coffee into his lap.

***

Fiona edged the MG out onto the Wenford Road. After days of unremitting gloom the sun showed signs of breaking through the cloud cover and she felt her spirits lift despite the previous night's debacle with Mike and the prospect of an extended lunch with her mother.

The winter sun shone milkily as she drove into the village, burnishing the prosperity that gleamed from the villas and renovated cottages and serving to remind her again of her privileged early years. Young mothers were driving children home for lunch from the primary school, and she recalled how she had pleaded with her parents to be allowed to join her friends there instead of being thrust, uniformed and straw-hatted into the private establishment in the town. But her mother had insisted that they had their position to consider and that Fiona would meet lots of new friends with whom she would have much more in common. The one advantage of her father's declining business fortunes was that when she passed the eleven plus it did not take too much argument to persuade him to let her attend the direct-grant grammar school in town rather than continue in private education. It was after all a single sex institution and her father had comforted himself with the thought that she would at least be free from the predations of adolescent boys, Fiona already at the age of eleven showing a precocious nubility.

She pulled into the drive of the house and saw, as ever, her mother peering expectantly out of the drawing room window. She had opened the door even before Fiona had extracted herself from the car, and with a 'Hello darling' proffered a powdery cheek to be kissed. Fiona obliged, and was ushered into the drawing room there to participate in the ritual of a pre-lunch sherry served from a crystal decanter. She knew better than to suggest that the drink and lunch be taken in the kitchen, which had the advantage of being warmed by the ancient Aga, the rest of the house being permeated by a deadening chill.

'Mummy, can't we have the central heating on?' she asked, 'it really does feel damp in here and it can't be doing your arthritis any good.'

'It's not at all cold today dear,' Mrs Smythe's hand trembled slightly as she poured the drinks, 'I do not have arthritis, just a touch of rheumatism now and again.'

She then began a litany of complaints about the local Conservative Association, of which she had been a member for over thirty years. 'I really think that I'm going to stop attending their meetings. It's just not the same as it used to be. So many of the new members aren't our sort of people. I've no objection to people making their way in the world: heaven knows I'm not a snob, but you would think that the nouveaux riche might acquire a bit of gentility and learn to speak the Queen's English.'

'Well, if you want to mix with people who speak with public school accents, why don't you join the Labour party? Tony Blair should be posh enough for you.'

'Don't be ridiculous darling and don't mention that awful man's name in this house. I can't stand him. Ever since you've been with that... *that man*... your head's been full of nonsense.'

'If by 'that man' you mean Mike, I think you'd find that he hates Tony Blair as much as you do.'

'If you've finished your sherry,' Mrs Smythe cut off further discussion, 'I'll serve lunch. Would you like to come to the dining room?'

As lunch progressed Fiona could feel the familiar numbness in her feet setting in as the draught from the hall began its stealthy attack. She confined herself to 'yes', 'no' and 'really' as her mother wittered on about her neighbours, her distant relatives, the iniquity of the council tax and the appalling rubbish that they showed on television these days. Watching her, she realised with a pang that she was becoming an old woman before her time: she was developing a stoop; the arthritis which she denied was clawing her hands, and the thick layer of powder failed to disguise the thread-veins and age spots on her face.

'At least let me make the coffee, mummy,' she said, longing for a few moments in the company of the Aga, and she leapt up to go to the kitchen before her mother could protest. Much to her surprise Mrs Smythe followed her, and sat silent at the scrubbed table while Fiona busied herself with the percolator.

'Simon came to see me last week,' Mrs Smythe blurted out, a hint of defiance in her voice.

Fiona was shocked by the news. She knew that in the months following their break-up Simon had been in frequent telephone contact with her mother in the course of which, according to Mrs Smythe, he had protested wounded innocence and had pleaded with her to intercede on his behalf, a request with which her mother had been only too happy to oblige. The phone-calls had tailed off when Fiona had made it clear there was no going back, and ceased altogether once Simon had sold the marital home and moved into a flat in Levington.

She took a deep breath, and as she busied herself with the coffee decided on a display of dispassionate interest. 'Oh, and how is he?' she asked, bringing the cups to the table.

'He looks very well indeed. He's lost weight. And he's driving a Porsche.'

'Well, I'm pleased for him. It's what he always wanted.'

'Don't you wish to know why he came to see me?'

'Well, you and he always got on well, didn't you? Why shouldn't he visit you?' She resisted the temptation to add that he probably wanted to show off his Porsche.

'He still cares for you, you know. After all this time and after all you did to him.'

Fiona poured the coffee, sat down, and decided that the time had come to risk further upsetting her mother in the hope that she might eventually come to understand.

'Mummy, listen. I'm not going to try and excuse my behaviour. Things go wrong in marriages, you know; things went wrong in ours. There was no future in it. Even if Mike hadn't come along the marriage would still have ended sooner or later, probably later when I'd have been too old to make a new life.'

'I still think you were very selfish, Fiona.'

'I'm *not* selfish!' Fiona raised her voice. 'Don't you realise that after ten years of being the dutiful wife I saw that I was turning into someone just like you? You spent your entire married life acting as daddy's social secretary and hostess, kow-towing to all those dreadful businessmen and their hard-nosed wives, and where has it got you? Sitting alone in a huge house that you can't afford to run, no real friends, no interests except those trashy novels you insist on reading - '

Mrs Smythe's lower lip began to tremble. 'I'm alone because your dear father died. He wore himself out trying to keep the business afloat; he did that for me and for you; how can you be so ungrateful?'

'I'm not ungrateful. You know I loved daddy. But suppose he'd lived? He'd be retired now, no business to absorb him, no colleagues to socialise with. Daddy didn't have friends, he had colleagues. Who would you be entertaining now? What would you be doing with your lives? What interests did he have outside work? He'd be sitting here day after day doing f... doing nothing, expecting you to run after him, organise his domestic life like you always did.'

Tears began to run down Mrs Smythe's cheeks. 'Don't you think that I'd give everything I've got to have your father sitting there? I loved him. I looked forward to looking after him in our old age. When you're my age you'll understand how important companionship is. When you lose your looks and your energy as we all do you'll end up lonelier than I am, no husband, no children...'

Fiona looked at the rivulets eroding her mother's make-up and was torn between pity and anger. She had never heard her admit to loneliness before. To embrace her, as part of her wished to do, would be embarrassing for both of them: theirs had never been a tactile relationship. She compromised by touching her mother's hand briefly. 'Drink your coffee, mummy.'

Mrs Smythe composed herself. 'Simon would like to see you, you know.'

'What on earth for? We've nothing left to talk about. We're worlds apart now in any case.'

'I think you'd find he's changed. He's not like he was, not so, so, oh I don't know, so self-assured.'

'What you call self-assurance was pure arrogance. This is all just a ploy to go over all the old ground again; I'm not doing it, mummy.'

'You've become very hard since you've been with that dreadful man. I suppose you need to be; you don't seem happy. I know he's not doing you any good. What do you do with yourself all the time he's at work? I don't hear any more about you continuing your education – doesn't he like the idea any more? I thought you were going on to do more A-Levels. What's happened to that?'

Fiona responded by asking if her mother wanted more coffee, and then re-asserted her determination not to meet Simon. 'So if you had any thoughts of a grand reconciliation, please forget it: you'd only be disappointed. Can we talk about you, mummy? I know you'll hate this, but don't you think it would really be much better if you sold this place and bought something smaller and more comfortable, maybe in town?'

Her question had the desired effect of diverting her mother into a discourse in which figured prominently the importance of living with one's happy memories, the need to keep up standards, the nastiness of poky rooms and pocket-handkerchief sized gardens and the desirability of retaining relationships with tradesmen whom knew their place.

Thus passed the remaining half-hour of Fiona's duty visit. On kissing her mother goodbye went straight to the car and drove off, not turning to give her usual wave lest she upset herself by seeing Mrs Smythe standing alone at the door wearing her usual sad valedictory expression. She always found these visits depressing, but on this occasion depression was overlain by a vague feeling of unease. As she drove down Bardon Hill, the town spread out before her, the streetlights already flickering on, she tried to pinpoint the reason for her mood. It wasn't the fact that Simon was, however obliquely, in the picture again: her determination not to renew contact was resolute. What else had her mother said which might have subliminally disturbed her? She could not put her finger on it. Shaking her head, she turned her attention to the shopping she had to do and the evening meal she had to cook – what particular favourite might improve Mike's mood, she wondered?

***

After clearing her post and dictating letters to her PA, Marcia called in Lucas Harper and put to him her idea that he should chair a working party of the SMT to draft a paper on re-structuring acceptable to the pedants amongst the Programme Leaders.

'Make sure that the proposals are based on financial savings and the need to cut out dead wood,' she said. 'Don't stand for any nonsense from Jay and Hickman. Jay's devious enough to try to water down any plan under the guise of turning it into a work of literature.'

Lucas, delighted at the further evidence that she valued him above the other members of the SMT, wondered whether it soon might be opportune to broach the possibility that he might be given the title of Vice Principal, or, even better, Deputy Chief Executive. An ambitious young man, he had his sights set on being a Principal before he was thirty-five, and, unencumbered by partner, friends or principles he was likely to achieve his objective.

The tête-à-tête concluded, they moved from the easy chairs grouped in front of Marcia's desk to the large table at the other end of the spacious room. She called her PA to ask her to send in the other SMT members for the weekly pre-meeting that was held prior to the meeting of Programme Leaders. The purpose of this gathering was to review the agenda and ensure, as Marcia unashamedly put it, that they were all singing from the same hymn sheet.

Paul Tasker, Charles Jay and Edgar Hickman entered, the latter two registering Lucas's presence and exchanging knowing glances.

'Sit down, please gentlemen.' Marcia still on occasion reverted to the formalities of the private industry boardrooms. 'I don't think there's much on this afternoon's agenda that need concern us. Only two PLs who've submitted items, and it's the usual whinges as you can see. All the other items are ours. Edgar, no items from you? You've gone very quiet recently.'

'Nothing at present Marcia. No doubt there'll be lots for me to do when your restructuring plans are implemented.'

'Yes. I want to talk about that now. I've decided that Lucas will chair a working party of you four where you will draw up a paper outlining the restructuring policy. I hope it'll only take one meeting. This is a matter of urgency as I'd like the paper to be tabled at next week's PL's meeting, yes, tabled. There's no way I want documents like that floating round the college; some of the PLs are as leaky as sieves. The staff don't need to know yet.'

There was no reaction to her statement; unusually for him, Charles Jay had gone ominously quiet.

'I'll get together with you three after the PL's meeting, then, to fix a time for us meet,' said Lucas.

'You three!' muttered Edgar to Charles. 'That puts us in our place.'

The meeting over, Marcia phoned through to her PA to say that they were ready for lunch to be brought in. Sylvia, who resolutely insisted on calling herself the Principal's Secretary despite the letter-heading which referred to her as PA to the Chief Executive, nodded to the refectory manager standing guard over the trolley on which was spread a finger-buffet.

'Her ladyship's ready for you now, Karen.'

Karen giggled. She wheeled in the trolley, was greeted by Charles and Edgar, nodded to by Paul and Marcia, and ignored by Lucas. She laid out the lunch, moving slowly in the hope that the conversation might reveal interesting tit-bits for onward transmission to her colleagues in the refectory, but they seemed to be talking about something called the Learning and Skills Council, whatever that was.

'Thank you Karen,' Marcia said eventually, 'That looks excellent: we'll do the rest.' After Karen's departure Marcia moved over to a side cabinet, extracted a wine bottle and five glasses, and placed them on the table.

A rush of blood came to Edgar's head. 'Haven't the regulations in your memo concerning drinking come into force yet, then?' he blurted out.

Marcia's heavy brows met in a thunderous scowl. She said nothing but glowered at Edgar.

Charles leaned towards Edgar. 'Well done,' he muttered.

'I'll live to rue the day,' Edgar whispered.

***

Adrian emerged from the Programme Leaders' meeting steeling himself for an uncomfortable afternoon. He had to inform his staff that he'd been unable to persuade Marcia to give further thought to her edict. In the event, Derek, Barbara, Graham and Rhodri received the news with resignation while Elizabeth, Heidi and Kelvin kept their counsel. Arthur, as expected, treated him to lengthy analysis of the merits of the Marcia's case before launching into a detailed history of previous Principals and their varying styles of management, all of which Adrian had heard before.

Much to Adrian's surprise, Carter, on hearing the news, failed to deliver the anticipated harangue: he merely nodded, collected his books and walked out without saying a word, his face expressionless. Adrian asked Rhodri, who was still in the workroom doing some last-minute reading before his evening class, whether he thought Mike might do something stupid, and was he alright, because he'd seemed to be in a strange mood for some time now. Rhodri replied that he was not his brother's keeper and he couldn't account for Mike's moods but that Adrian shouldn't let it worry him.

'And what about you?' asked Adrian. 'Are you going to compromise? Couldn't you at least tidy yourself up a bit?'

Rhodri peered at him intently through his granny-glasses and stroked his beard. 'You're the second person in as many days who's asked me that. The first one indicated that she might fancy me if I did; feel the same way, do you?'

Adrian's single status sometimes invited innuendos such as this, but he had learned how to deal with them. He contented himself with 'Rhodri, at your time of life there's nothing you could do that would ever make yourself attractive to anyone of either sex,' and left the room.

Rhodri thought for a while before continuing his reading.

Tuesday evening

Rhodri ambled into his classroom and noticed with satisfaction that all his students seemed to be present. He'd lost only one of the original eighteen who had enrolled the previous September. His Literature group was one of only two A-Level evening classes that the college still ran. The advent of Access courses a few years ago, offering mature students a modular, faster and easier route to Higher Education, had had the effect of decimating the former wide range of part-time A-Level and GCSE courses. The fact that Rhodri's had survived was a testament to its habitual large enrolment, high retention rates and excellent examination pass rates, these being the performance indicators that were scrutinised by management in their continual drive to maintain government funding levels.

'Good evening,' said Rhodri as he took his seat, and his students responded with enthusiasm, eager for the evening's entertainment to begin. They were a mixed bunch and the group included a few 19-year-old re-sit students, pensioners seeking company as well as stimulation, lonely bachelors of indeterminate pedigree on the look-out for possible partners, and, overwhelmingly in the majority, middle aged, middle class housewives there for a variety of reasons; some of which they would be unlikely to admit to.

Rhodri was on form this evening, and the class responded. When not hung-over he was an enthusiast for teaching, and with responsive students he lost himself in the sheer joy of debate. He'd once said to Carter that the high he experienced on these occasions was as good as that provided by booze or dope, and nearly as good as sex, but Carter had looked at him uncomprehendingly, and it was then that Rhodri had begun to wonder whether Carter, though articulate, persuasive, challenging and amusing, might perhaps be too self-aware to ever forget the image that he was trying to portray.

His two-hour class passed quickly. Tonight he had been repeating his earlier session on *Middlemarch*, the evening students more receptive to his notions than had been the teenagers. In particular Christine Fitzroy, a mousy-haired thin young woman and a late entrant to the class, had begun to participate enthusiastically when he had broached the idea of the underlying eroticism in the novel.

At the end of his classes a number of the students liked to remain behind to try and engage him in further discussion, something from which he always tried to disengage himself, as by nine o'clock he was desperate for a cigarette and eager to get to the *Woodman*. This had not been a problem for him until the current academic year: previously all evening classes had taken an extended coffee break in the Refectory. It was a long-standing practice stretching back to the era of old Jefferson, the much-loved Principal of the 1970s and which had survived the succeeding Principal before being stamped on by Marcia Martell.

81

This week the usual suspects crowded round him as he began stuffing his books into his bag, but for the first time the group included Christine Fitzroy. She stood silently as the others propounded their ideas to which Rhodri listened but did not respond, until with a hint of impatience he said that if they didn't mind he'd address their interesting suggestions the following week but that he'd really like to get a few pints in before closing time. The group immediately made for the door, all its members being slightly in awe of him and not wishing to incur his displeasure.

Christine Fitzroy, however, moved in the opposite direction, closer to him.

'I'd just like to say, Rhodri, how much I enjoy your lectures.' Her voice was well modulated and husky, with a slight midlands accent lurking under the received pronunciation.

'Very kind of you to say so,' said Rhodri, picking up his bag.

'I was so pleased that you find parts of *Middlemarch* erotic; I do as well. In fact I found it so at school, but I was the only one who did, or at least the only one who would dare to admit it, not that I *did* admit it to my teacher. It was a single-sex school.'

'Well, I'm glad we're of like mind, Christine.' He moved towards the door. There had been a hint of sarcasm in his voice, but she seemed not to have noticed.

'It's erotic because the sex is so understated, don't you think?'

Rhodri stopped. He could not let this go unchallenged. 'I don't think you can say that. Sex per se isn't understated; it's not alluded to at all.'

'Well maybe not, but it's there, underneath, isn't it? Perhaps one has to be particularly sensuous to pick it up.'

'Or even sensual,' said Rhodri, but the rebuke was evidently lost on her. She moved closer to him.

'You're obviously in need of your drink,' she said. 'I won't keep you any longer, but you don't mind if I walk down to the town with you, do you? I've left my car there. It's impossible to find a parking space at the college.'

Rhodri looked at her closely for the first time. She was almost his height: she wore no make up, her complexion was creamy and her large brown eyes were gazing intently at him. At close quarters she was not unattractive, he realised, and she had youth on her side. 'Why not?' he thought. It was some weeks since Tracey's hurried departure, and apart from missing the comfort of a woman's company he was ready for a new challenge, the thrill of the chase often providing more excitement than the actual kill.

'Where are you parked?'

'In Market Square'

'That's on my way: ok, let's go.'

On the walk into town she kept up a stream of chatter. By the time they reached her car Rhodri was having second thoughts about the possibility of an evening's dalliance. Her knowledge and appreciation of literature was obviously limited, not that it bothered him in this context, but her talk exhibited all the self-absorption and lack of irony of the social misfit, combined with the arch innuendos of the sexually frustrated. In Rhodri's experience the latter characteristic was rarely a precursor to a night of extended experimentation, while the former usually resulted in protracted agonised self-analysis before, during and after the event.

She stood by the car door. 'Well, Rhodri,' she said. 'Here we are, but the night is still young.'

Rhodri winced. Perhaps at last this was the touch of irony so lacking in her conversation hitherto? He examined her features for a hint of a smile but there was none, but the length of his gaze provided the opportunity for which she had evidently been waiting: she pulled him to her and said in his ear, 'Are you taking me for a drink, then?'

Any doubts he had been experiencing were dispelled by contact with her body: though thin, it was firm and inviting under her suede jacket and jeans. He stood back and looked at her appraisingly.

'Up for a long session in the pub are you then?'

'To start with, anyway.'

Her riposte reconciled him to the necessity of conversation before consummation, and that this would best be leavened by the company of Mike, Stu and Geoff.

'Come on then. I always meet some friends in the *Woodman* on a Tuesday evening. It's only five minutes away.'

'I don't think I've ever been there,' said Christine, 'is it the haunt of intellectuals?'

Rhodri snorted with laughter. 'It's not the Left Bank, but it has its moments. Hope you like real ale.'

***

The *Woodman* was the regular evening haunt of a clientele that had been disenfranchised by the tourist-ridden olde-worlde pubs, yuppie wine bars and the alcopop drinking shops that constituted the majority of licensed premises in the town. It remained comfortingly scruffy with a flagged floor, unpolished wooden tables and nicotine-stained walls.

Geoff was sitting listening to a Carter monologue about how he was faced with the prospect of revamping all his lecture notes to introduce anecdotes and analogies that might have resonance for twenty-first century teenagers.

'But, shit, man, it's been years since I had to do systematic lesson preparation. I tried to get down to it this evening, but it's a drag; Christ, you expect to have to do it when you're starting out, but now? In my fifties?'

'Don't tell me you're feeling your age, Mike?' Geoff asked, expecting an emphatic denial.

Carter dragged at his roll-up. 'This morning it hit me that the 1960s are as alien to the students as the 1920s had been to me when I was in the sixth form. Did me old mum and dad feel like I do now? Sometimes I feel like a stranger in a world that knows little and cares less for the things that turn me on. Sometimes I wake up in the morning and it hits me – I'm not forty or even fifty, but getting on for fuckin' sixty, and it scares me shitless man, I don't mind telling you.'

Bloody hell, Geoff thought, this'll be something to tell Julie.

As if regretting his confession, Carter ground out his cigarette aggressively and suggested that they had a game of pool before the pub got too crowded.

Carter potted his remaining balls with panache, winning the game. The leather-jacketed, balding man who'd been standing watching them play approached and indicated that it was our turn, mate, to which Carter replied 'Sure' and handed him his cue. They picked up their glasses and occupied seats in the alcove away from the draughty doorway. Carter lit a cigarette.

'*Was* it old Todger's turn?' asked Geoff, nodding towards the pool table where the balding man had been joined by a friend, more hirsute but similarly clad.

'Dunno, I wasn't sure, but you don't argue the toss with Todger and his mates. Remember that time when Stu insisted on having one more game and nearly got a cue rammed up his arse?'

Geoff grinned. 'Aye, but that were years ago, when old Todge had a full head of hair and was leader of the pack. Look at the gut on him now. Where's Evans got to? Isn't he coming tonight?'

'Didn't say he wasn't,' said Mike 'He's probably been buttonholed by the seekers after enlightenment. That'll piss him off; he'll be gasping for a pint.'

'Time was when you and Evans used to bring some of your adult students to the pub after your classes: some of them were right fit as well. I reckon when you brought Fiona was the last time that happened, wasn't it?'

'Yeah, but you know what adult students are like. Middle-class bitches, most of them. They'd go to the *Swan* or the *Falconer* but you'd never get 'em coming into a place like this, and anyway Evans has been barred from most of the poncy pubs. Doesn't bother me anyway, since fuckin' Ski-slopes put an end to my evening History class.'

Geoff was ready with an instant response to divert Mike from a monologue about the Principal. 'And anyway, you've got Fiona now.'

Mike looked away, took a drag at his cigarette and muttered, 'Oh yeah, I've got Fiona all right,' before asking Geoff if he wanted the same again.

Carter took the two empty glasses to the bar. George, the landlord, was being chatted to by Rita, a faded frizzy-haired bottle-blonde of advancing years who liked to perch on a bar stool, crossing and uncrossing her varicose-veined legs and talking in a cigarette-roughened rasp to anyone who'd listen.

'Same again?' said George to Carter, interrupting Rita's flow.

'Please,' said Carter. 'Hi Rita, how ya doin?'

'Can't grumble darlin'. Bloody cold, innit? I was saying to George here, could do with a nice hunk to keep me warm tonight. How're you fixed, Mike? Can't that lovely Fiona let you off the leash tonight?'

'Sorry Rita, your luck's not in. Why not try old Todger over there?'

'That greasy fucker? I've got me standards, I'll have you know. Anyway the bugger's more interested in his motorbike, it's the only thing he can get his leg over.' This was said with a cackle followed by a phlegmy cough.

Todger heard the end of this comment and glowered at her from across the room before, with studied deliberation, chalking the end of his cue. Geoff, who'd been listening to the exchange at the bar, noticed Carter, doubtless alerted to the possibility of trouble, starting to pay avid attention to George's manipulation of the beer pumps. Though it was Rita who'd made the remark, it was well known that Todger and his crowd still adhered to the bikers' code of honour which held that chicks were immune from retribution for slights, revenge to be exacted instead from their male companions.

Carter's luck was in: Todger's attention was diverted by the entry of Rhodri, who held the door open behind him for a slim young woman dressed in boot-cut jeans and a suede jacket. He led her to the alcove where Geoff sat, effected hurried introductions, then walked over to Carter.

'One for me while you're there, and a half for the lady,' he said, and went back to the alcove.

'Bloody hell,' muttered Carter, 'the bastard's pulled again already.'

Christine felt ill at ease. Rhodri was ignoring her and deep in conversation with the man he'd introduced her to as Geoff. And the pub was shabby, not a nice place at all. The bearded man to whom Rhodri had spoken at the bar approached, placed a half pint in front of her and sat down beside her.

'Fuckin' hello!' he said with a smile, 'I'm Mike; who are you?'

Though taken aback by the greeting, she held his gaze. 'I'm Christine,' she said, 'Christine Fitzroy. Are you one of Rhodri's colleagues?' She took a dainty sip from her glass.

'Yeah. I suppose you're from his evening class?'

'That's right. We were discussing *Middlemarch* tonight, one of my favourite books, and Rhodri suggested that we continued the discussion over a drink.'

'I bet he did,' said Mike. She noticed he was looking not at her face, but giving an appraising survey of her body. 'Where are the rest of the class then?'

'Oh, they didn't seem too interested in pursuing the topic. You see, Rhodri and I are kindred spirits when it comes to Eliot.'

'Kindred spirits eh? Is that what he told you?'

Christine was puzzled by the sarcasm in his voice. She thought for a moment then said, 'Some things don't need to be made explicit, do they?

One can sense when one's on the same wavelength.'

Rhodri turned to them. 'This is Christine... Mike Carter... Christine Fitzroy. Mike teaches history. Christine's - '

'Yeah, we've got that far. I hear you and Christine are kindred spirits then?'

A pained expression flickered momentarily across Rhodri's features. 'See you were getting your usual come-on from randy Rita then?' he said.

'Diverted her to old Todger, but she doesn't think he'd get it up. Glad you came in when you did.'

Christine was finding it hard to hold her look of bright, alert interest. On the way to the pub she'd prepared herself for a conversation about literature or politics or art, hoping that any contribution she could make would not be ill-judged. But after only five minutes in the place she'd been greeted by a four-letter word, heard reference to the sexual mores of a customer, and been indirectly informed of the deficiencies of another whose nickname must surely be an ironic reference. Perhaps this was how intellectuals chose to relax, she thought? After all, one couldn't live cerebrally all the time. She thought Mike Carter was a bit strange: she wasn't certain whether he was friendly or not and he was too conscious of his good looks; she'd seen him eyeing his reflection behind the bar while he was waiting to be served. Somebody ought to tell him that patchouli oil was no longer fashionable.

'Hope you're going to accept that you've lost the battle over Ski-slopes's dictat,' Rhodri was saying to Carter. 'It's just not worth the hassle.'

'No way,' said Mike, 'I'm going to have a go at the Union meeting, and if I don't get support there then I'm gonna make an appointment to see her. Just because Adrian hasn't got the guts to stand up to her doesn't mean the bitch is immovable. I reckon a reasoned approach might get her off our backs.'

Ah, this might be more interesting, thought Christine; they're going to discuss college matters. But as she settled down to listen she was immediately disappointed by the diversion created by the approach of Todger, who'd finished his game.

'Come on then,' he grunted, 'Me and Wally will take on any of you two. Five quid on it.'

'You're on,' said Rhodri. 'Are you up for it, Geoff?'

Geoff looked at his watch. 'Just one, then,' he said, and the two got up, leaving Carter and Christine together.

'So, Christine,' Carter said, looking at her intently, 'what motivated you to join Rhodri's evening class?'

'Oh, a love of literature of course. I liked it at school, but I didn't fully appreciate it. The teacher was a dry old stick. I've read an awful lot since then and –'

'What's your job?'

'I'm a senior clerk in an insurance company. I organise the whole office; the partners say I'm worth my weight in gold, but there's no stimulation there. All the young girls are very empty-headed. I try to talk about literature sometimes but they don't really appreciate what I'm saying. I give them lots of advice on their love lives, based on what I've read of course; wide reading is such a help in life isn't it? You must have found that?'

'I bet your advice is based more on your own experience, good-looking lady like you. Do you live in town? Haven't seen you around before.'

Christine simpered. 'I moved back into town six months ago. I lived for a while in Levington, but it's getting very rough there, lots of, well you know, immigrants, not that I'm prejudiced of course, but you meet a nicer class... a more intellectual class of people here.'

Carter was silent for a moment, as though considering his next course of action. For a moment Christine thought he was about to get up, but he turned to her and suddenly asked if she had a partner. She coyly responded that wouldn't he like to know, at the same time fluttering her eyelashes.

She was beginning to relax and enjoy herself when a couple entered. The female half immediately sat down next to Carter: her partner stood over him and said saying grudgingly that he supposed Mike wanted a pint.

'Yeah, cheers, I'll have a pint of the usual.'

'And what would your young lady friend like?' There was the hint of a sneer in the man's voice.

'I'm ok, thank you,' said Christine.

As the man went to the bar, Carter introduced the woman as Lisa, and said that her husband was Stu.

'Hello, I'm Christine. Are you a regular at this pub?'

'What do you mean by that?' said Lisa. 'I'm not here every evening if that's what you're getting at, in fact I hardly come here at all except sometimes on Fridays. Has Mike been talking about me? You don't want to believe everything he says.'

Christine, taken aback by the venom in Lisa's voice and the wine on her breath, was unable to respond. Carter came to the rescue. 'Cool it, Lisa, Christine's new to the *Woodman*; she was just making conversation, and no, I haven't bloody mentioned you, why should I?'

Lisa drummed her fingers on the table and looked away. Christine wondered why this seedy woman seemed so agitated and why she had been so unpleasant. She felt a sudden lurch of insecurity in this rather sordid environment, its low life ever more in evidence as the room had begun to fill up. Rhodri had not paid her any attention since starting his game: does he want me or not, she wondered?

Stu returned with the drinks and sat down next to Lisa, facing Mike and Christine. Lisa grabbed her wine glass and half emptied it with a couple of swallows; Carter acknowledged his pint with a 'Cheers' and lit a cigarette, then offered one to

Christine, which she refused, saying that she didn't smoke.

Stu laughed and addressed Christine for the first time. 'If you don't smoke then you're in for an uncomfortable evening with Carter. He's got a wealth of dirty habits, has Carter: hope you're ready for them.'

Carter glowered. 'You don't often bring Lisa here midweek. What's happened, run out of wine at home?'

'Fuck off. Anyway, where's Lady Fiona? Keeping her well hidden lately, aren't you? Or isn't this place classy enough for her? Still, I suppose it gives you the chance to try your luck with a bit of rough. Getting a bit past it, though, aren't you?'

Lisa joined the fray. 'But at least you had it at one time, didn't you Mike? Unlike some I could mention.' She emptied her glass. 'You'll get me another, won't you Mike?'

Carter grabbed her glass and marched off to the bar. Christine's discomfiture turned to something approaching panic, left to sit with a couple who were bereft of manners and whose appearance was moth-eaten to say the least.

Stu, without looking her in the face, said 'So Carter's not told you about Fiona then?'

'No, why should he? Who's Fiona?'

'Fiona's his bitch, of course,' said Lisa, 'She's older than you, but better looking and posher, she went to the local snob school. You might be all right for a one-nighter, but Mike knows which side his bread's buttered in the long term so don't raise

94

your hopes, sweetheart. Where the fuck is he with my wine anyway?'

Christine had had enough. She rose and marched over to the pool table where Rhodri and Geoff had just finished their game. 'Rhodri, I don't want to stay here any longer,' she said, her voice tremulous. 'Can we go now?'

Rhodri glanced over to the table where Stu and Lisa had obviously begun one of their public disagreements, then to the bar where Carter's expression spoke volumes. Realising that exposure to a rancorous interchange between the three of them would do little to enhance Christine's libido, he decided that it was indeed time to go. He nodded his assent, said 'I'm off' to Carter, still standing at the bar, and led her to the door.

Carter took the wine over to Lisa, told her he felt like getting an early night and hurried to the door, not quickly enough to avoid hearing Stu's shouted comment that it looked like he was on a loser tonight.

Geoff, somewhat reluctantly, sat down with Stu and Lisa.

'So, Geoff,' said Stu, 'That was an interesting little scene. Where did Carter pick that one up? How come she left with Evans? D'you reckon Carter's off to mount a challenge, or perhaps he has a threesome in mind?' He grinned lasciviously.

A feeling of weariness overtook Geoff at the prospect of having to explain the evening's events. He swallowed the remains of his pint, said that he hadn't been party to anything that had happened and that in any case he'd promised Julie he wouldn't be late, wished them goodnight, waved goodbye to George, and departed, leaving Stu and Lisa to the delights of each other's company.

***

After Mike had left for the pub, Fiona bent determinedly to the task of ironing to the accompaniment of an 'Abba' CD which she was not allowed to play in his presence. However the repetitive movement of the iron and the cheerful harmonies failed to soothe her. The news that Mrs Smythe had been in contact with Simon had rattled her slightly, but there was something else about her visit that had produced this vague feeling of unease; something that she couldn't put her finger on, like a dream that is so elusive on waking, a dream that cannot be remembered but retains its power to disturb throughout the day.

She finished her ironing and sat down. It was not a room in which to sit alone, despite all her efforts to brighten the place. The serried ranks of books loomed at her gloomily, and she felt a swell of resentment that Mike was so unwilling to compromise in the matter of décor. If they had a larger house, she thought… she stopped, realising the impossibility of ever moving to a larger house on Mike's salary. She thought of her old house in Benton that she and Simon had so lovingly restored, with its spacious living room with French windows opening onto the terrace where they'd sat on summer evenings in the early years of their marriage before things had turned sour and she'd begun to pace the rooms in frustration and boredom.

She could never go back to that, she told herself firmly. But thoughts of the house served to remind her that Simon had re-established contact with her mother, and that from now on Mrs Smythe would continue to harp on about it, and that having once called on her Simon was likely to do it again, and – oh God! that her mother wasn't beyond conspiring with him to arrange for him to be present at a time when she knew Fiona was due to come.

The thought caused her to leap up. A meeting with Simon in her mother's company would be so excruciatingly embarrassing: she couldn't cope with it! Was it this scenario, she wondered, that had been in her subconscious and had been making her so ill at ease?

Shit. How could she resolve this? She sat frowning, running her fingers through her bob, her mouth contorted as she chewed her bottom lip: *I've been bloody trapped*; trapped into making contact with Simon.

I'd better do it immediately, she thought, otherwise I'll have a sleepless night. She glanced at her watch; Mike wouldn't be home for a good hour yet. Where had she put Simon's phone number? She ran upstairs to the bedroom and groped around in her knicker drawer to find the old address book in which she'd ashamedly scrawled his number several years ago when he'd moved to

Levington. Not giving herself time to think she charged back downstairs and grabbed the phone.

'Four nine one five oh six,' said the familiar assertive voice.

'Simon, it's me, Fiona,' she said briskly.

'Fiona! Long time no contact. Have you been to see your mother by any chance?'

'Yes. That's why I'm phoning. There's no point in all this. You must know there's no chance of –'

'Look, Fi, I can't talk now; I've got colleagues round. Let's meet for lunch.'

'No! There's only one thing I want to say, you must get it straight –'

'Fi, darling, I'm sorry but I really can't talk now. If it's important, meet me for a quick lunch on Thursday in the *Fox* at Loxton. I'll be there at 12.30. See you then I hope. Bye, Fi.' The line went dead.

Fiona had time only to realise that she had been trapped into having to make another decision when Mike's key rattled in the lock and he entered, earlier and more sober than expected but wearing the same disgruntled expression with which he had left. She prepared herself for an uncomfortable night.

***

Marcia was spending the evening giving thought to the agenda for the forthcoming meeting of the College Corporation. Her restructuring proposals would of course be the main item for discussion: by the time of the meeting, a month away, she would need to have informed the Programme Leaders, put the plan to the Academic Board, and gone through the motions of consulting the unions.

The Corporation Meeting should present no problem. The only possible complication that might arise was if the Academic Board were to fail to endorse the proposals, because the minutes of Board meetings were scrutinised by the Corporation. There was no danger of the Corporation challenging her proposals, but evidence of dissension would be an embarrassment and might result in delay.

Much, therefore, depended on the paper that Lucas and his working party had been delegated to prepare. Too baldly factual, too much emphasis on the financial imperatives, and the Board would react adversely and might even vote against it. If it was too discursive the Board would assume it was a consultative document and start a protracted discussion that might result in a dilution of the plan. She had faith in Lucas to deliver the goods, but left to himself his paper might be too brusque. If, however, he could incorporate a précised version of the best of Charles Jay's probable observations then the resulting compromise might be acceptable to all parties.

But Lucas needed watching. Although he looked like a geek with those silly horn-rimmed glasses and short-back-and-sides, he was obviously an ambitious man, probably without scruples, and though apparently eager to please her, she was sure that he was the sort to seize on any opportunity for self-advancement; if necessary, at her expense. She'd come to realise that the ruthless in-fighting and back-stabbing amongst senior managers that she'd experienced in private industry were these days replicated in the semi-privatised public sector, now that the financial rewards were sufficient to act as an incentive.

She poured herself a second glass of wine. Not for the first time in recent weeks she had to fight down a growing restlessness. I'm still a young woman, she thought, a successful hardworking one, surely I deserve some relaxation? No, more than that; excitement, as a reward for my labours? She wished that some of her former colleagues lived closer: a raucous night with them in a wine bar suddenly seemed an inviting prospect. After nearly six months in Streetbridge perhaps it was time to start cultivating some social contacts?

Why is it, she wondered, that forty years of the women's movement had still not resulted in a situation where a self-confident assertive female could walk alone into a pub at night and sit at the bar or in a corner without some feelings of discomfort? One night, a few weeks after her arrival in Streetbridge, she'd walked round the town. Most pubs seemed to have metamorphosed into dens from which blared the over-amplified accompaniment to youthful revelry. The few quieter ones, with older clientele, appeared to be the haunt of regulars for whom the entry of a lone woman would cause a sudden halt to their conversation, the resulting silence being more

100

intimidating than any shouted vulgarity by a half-drunk teenager.

Swallowing her wine, she cursed. No, I'm not lonely, she told herself, just temporarily alone. But it would be nice, on occasions, to have a well-presented man in tow when the need for chivalrous company arose. She cursed again at having permitted herself such a heretical thought.

***

Heidi had dragged Kelvin to the *Waggoner*. It wasn't her sort of pub, but Kelv had been like a fish out of water in the *Eagle*, standing there amongst the gel-haired youths and the bare-midriffed girls. In any case, she'd begun to be embarrassed to be in his company: he was still in the anorak, sweater and cheap jeans that he wore to college, and had begun to attract disparaging asides from the clientele. He'd clammed up, not that it was easy to converse once the music started. He'd responded with evident relief when she suggested that they find somewhere quieter.

The *Waggoner* was indeed quiet. She pointed to a vacant table, told him to sit down, and marched to the bar, returning with two bottles of lager and one glass in deference to his requirements. She sat beside him, took a swig from her bottle and immediately launched into an interrogation. Where was he brought up? What did his parents do? Why did he chose to study Geography 'cos it was, like, so boring? Did he have a wicked time at Uni? Did he have lots of girls there? What sort of music did he like? Did he go to clubs? Had he taken E? Or weed perhaps? What did he do every evening?

Kelvin began a hesitant response and revealed that he was raised in Henley-on-Thames, that his father was a vicar, that Geography was his best subject at school and that he found it interesting, that he enjoyed studying at university but he didn't really enjoy the social life apart from walking trips with the Geography Society, and that no (blushing) he had never really had a steady girl friend though he had taken a few to the cinema, that he wasn't at all musical and had never really liked dancing so he'd not gone to clubs, and did she mean Ecstasy? No, he didn't mix in those sorts of circles, though he had tried marijuana once because one of his geography friends was a bit wild and had acquired some, but it didn't do anything for him because he didn't smoke and inhaling made him cough, and now most evenings he spent preparing and marking because he was finding teaching quite demanding.

Heidi looked at him expectantly. Kelvin evidently remembered his manners, and asked her about her history. This was the chance for which she'd been waiting. She launched into a lurid and only slightly exaggerated account of the wild times that she'd enjoyed since the age of sixteen, sparing him no details and watching with ill-disguised amusement as his reactions progressed from mild discomfort through distinct unease to wide-eyed horror. She ended with 'Life's for living, Kelv; like, I think our generation's gonna cop it through terrorists or global warming. You don't want to die a virgin, do you? You *are* a virgin, aren't you Kelv?'

He looked so miserable that she felt a momentary twinge of pity and decided she'd probably gone too far.

'How about another drink then?' she said.

As he went to the bar she decided to revise her strategy: there was no point in reducing the poor little geek to abject silence if there was no-one else around to talk to. When he returned with the drinks she began to chat about their colleagues, but even this proved to be unsatisfactory. Kelvin was one of those who were determined to see the best in everyone and was unresponsive to her witty put-downs. He introduced the topic of the Principal's memorandum and the varied reactions of the staff to it. Heidi said that so long as Marcia didn't object to miniskirts the edict wouldn't affect her 'cos she didn't smoke, didn't visit the pub at lunchtime and didn't swear at the students 'cos most of her classes were conducted in German anyway, and, thinking about it, Marcia wouldn't object to mini-skirts because *she* wore them well short herself, didn't she, she had a good pair of legs on her for an oldie.

'Mike Carter seems really upset by it, though,' said Kelvin. 'He's a strange fellow, isn't he? He's obviously very intelligent, and by all accounts he's a good teacher. I don't really understand his objections to what the Principal wants.'

'Oh, Mike's quite a guy,' said Heidi. 'I reckon he was a real cool dude when he was younger. I'm not one for the wrinklies, but Mike's got something about him.' She paused. 'Pity he's getting past it'.

'What do you mean, past it?'

Heidi hesitated for a moment.

'Can you be cool and keep a secret, Kelvin?'

'Yes, of course.'

'You remember the piss-up when classes ended at the end of last term? You were there, weren't you, in the *Blue Boar?*

'Yes, but I only stayed for an hour.'

'You should have stayed on: it got interesting. Mike came and sat with me and we both got rat-arsed, and towards the end when most people had left we started, like, snogging.'

'With Mike Carter?' Kelvin looked horrified. 'But he's *old*!'

'But he's still quite fanciable. He's got a good body on him. Anyway, we were snogging, sort of secret, like, don't think any of the others saw, and Rhod was at the bar, but when Rhod came back Mike stopped and was like – 'let's get out of here,' and I was like – 'ok, I've got some booze in my flat,' so we went back and, like, started getting down to it.'

Kelvin's mouth opened and remained agape.

'He started off great, knows all the tricks, but when it came to the point he couldn't get it up! I was well pissed off 'cos he'd really got me up for it. He was really upset, kept saying it had never happened to him before, but that's what all you guys say when you get the droops, don't you?'

This was a question to which Kelvin evidently had no answer. He swallowed. 'Have you and Mike been out, I mean, been together, since then?'

'No way! He's scarcely been able to look me in the face after that night. Pity really, he can be good fun once he stops talking about what things were like when he was young. I mean, all we hear about from the wrinklies is how good the 60s were. Mike goes on about it a bit, but he can be well funny if you get him talking about other things. He can even make politics sound interesting.'

'But do you want to, um, have a relationship with him?'

'It was just a fun-fuck, Kelv, or would have been if he'd have made it. It's no big deal.'

***

Walking back to her car, clutching Rhodri's arm, Christine was subdued. Rhodri also was in no mood to talk, resenting the fact that his evening's drinking had been curtailed. At least this woman had ceased her inane chatter, he thought; perhaps she's having second thoughts; wouldn't bother me too much if she has. Perhaps a quick kiss goodnight when we reach her car would give her the message?

It was not to be. Christine asked if there was a parking space outside his house and if it was safe to leave her car there overnight, and such was his annoyance at the inference of her question that he passed by the opportunity to reply in the negative, finding himself in the passenger seat and being driven at some speed towards Waldron Street.

'In a hurry are you?' he enquired mildly.

Christine replied archly that she believed in striking while the iron was hot, to which Rhodri responded with a groan of anguish.

'You're not having second thoughts, are you?' she asked.

'Just so long as there are no clichés during intercourse.'

'Whatever do you mean?'

'Oh never mind. Look, park in that space, see?'

They entered the house. Rhodri blinked in surprise when the light revealed moderately tidy rooms, and he remembered with a surge of pleasure Megan's imminent arrival. It also saved him the bother of having to make excuses to Christine for its usual squalor.

'Shall we go straight up, then?' he said.

'I'd like a coffee first. Anyway, we've not really spoken much; you were with your pool-playing friend all evening. We've got lots to talk about.'

Rhodri reluctantly busied himself with kettle and mugs, Christine hovering round him as he did so.

'Why is that woman Lisa so objectionable? She was very rude to me and I can't think what I did to offend her.'

'Oh, Lisa's neurotic; don't worry about her. She's got problems.'

106

'Her husband – is it her husband? Stu? He doesn't seem very nice either. And they don't seem to like each other very much.'

'They have histories, bach. When you get to our age you'll have one too.'

'And that man Mike Carter; he's an odd one isn't he?'

'Rush to judgement, don't you?' retorted Rhodri. 'Mike and I have been colleagues for years. He's all right. Let's go through to the sitting room.'

Christine took her mug and cosied up to Rhodri on the settee. 'But he was trying to chat me up, you know. He can't be much of a friend if he tries to take your girl.'

'You're not my girl. He was just being friendly.'

'But he knew you were with me. And he has a partner doesn't he? Lisa was going on about her, someone called Fiona. She said she went to the local snob school; did she mean a private school? Mike Carter doesn't seem the sort to live with a type like that.'

'I think Fi went to the local Direct Grant Grammar.'

Christine sat upright.

'Then she went to the same school as me. How old is she?'

'Fiona? Mid thirties I think.'

'What's her surname?'

'Lewis. But she was married; still is, I think: that would be her ex-husband's name.'

'What does she look like?'

107

'She's very sexy if you must know. Blonde hair, tallish, long legs, nice neat bum, good breasts. Talks with a bit of a plum in her mouth, but that adds to her charm somehow.'

'Fiona Smythe! Yes, it must be her! She was in the sixth form when I joined as a first year. She lived in Wenford.'

'Yes, I think Mike *has* said her mother lives there.'

'Well, well; Fiona Stuck-up Smythe. Living with a college lecturer.'

'What's wrong with that?'

'Oh, nothing of course, Rhodri. It's just that Fiona was part of the sports-car set even when she was at school, she used to go out with Hooray Henries. She really fancied herself, but she failed all her A levels. After she left school I think she moved to London, I never saw her again after that, though I seem to remember one of my friends saying she came back here and got married. I bet she married one of the county set.'

'Look, are we going to sit here all night gossiping? Do you want a cuddle or not?'

Christine giggled. 'Am I getting you excited? Do you want to go upstairs now, then?'

'Yes, let's go.' He pulled her to her feet and led her towards the stairs.

Christine would normally have put on a show of pretend-resistance, but her mind was still digesting the possible re-emergence of the hated Fiona into her life. As Rhodri began to undress her she was

108

still considering the interesting possibilities that this might hold.

Wednesday daytime

Sylvia was relieved to see that Marcia hadn't yet arrived. She liked to be at her desk at least ten minutes before the arrival of the Principal, to open the post, bin the junk and leave the substantive items in a neat pile on her boss's desk, having first scan-read them in an attempt to guess what responses might be forthcoming. She was finding it hard to reconcile herself to Marcia's methods of working.

In Jefferson's day it had been predictable and simple. He was a sweetie. She had enjoyed a close but professional relationship with him and was saddened when he'd retired on grounds of ill health in 1984, having made her first six years as a Principal's secretary tolerable to the point of enjoyment.

She had been less enamoured of his successor, Sparrow, but he spent his time mainly on external matters, leaving her to deal with the administrative requirements of the day-to-day running of the college. This suited Sylvia: her talents were much more suited to administration than mere shorthand-typing, and during this period she won the respect of staff at all levels for her efficiency and expertise. Sparrow developed a high profile in the world of FE and served on numerous committees and working parties, as a consequence spending less and less time at the College until, to no-one's surprise, he left, having secured the post of principal in one of the largest colleges in the region.

Now, at the age of 55, Sylvia found herself for the first time in her life working for a female, and one much younger than herself. She was finding it hard to adapt to Marcia's style. While she was pleased that a woman should have reached the top of the pile, she was unimpressed by the short skirts, disquieted by the click-clack of stiletto heels along the corridors, discomforted by the proximity of cantilevered breasts under the tailored jackets and disturbed by the wafts of expensive perfume that followed Marcia on her tours of inspection of her empire. An attractive woman herself, Sylvia's style was nevertheless understated. This had not seemed to bother her male bosses, and had in fact served to render her the more attractive to many of the junior staff. In her early days there had been no shortage of offers, but, happily married as she was, she had, with one exception that she sometimes regretted, laughingly brushed them aside.

Initially Marcia had made no comment on her secretary's appearance, but Sylvia more than once had found herself being looked over with mild disapproval. After two months in post Marcia had called her into her office, complimented her on her work and said that as she, Marcia, now had the title of Chief Executive it would be appropriate for Sylvia to be dignified with the title of Personal Assistant, and, with the small increase in salary that she could bestow to accompany that title, perhaps Sylvia might consider modifying her dress in accordance with her new status?

Sylvia had almost told her to get stuffed there and then, but her husband was nearing retirement and she was in no position to sacrifice her salary. She'd swallowed her pride, made a few minor modifications to her dress, and resolved to demonstrate through her efficiency and expertise that Marcia had a lot to learn about being in charge of an educational establishment.

She turned her attention to the post, sorting it into external and internal correspondence. Today there were only three items of internal post. There was a handwritten note from Colin Ward, Programme Leader for Creative Arts, apologising in advance for his absence at the next PL's meeting; he would be attending an external examiners' conference. Next was a request from Karen asking permission to close the refectory an hour early the following Friday so that she could complete her Safety Audit. Fat chance, thought Sylvia, she'll be told to do it after normal closing time.

The third item was contained in a brown envelope, slightly crumpled, on which was written in red biro 'The Boss'. Sylvia ripped it open, recognising instantly the memorandum sent out to all staff on the first day of term, a memorandum that Marcia had insisted she type out word for word from her handwritten original. The paper was even more crumpled than the envelope and was disfigured by a large brown stain: it was scrawled over in the same red biro, not easy to decipher, but the capital letters at the bottom proclaimed clearly – *'Meaningless semi-literate management-speak. Use English next time.'*

112

'Bloody hell,' Sylvia said under her breath. A grin spread over her face as she thought of the entertaining morning that would be forthcoming; how's the bitch going to handle this, she wondered? Then through the windows she saw Marcia's BMW swinging into her Chief Executive's parking space by the front entrance. Hurriedly she collected the post, entered the inner sanctum, placed the papers on the large mahogany desk and returned to her own office, managing to turn on her PC and begin tapping at the keyboard just before Marcia swept through with her usual 'Good Morning, Sylvia'.

Sylvia sat, hugging herself in gleeful anticipation, waiting for the explosion.

Marcia was in fact in good spirits, looking forward to a day free of meetings and a lunch with the Chair of the Corporation at the *Swan* hotel. Fred Bradley was the managing director of a small local engineering company, a self-made man in late middle age and unused, it was evident, to dealing with female executives. She wasn't ashamed to flirt mildly with him, having found that it had the effect of making him more ready to go along with her suggestions about the governance of the college. She had dressed with special care this morning. She knew by now that Fred, a man of the old school, appreciated a hint of breast but was distracted by too much leg, so her skirt was less brief than usual, but the white shirt under the tailored jacket had sufficient buttons undone to maintain his interest without inducing palpitations.

She hung the jacket carefully over a hanger, smoothed down her skirt, and sat down at her desk.

It was her practice to read the mail before calling on Sylvia to bring her the first cup of coffee of the day. She read the memo from Colin Ward, writing 'OK' on it while thinking that he'd have less time to devote to his examiners meetings after his precious Creative Arts area had been subsumed into a larger faculty resulting in his having to take on a full teaching timetable. She glanced at Karen's request and mentally began to compose a response that was exactly as Sylvia had predicted. Half way through, her attention was diverted by the red ink on the remaining paper in front of her.

She snatched it up, read the capitalised enjoinder at the bottom and felt her guts turn. What the hell was this? She began reading the annotations; *Cliché! Split infinitive! Plural pronoun referring to singular noun! Clumsy!* Her dark brows met in a ferocious scowl, her ample breast heaved as she began to hyperventilate with rage, and under her breath she swore ferociously, dredging up all the words of her Essex adolescence. The bastard! The impertinent little prick! Who the fuck did he think he was? The little shit deserves instant dismissal! It's bound to be one of those hippies from Humanities: the whole rats' nest needs clearing out. That ineffective little pillock Adrian Haver has no control over them.

Shaking with fury she jabbed at her phone. 'Sylvia! In here, please. No, I don't want coffee.

Just get in here.' *Mistake*, she thought: *Should calm down first.*

Sylvia entered, her features an expression of alert neutrality. She was not invited to sit down. 'Are you alright, Marcia?'

'All right? Yes of course.'

'It's just that you look a bit flushed.'

'Nonsense.' Marcia's voice was pitched higher than usual, and shook slightly.

'You can get some very good tablets for them, you know. They did wonders for me: would you like me to - '

'What on earth are you talking about, Sylvia?'

'Hot flushes, of course. Had them for long, have you? You're of an age.'

Marcia fought down the urge to scream abuse at the presumptuous bitch, swallowed, took a deep breath, remembered that she should keep her voice low, and said, 'I didn't call you in to discuss my health, Sylvia. Have you kept the envelopes that today's mail came in?'

'Envelopes? Well, no; I've binned them.'

'Well, would you delve into your wastepaper basket please and retrieve them?'

'What, all of them?'

'Yes, all of them. Could you do that now please, and bring them in along with my coffee?'

Sylvia stood still for long enough for it to verge on impertinence before she turned and went back to her outer office.

Marcia, pleased that she'd not only found a way of gaining time alone in which to recover, but also to have given Sylvia a task that was both germane

115

and demeaning, sat back to consider her possible course of action. It was gross misconduct on somebody's part of course, and gross misconduct would lead to instant dismissal, after the required disciplinary hearing, of course.

She began to read again the annotated memorandum, and as she did a feeling of unease began to undermine her determination to exact retribution. Was her English really that bad? After all, the memo said what she'd wanted it to say; she thought she'd expressed herself very clearly. Then she thought of the document being produced as evidence at the disciplinary hearing. Oh God, she could imagine the field day that the union rep might have with it, and then reports of the proceedings would spread round the College. But in any case, the matter of the annotated memo could well be the focus of staff room gossip long before it came to the hearing.

Shit! She banged the table in frustration, just as Sylvia entered with the pile of opened envelopes. 'Thank you, Sylvia. Just put them there. You haven't forgotten the coffee?'

'It's percolating. It'll be with you in a minute. Is there anything I can help you with in the meantime?'

'No.'

Sylvia turned and left, this time without hesitation.

Marcia rifled through the envelopes, almost instantly finding the offending article. It did not of course tell her anything further. How best to deal with this? It occurred to her that it was possible that currently the only people who might be aware of the document might be just herself and the miscreant – oh, and Sylvia of course. Damn. She was going to have to ensure that Sylvia remained discreet. No reason to assume she wouldn't be of course: both her predecessors had sung Sylvia's praises when it came to confidentiality. But there was a slight edge to their relationship: sometimes she felt that Sylvia viewed her with something less than the respect demanded of her office. The request that she dress somewhat more smartly had been complied with to such a minimal degree that it verged on the insubordinate. Best to make sure she was onside. She buzzed her.

'Sylvia, when you bring my coffee, bring one in for yourself, will you?'

Sylvia entered with her shorthand notebook and pen balanced on the tray that held the coffee pot and Marcia's bone-china cup and saucer.

'I've already had my coffee. I prefer instant.'

'As you wish. Sylvia, I've decided that it's not necessary for me to dictate responses to every item of mail. I'm aware that you are more than capable of drafting letters and memos so long as I indicate what I have in mind. Does that suit you?'

'That's fine by me. In fact you could leave much of the day-to-day stuff for me to deal with on my own initiative. I *have* acquired quite a bit of know-how in the past 25 years you know. Mr Sparrow used to -'

117

'I'm not Mr Sparrow, Sylvia, but I hear what you're saying. We'll take it stage by stage, shall we? OK, let's start with the external stuff.'

As she went through the assorted circulars, briefing documents, statements of policy, magazines, journals of professional bodies and even the occasional letter, Marcia was true to her promise, only once starting to dictate before noticing that Sylvia was merely making the odd note in longhand. She turned at last to the internal mail.

'Email Colin Ward and tell him it's ok for him to miss the PL's meeting; email Karen and tell her that I expect Safety Audits to be completed without any detriment to the service we provide and that no, she can't close the refectory early'

There was a pause. Marcia glanced at the one remaining item in front of her: she picked up the offending document, waved it in front of Sylvia and said, 'I take it you've seen this?'

'Well, I opened it, of course.'

'Yes, yes, but did you read it, Sylvia?'

'It was the memo you sent out to all staff, wasn't it, so yes, of course I've read it.'

Marcia fought back the urge to tell her not to be deliberately obtuse.

'No, did you read what was written in red ink?'

'I couldn't help seeing what was written at the end, but I didn't read the rest of it.'

'What do you think of what you *did* read?'

'It wasn't very polite, was it?'

'That's an understatement, Sylvia. However, I don't want to make a mountain out... I don't want

118

to give this a high profile, so I'd like you to forget you ever saw it.'

'Forget? What do you mean?'

'I mean that this incident should remain absolutely confidential between the two of us; I don't want anyone else to know about it until I've decided my course of action. I can trust you on this, can't I?'

Sylvia placed her pen and notebook slowly and deliberately on the desk and was silent for a moment before speaking.

'Ms Martell, I strongly resent your implication that I would ever behave in any way other than professionally, No, wait,' (as Marcia began to interrupt) 'Neither Mr Jefferson nor Mr Sparrow ever felt the need to question my discretion or integrity. I have been Principal's secretary in this college for over 25 years. Do you really think that a trifling incident like this is of the slightest concern to me, and even if it were, that I'd let any inkling of what's been written pass outside this office? What do you take me for? How dare you presume to ask whether you can trust me?'

Marcia was left reeling from this onslaught, the longest speech she'd ever heard her secretary deliver. She knew that Sylvia was good with words on paper, but she'd just demonstrated an unusual verbal fluency. Normally her delivery was rapid and slightly mumbled, but on this occasion she seemed to have acquired a cut-glass accent, her declamation enunciated slowly, deliberately and clearly. Perhaps she had underestimated her; even as she sat groping for a response she resolved to

119

examine Sylvia's curriculum vitae to find exactly what sort of background she had. In the meantime, a tactical withdrawal was called for.

'Sylvia, I'm sorry if I offended you. It wasn't my intention, I assure you. I think maybe you misinterpreted what I said.'

'You asked me to keep the matter confidential and then asked if you could trust me. Seems pretty clear to me what you meant.'

'Perhaps I expressed myself badly.'

'Perhaps you did.'

'OK, let's forget it for the moment, shall we? I think we've finished with the mail haven't we?'

Sylvia got up, picked up the tray with its lipstick-smeared cup and moved to the door.

'Oh, just one thing, Sylvia.'

'Yes?'

'Did you by any chance recognise the handwriting on the memo?'

'Sorry, can't help you there.'

As the door closed, Marcia sat back in her executive chair and sighed deeply. The day, once so promising, had been spoiled for her. Even the prospect of lunch with Fred no longer held an appeal. There was so much important work to do; the reorganisation, the Corporation meeting, the forthcoming OFSTED inspection, but she knew she could not give these her full attention until she'd found who the culprit was and had decided how to deal with him. Or perhaps it was a her? Lurking beneath these concerns her old self-doubts began to stir.

***

One door down the carpeted corridor of the management suite, Lucas Harper sat at his desk, brows furrowed, rubbing his palms together in the gesture that had led to his being christened 'Uriah' by the literati of the college. A spreadsheet of projected expenditure on salaries was displayed on his PC and there was a list of staff in each Programme Area on the paper on his desk. He was ready to begin.

Not quite, though. He needed to be sure that he would be free of interruptions. He phoned Joy, the secretary whom he shared with Paul Tasker, and directed her to block all phone calls, except those from the Principal of course. He then opened a desk drawer, retrieved a 'Do Not Disturb' sign, and blu-tacked it neatly to the outside of his door.

He returned to his desk and gave thought once more to the hurried telephone instructions that Marcia had given him after yesterday's SMT meeting. 'Five Faculties are what we want, Lucas. They should be of similar size in terms of staff and student numbers. Try to make as big a saving in salaries as possible. You might also think about the dead wood that we can dispense with. Oh, and we should reward the income-generators.'

He approached the exercise with relish. This was what he'd enjoyed so much when he'd been Finance Director at Marville-Grentham plc in Birmingham. He'd proved to be an asset to the company, or at least to the managing director and the shareholders. He hadn't cared that he'd been known as 'Hatchet' Harper, hadn't been concerned about the animus of the junior managers, hadn't given a toss for the trade unionists. Efficiency, effectiveness, profit: that was all that mattered in business. His future had seemed assured until that cow in the personnel department had made that complaint about him. The MD had promised him an excellent reference, saying that he couldn't afford the adverse publicity of an industrial tribunal, and that it would be better if Lucas took his talents elsewhere. Jobs weren't easy to find in the recession of the early nineties, and he'd resorted to the public sector with much reluctance, but at that time there was a demand in Further Education for finance experts and he landed his present post with ease. To his surprise he found the job enjoyable. He'd been able to blind his senior colleagues in the college with his financial expertise, and Sparrow had soon come to depend on him, though remaining reluctant to take the more drastic measures to economise that Lucas had advised.

He'd been very apprehensive when Marcia had been appointed, not being comfortable with women and never having had one as his superior. He'd soon come to realise however that in terms of management style she was his kind of person, and he'd set about making himself even more indispensable to her than he'd been to Sparrow. Now she'd given him his wings: her initial thoughts on restructuring were so sketchy as to provide him with the opportunity to devise his own blueprint for the future shape of the college.

Hickman and Jay would have to accept that on this issue, one dictated by financial imperatives, his views would have to take precedence.

He began transcribing the salaries of the Programme Leaders from the spreadsheet onto the staff lists in front of him. They were all on the management salary spine of course, but with significant differences resulting from the varying numbers of students in their Areas. The simplest solution would be to merge the smallest Programme Areas with the middle-ranking ones, but this wouldn't necessarily meet Marcia's other criteria. Who were the main income generators? Who represented the dead wood?

He began to map out the possible permutations in detail, factoring in staff salaries, student numbers, potential for income-generation, savings made by redundancies. He swivelled round to face the PC screen and was about to open a new document when he realised he needed refreshment. He keyed in his secretary's number.

'Joy, I'd like some coffee please.'

***

'Did you shag her, then?' Carter asked Rhodri, as, clutching their sandwiches obtained from the machine in the staff room, they made their way to the NATFHE meeting. 'All right, was she?'

'OK. I've had worse. She was a bit pissed off by Stu and Lisa earlier, though. Kept going on about them when we got back to my place; delayed things a bit.'

'Seeing her again, are you?'

'She's in my evening class so I'll have to, man. But if you mean more shagging, then no way. She's bad news. Neurotic I reckon.'

'Yeah, I thought she was a bit intense when I was chatting to her in the pub. Did she stay overnight?'

'Yes, unfortunately. Had a job getting rid of her this morning, as well; told me she could take the day off work and stay in the house ready for a lunchtime session.'

Carter grinned. 'Think you might have problems there, boyo.'

They entered the wired enclosure, once tennis courts, which housed ranks of temporary classrooms in one of which the Principal permitted the union to have its branch meetings. Entering the hut, they found it already half full, the furniture still arranged as for a lesson. Derek Surman was sitting at the lecturer's desk at the front with Terry Whelan, business studies lecturer and branch secretary sitting beside him. The meeting had been scheduled to start at one o'clock, but it was already ten-past, Derek as usual having forgotten that many of the staff had to collect sandwiches after their morning lectures ended.

Derek, with 35 years service under his belt and beginning to long for retirement, sat watching his colleagues file in. A rather sad, ageing, down-at-heel bunch, he thought, apart from the smattering of young recent appointees (most of the newcomers never attended Union meetings) who

124

had the fresh faces and fashionable clothes that spoke of an unwillingness to be tied down by families and crippling mortgages. The age profile of the place had certainly changed since his early days – in the early 70s there had been an influx of young entrants, recruited in haste by old Jefferson to teach liberal studies to vocational students and to service the college's burgeoning GCE provision. He remembered the hostility that had rapidly developed between the vocational and academic staff, a real clash of cultures, the vocationals being outraged by the clothes, hair-length and teaching methods of the academics, and loathing the fact that those dirty hippies were allowed to brainwash the vocational students in liberal studies lectures. The mutual mistrust had extended up to Management level, with rancorous memoranda apparently being exchanged between the Head of General Studies and his Catering and Engineering counterparts, old Jefferson trying ineffectually to keep the peace.

That seems like another lifetime, Derek mused. A lot of the animus had disappeared with the demise of liberal studies and the requirement that general studies lecturers conform to the teaching requirements of all the numerous training initiatives, each with its own arcane acronym, produced over the years by the Department of Education and various quangos. These of course would probably be replaced by yet another headline-catching government brainwave in the near future. There were still the occasional jealousies and disagreements, but those of the 70s intake who remained had grown middle-aged together. Listening to their banter as they took their seats in front of him, it struck him that the older lecturers were now bound together by an affectionate generational solidarity that crossed the vocational-academic divide: even the likes of Mike Carter and Rhodri Evans seemed to rub along well enough with the older caterers and engineers. Ironic, he thought, not just that the cultural clash was now between the old and young, but that the latter were often the new puritans who railed against the educational permissiveness of their seniors.

He was nudged by Terry. 'Better make a start, Derek: half the buggers'll have two o'clock lectures.'

Forty-five minutes later there was a vote. It was 21 in favour of the Executive's proposal to claim a modest 3% pay increase, 20 against, with one abstention. Derek's heart sank. It had been bad enough having to listen, with benign neutrality, to the rancorous, repetitive and utterly predictable arguments that had raged amongst his members. He knew what was coming next.

'Too close!' shouted Sam Garner, an Engineer. 'This calls for a ballot of all members. Lots of people couldn't be here; blimey, only 40 votes have been cast and the membership must be well over 70. You don't have a proper mandate.' Murmurs of assent.

'OK Sam, I take the point. I'll consult with the exec and we'll report back. I declare the meeting closed.' Derek hurriedly gathered his papers together and stood up, anxious to avoid any further debate.

The meeting broke up, some hurrying out to deliver their next lecture, others beginning the usual ill-tempered post mortem. Carter, Barbara and Rhodri sauntered out together.

'Pretty predictable,' observed Rhodri. 'Derek'll have to have a ballot; he'll be on a hiding to nothing otherwise. Don't know why he didn't put the issue to a ballot in the first place; would have saved him a lot of hassle. Still, I suppose he feels he has to let the windbags have a go. How d'you think the final vote will go? Carter?'

'What? Oh, I dunno. I was hoping there'd be time left over to raise the issue of Ski-slopes' memo.'

Rhodri and Barbara exchanged raised eyebrows.

'Bloody hell, Mike,' said Barbara, already half-way through the cigarette that she'd lit at the door, 'where are you at these days?'

'On my fucking own, it would seem.'

Carter turned on his heel and set off towards the administration block. As he mounted the stairs to the management suite he was nearly knocked over by Edgar Hickman, apparently deep in thought, hurrying down.

'Hey, Ed,' he said, 'What's the scene along the golden mile, then?'

A degree of empathy existed between Carter and Edgar, dating from the time when the latter had been Head of General Education, before reorganisation had resulted in his somewhat unwilling promotion to the Senior Management Team.

'Golden mile? More like Desolation Row, mate,' said Edgar before scuttling away.

Carter strode along the carpeted corridor, noting as he did the *Please Do Not Disturb* notice on Lucas Harper's door. 'Wanker,' he muttered, and on reaching Sylvia's door he knocked and walked in.

'Hi Mike,' she said, looking up from her PC screen, 'Don't often see you in this neck of the woods.'

'I try to give it a wide berth, Sylvia, even though you're up here. How're things?'

Sylvia grimaced. 'As usual.'

'You don't give much away, do you?'

'More than me life's worth, Mike. Anyway, what can I do for you?' She coloured slightly.

'I want to see the boss. I suppose I have to make an appointment?'

'Too right.' She consulted Marcia's diary. 'Looks like she's free on Thursday afternoon, but she'll want to know what it's about.'

'It's about her memo, the one to all staff. She invited people to come and discuss it with her.'

'OK, I'll pencil you in for 2.30. Assume that's ok unless I contact you.'

'Thanks Sylvie.' He turned to go.

'The best of luck, Mike. Reckon you'll need all your charm.'

He winked at her and left. Sylvie sat motionless for a moment, a slight smile on her face, before resuming her keyboarding with a sigh. It had been an incredible night, her one fall from grace, but so long ago now.

***

Shaking with an emotion she could not define, Fiona slammed down the phone. For the first time in her life she'd told her mother exactly what she thought of her, and expressed her feelings using the sort of language that Mrs Smythe loathed. Perhaps it had had the desired effect: perhaps her mother now finally understood her feelings about Simon. But the exchange of insults had left her unsettled. She couldn't face the housework, couldn't face Belinda and Charlotte, couldn't think how to occupy herself. A bath, a long hot soak, she thought, and ran up the stairs, turned on the taps, mixed in the oil and finally with a sigh of relief submerged herself in warmth. It helped a bit – her angst, if not dispelled, was dulled, rather as the treadmill thoughts of the insomniac are quietened as the sleeping pill begins to take effect.

Half an hour passed. Reluctantly she hauled herself out, grabbed a towel from the airing cupboard and vigorously scrubbed herself dry. She wiped the condensation from the mirror and peered at herself critically. She'd always been aware of, but not obsessed by, her attractiveness, and had never bothered with long titivating sessions. She'd remarked on many occasions that Mike spent more time preening himself than did she. She scrutinised her face more closely; yes, the beginnings of fine lines round the eyes, the trace of thread veins on her cheeks. She stepped back, dropped the towel and examined her naked body, turning from side to side. Not bad, but was that the beginnings of cellulite at the back of her thighs? She breathed in and pulled back her shoulders: tits still ok, she thought, thanking God that they'd always been small. Hips still narrow, bum still firm. Not much to worry about there then, but perhaps she ought to start taking pre-emptive action and join Mike in his daily exercises.

Feeling less unhappy, she dressed quickly, applied minimal make-up and brushed her hair. She pulled on her suede jacket, grabbed her bag and left the house, banging the door behind her. It was drizzling again. She walked quickly down the street, not knowing exactly what to do or where to do it, and found herself in the town centre gazing into shop windows. The clothes shops brought retail therapy to mind but she had not the means to indulge. Perhaps she ought to get a job? She'd tried a bit of agency secretarial work after moving in with Mike, but had been brought to screaming pitch by the inanities of her young colleagues and the patronising, leering chauvinism of her bosses. And the work was mind-numbingly boring.

She began to feel hungry. The thought of buying a sandwich and taking it back to the house was unappealing and a restaurant was out of the question, but a pub lunch seemed attractive. I need a treat, she thought, and an aperitif of whisky would give me the lift I need. But the *Waggoner* probably contained Mike and Rhod, assuming that they were still ignoring the Principal's memorandum. Hang on, though, hadn't Mike said something about a lunchtime Union meeting? Yes, he'd been going on about the pay-claim. Great, and it's not Monday so Stu and Geoff wouldn't be there either. She shook herself out of the slouch that she realised she'd been adopting all morning, assumed her usual erect bearing and strode towards the pub.

The *Waggoner* was in its usual winter lunchtime torpor, which suited her fine. She went to the bar, ordered her whisky and was looking at the sandwich menu when from the alcove behind the redundant chimney breast came - 'Well, well, if it isn't the delightful Fiona.'

She knew only too well who it was, bloody Stu. What the hell was he doing here? She was tempted to leave, but was prevented by the fact that the barman had proffered the whisky and was waiting for payment. Stu joined her at the bar while she was paying.

'I thought Monday was your day for lunchtime drinking,' she said evenly.

'Was hoping to see Mike and Rhod. Wanted to know how they got on last night,' this said meaningfully.

'They're at a Union meeting.'

'Oh, so you decided to slip in a few in Mike's absence, did you? Didn't know you were a secret drinker.'

'That's not one of *my* vices.'

Stu glowered. 'You're eating, I see,' he said, glancing at the menu in her hand. 'Can you bear to join me?'

The events of the day seemed to be conspiring against her. She was about to retort that she wasn't intending to eat, then realised that Stu would have a field day if she were merely to down her scotch and leave. She could imagine his gleeful recounting of the event to Mike.

'OK,' she said, 'I'm just having a quick sandwich. I'll join you in a minute.'

She ordered her sandwich and took her drink over to his table.

'Oh, this *is* cosy, isn't it? he said, ostentatiously making room for her next to him. She sat down on the chair opposite.

'How's Lisa?' she asked, 'Mike said she was in the *Woodman* with you last night.'

'Oh he told you that, did he?' He crammed the remainder of his toasted sandwich into his mouth, masticated untidily, swallowed, and, suppressing a belch, added 'Was that *all* he told you?'

Fiona said nothing, thinking what a singularly unattractive man he was. He took a swallow from his glass.

'Got home late, did he?'

'Not particularly: no, in fact he was quite early.'

'Ah, must come hard on old Mike, not being able to score like he used to.'

Fiona's ham sandwich arrived, and the process of receiving it, disentangling the knife from the paper napkin and asking for more mustard, English please, gave her the opportunity to gather her thoughts and prepare her speech. She took a sip of scotch.

'What is it with you, Stu? Why is it that you never have a pleasant word to say about anyone? Why do you always make snide hints and innuendos about everything? Why not just come out straight with what you mean? I know you don't like me because of my upbringing, but what have you got against Mike? Just because you've got problems that doesn't give you the right to make life a misery for everyone around you. Christ, no wonder Lisa hits the bottle.'

She regretted the last sentence, but was pleased with the rest, feeling remarkably calm, though she could have done with a cigarette. Stu's response was not long in coming.

'You fucking arrogant middle-class bitch.' He spat the words out with venom. 'Don't you think we haven't noticed how you always sit there aloof except when you're making disparaging remarks in that bloody finishing-school voice of yours? God, I bet Mike regrets shacking up with you; no wonder he's always on the lookout for a bit of comfort on the side. That's what he was doing last night in the pub, since you seem to want me to be explicit, with a woman much younger than you, before she left with Evans.'

He downed the rest of his beer in one gulp and started to get up.

'Well, Stu,' Fiona said calmly 'if this woman left with Rhod, why did you imply that Mike might have made it?'

'Because,' he leaned over the table and put his face close to hers, 'because, when Evans left with the young lady, your beloved Mike followed them out, and we all know what that could mean, don't we? But it looks like Evans didn't fancy sharing the spoils.'

'You're sick and disgusting Markham, and your breath smells. Don't judge others by your own beastly standards.'

Stu pulled on his coat. 'Beastly? You'd better ask Mike about that, though I don't think he'd have resort to bestiality, not yet, anyway.' He walked out.

Fiona slowly began to eat her sandwich. Her day was not getting any better.

***

The trouble with having lunch with Fred Bradley was that he clung to the old way of having a businessman's lunch; three courses, wine, coffee, and in the *Swan,* where prompt service wasn't on the menu. Sometimes the time thus spent was profitable, particularly when Marcia was able to inveigle him through flattery into support for a course of action to which she was committed but for which he had reservations. Today, however, there was no such imperative, and she had to sit and listen while, between mouthfuls and surreptitious glances at her cleavage, he gave her the benefit of years of accumulated experience of man-management. She was still distracted by the events of the morning and gave only monosyllabic responses to his assertions, such that at one point he interrupted his own flow to ask her if she was feeling all right. She'd pulled herself together then, and thereafter managed to give him three-quarters of her attention.

Over pudding he began to tell her the secret of the success of his company's staff appraisal system, saying that it had all been made so much quicker and easier by dispensing with time-wasting one-to-one appraisal meetings and replacing them with a simple form to be completed by managers on-line for electronic transfer to the personnel department, and how the system had been dreamed up by this new IT whizz-kid he'd had the foresight to appoint a couple of years ago, and didn't Marcia think this was something that might be adopted by the college?

Half way through this peroration, a way forward in dealing with the Great Annotated Memo Problem came to Marcia in a sudden flash of inspiration. It was Fred's mentioning computerised appraisal forms that ignited it.

'Yes, Chairman,' she said at the end of his speech, 'You're right. In fact I put something along these lines to the Programme Leaders last term, only it was in the context of student reports, but yes, the idea can be extended to staff appraisals. Fred, I don't wish to be rude, but I have an important meeting with one of the PLs this afternoon which I need to prepare for, so would you mind if we dispensed with coffee? I really do need to get back immediately.'

Fred looked offended. She'd never been so eager to leave his company before, but he was evidently mollified by her touching his hand and saying 'I'm always very grateful to you for your

135

advice Fred, and today's been particularly useful. Bless you. I'll contact you on Friday about the next meeting.'

Before he could reply she rose, smoothed down her skirt and walked purposefully out of the dining room, leaving him to order coffee for one and no doubt ponder on the impetuous ways of the newer generation of executives.

'Good old Fred,' Marcia said the words out loud as she pulled the BMW out of the hotel car park and headed back to the college. Impatient to act, she drove faster than was wise through the town and turned off into the college with a screech of tyres. She jerked to a halt in her reserved space, got out, slammed the door, zapped the central locking system, clacked on her high heels through the entrance foyer and mounted the stairs two at a time before remembering the need for dignity and walking at a rather more measured pace along the corridor to her office.

'Could you buzz Adrian Havers please, Sylvia? Ask him to come and see me immediately; tell him to drop anything else he's doing, and see I'm not disturbed for the rest of the afternoon. And I'd like a coffee.'

She sat waiting for Adrian. Fred's reference to computerised appraisal forms had reminded her of the time, last November, when Paul Tasker had suggested that the college adopt a single computerised student report system. Adrian had raised strenuous objections: he'd gone on at length about how in Humanities teachers needed the freedom to write about student strengths or weaknesses, and how progress in academic subjects couldn't be reduced to a system of ticking boxes. He'd urged that in his area tutors be allowed to continue hand-writing reports; in any case not many of his staff had instant access to a computer. It was Adrian's final observation that had persuaded Marcia, reluctantly, to put Paul's proposal on hold, though she had warned Adrian that as soon as more computers became available his staff would have to grasp the technological nettle.

Her phone buzzed. 'Adrian's here, Marcia.'

'Send him in, Sylvia: better make it two coffees.'

Adrian entered, looking none too pleased.

'Thanks for coming Adrian. Sorry to call you at short notice, but I think you might be pleased about what I have to say.'

'Really,' said Adrian, and it was an observation rather than a question.

'You'll remember Paul Tasker's proposal last term for the computerisation of student records? Well, I've been having second thoughts.'

'Really?' This time the word expressed mild disbelief.

'Well, I want to investigate further the advantages of *your* system before throwing out the baby... before rushing ahead with implementing a new one. But I don't have first hand knowledge of your system of student reports, and quality is an issue here, so I'd like to have a look at a representative sample of the reports produced last term.'

'In what way, representative?'

'I'd like to see ten reports written by each lecturer in your area, just to see if there's any variation in approach.'

'That's no problem. I can get them to you tomorrow.'

'Not soon enough, Adrian, I want to take them home tonight. Could I have them by five thirty please?'

'That's a bit short notice, Marcia.'

'Five thirty, I said, Adrian. That's what I require.'

'Well, if you insist.'

'I do, Adrian. You'll have them back first thing in the morning.'

After Adrian had left, before his coffee had been forthcoming, Marcia sat back and relished the prospect of an interesting evening of handwriting analysis.

Wednesday evening

Stu was still smarting from the verbal mauling that he'd received from Fiona during his lunch break. He entered his house ready for trouble should Lisa have reneged on her promise to go easy on the wine. They'd come to an agreement that she'd try to cut down on her day-time drinking in return for his taking her to the pub on the odd evening during the week rather than just on Saturday night; hence her surprise appearance in the *Woodman* the previous evening after a day of relative abstinence. Stu knew that her sobriety was unlikely to be permanent: he'd seen too many cases of alcohol dependency in his caseload to hope for that.

The kitchen was moderately tidy. There was the usual patina of grime over the work surfaces but at least there was no washing-up piled in the sink, and this boded fairly well for Lisa's level of sobriety. 'It's me,' he called unnecessarily and was rewarded by a shout of 'Hi!' from the living room. Relieved at the response, he entered the living room to find his wife sitting on the settee surrounded by glossy magazines. There was a glass and a re-corked bottle of wine on the coffee table, but the liquid level pointed to only one glass having been consumed, and on seeing that she had brushed her hair and applied some make-up he dismissed the uncharitable thought that this might be the start of the second bottle of the day. In subdued lighting she could still pass as an attractive woman: under the floating hippie-style dresses to which she had reverted her figure remained neat, hardly surprising as she ate so little, and her features were regular.

He slumped in a chair opposite her. 'Good day?' he asked.

'If you mean have I kept off the booze then yes, I suppose so. I just had one after lunch. Can we go to the pub again tonight?'

'Oh, I dunno,' he said, 'I'm shattered; let's see how I feel after we've eaten. Anyway, I've got some news for you.'

'The meal's a take-away; I'll heat it up in a minute. What's the news, then?'

'Don't heat it up yet, it's only six for God's sake.' He knew that her one thought was to get to the pub as early as possible. 'Guess who I saw in the *Waggoner* this lunchtime?'

'Oh, so you've already had a visit to the pub have you? All right for some.'

'Don't start: I had one pint; that equals your glass of wine, ok?'

'Suppose so.'

'Anyway, I was sitting there having a sandwich, when who should walk in but Lady Fiona. She ordered a scotch before she saw me. Ever seen her drink alone before? I reckoned she was about to drown her sorrows. I bet she'd had an almighty row with Mike after last night's little episode.'

The previous night, on returning from the *Woodman*, Stu and Lisa had discussed at length the incident involving Mike, Rhodri and Christine. Apart from their prurient interest in how the three might have ended their evening, it was always a relief to have third parties to discuss. Mike was

140

dangerous territory, but Stu had no qualms about introducing the topic of Fiona: they both disliked her, Stu for her youth and unattainablity, Lisa for her youth, clear skin, burnished hair, white teeth, and long smooth legs.

'Did she say anything?' Lisa asked.

'I said I expected Mike was home late last night. She said he was early, but then she would say that wouldn't she?'

'God, you asked her, did you? I bet she was pissed off about that.'

'Too right. Called me all the names under the sun in that fuckin' posh accent of hers. It obviously got to her.'

Lisa grinned at this and reached for the bottle of wine.

'Thought we agreed you'd keep off it until we go to the pub?' Stu tried to ask the question neutrally.

'You said you were too tired to go.' Lisa's voice was instantly shrill and accusatory. 'Anyway, if fucking Fiona can drink whisky at lunchtime there's no harm in me having a wine before we eat, is there?'

'Ok, ok, just make it a small one, can't you?' Stu wanted a drink himself, so could not really object. 'Pour me one while you're at it.' He went to the kitchen to fetch another glass.

Lisa poured herself a generous measure, gulped it down and was in the process of refilling her glass when Stu returned.

'There's one way we might find out what went on last night,' she said.

'How's that, then?'

'Ask Geoff. He was in the pub with them all when we arrived; he must have seen what had been going on between those three.'

'But I *did* ask him, after they'd left; don't you remember? He wasn't saying anything.'

Lisa didn't remember.

'Oh, I didn't mean ask Geoff *directly*. But he'll have told Julie all about it, won't he? You can ask her.' She took a generous gulp of wine.

'Oh, I dunno. I don't really want to involve Geoff and Julie, 'specially if Geoff doesn't want to talk.' Stu was becoming increasingly conscious that Geoff was the only person in the group that seemed to welcome his company, and he was reluctant to push him where he didn't want to go.

'Well if you're too fucking scared to ask her, I will.'

'No! Just leave well alone, can't you.'

'What are you so uptight about all of a sudden?'

'I'm not uptight. Look, let's eat. I'm bloody starving.' He wasn't, but eating might make her forget her wish to phone Julie: he'd noticed that her lapses of memory were becoming more frequent. He was beginning to regret ever having mentioned seeing Fiona.

'What *is* the take-away, anyway?'

'A Chicken Tikka Bhuna for me and I've got you a Madras as usual.'

'Well, I'll get some beer to go with it. I'll just go round to the offie while you're heating it. Look, if I get a few cans in, how about we spend the

142

evening in instead of going to the pub? Is there anything on the box?'

Lisa evidently recognised the peace offering. 'Not a lot. Ok, you go and get the beer.'

As soon as he was out of the door, she hurried to the kitchen, turned on the oven, inserted the cardboard trays of curry, then, stumbling in her haste, re-entered the living room, grabbed the phone and dialled Julie's number.

***

'How was your dad today?' Geoff asked as he took his usual stool in the kitchen to watch Julie prepare the meal.

'Okay, I suppose, but you're right, he is slowing up a bit. Usually he asks me about the business, but he didn't say a word about it today, except to say it was good to know you were running it well. Mum's quite worried about him: she says he's getting very vague and forgetful. D'you want your potatoes mashed?'

'Aye, please love.'

She busied herself around the hob. Geoff continued watching her, thinking how little, apart from the extra pounds, she'd changed in the 25 years since they'd first got together. His friends had all warned against a hasty marriage made on the rebound, but he'd never regretted it. Occasionally, when being told by Mike or Rhodri of some orgy in which they claimed to have participated, he wondered whether he'd missed out on the wild oats scene, but on returning home to

Julie he knew he'd made the right decision. Their spacious house had all the trappings of middle-class comfort that he'd once mocked when a young lecturer at the college, a comfort he'd since come to relish, especially after visits to Stuart's grimy semi or Rhodri's squalid lair. Even Mike's terrace, neat and well-ordered as it was, seemed depressingly dark and poky. Mike had mocked him mercilessly when he'd first moved to Rowley Road, saying he'd sold out to bourgeois convention, not that his views had ever prevented him from accepting Geoff's invitations to parties there.

The phone rang. Geoff answered it. 'Oh, hello Lisa.' He grimaced at Julie. 'Well, she's cooking supper at the moment. Hang on a minute.'

He put his hand over the mouthpiece. 'She wants to talk to you. Says it won't take a minute.'

'Does she sound pissed?'

'No, not pissed; a bit excited though.'

'Ok, I'll take it. Watch the spuds please babe, they're almost at the boil.'

She took the receiver. Geoff, standing over the hob, listened to her end of the conversation.

'Hi, Julie, how are... What? Sorry, didn't catch that: slow down.' Evidently a long monologue: Julie frowned as she listened. Eventually – 'I don't know anything about this, Lisa, Geoff didn't mention it.' Obviously another long monologue, during which Julie's frown deepened, then – 'I think you're jumping to conclusions... no, wait, Lisa, you can't possibly know that for a fact. And even if it did happen, what's it got to do with us?

'...Oh, rubbish. Look, I've got supper to prepare... no, for God's sake don't do that, it's none of your business... I'm not listening to any more. Bye.'

She replaced the receiver on its stand and, scowling, marched back to the hob.

'God, she's a bitch.'

'I can guess what that was about. Last night in the *Woodman*, yes?'

'That's right. I told her you'd said nothing about it to me.'

'What did she want to know? She was there, for God's sake.'

'First she wanted to know whether that woman came with Mike or with Rhod or with both. She said you might know 'cos you were there before she and Stu got there.'

'Bloody hell, I told 'em at the time that I didn't know anything about it. I never tell Stu and Lisa anything, they're such vicious buggers. When they're not tearing each other to pieces they take every chance to make trouble for someone else.'

'I don't know why you bother still seeing Stu. Anyway, Lisa's got it in her head that it was a threesome and that's why Mike left immediately after Rhod.'

'That's bollocks, I reckon. D'you want some wine?' He rummaged in the drawer for a corkscrew.

'Please. Supper'll be ready in about ten.'

Geoff poured two glasses of wine. He was beginning to find the antics of some of the *Woodman* crowd as boring as their constant moaning about life at the college. Perhaps it was

145

time to cut them adrift? He'd begun to develop a rapport with some of the fellows from the Chamber of Commerce: evenings in their company were becoming more to his taste than the adolescent behaviour of his former colleagues.

'Fuck 'em all, I say, let'em get on with it.' He passed his wife a glass.

'Cheers, darlin'. But that isn't all. Lisa says she's thinking of calling on Fi.'

'Bloody hell; why? She can't stand Fi.'

'To do some stirring of course, the malicious bitch. She's says she's going to drop into the conversation something about seeing Mike in the *Woodman* with a young woman just to see what Fi's reaction is.'

'I don't see Fi even letting her in the door, let alone having a conversation with her. They don't even acknowledge each other's presence in the pub.'

'I dunno. Fi's got manners; it's her upbringing. She'd probably be so surprised at seeing Lisa on her doorstep that she'd invite her in. I like Fi; I don't like the idea of her being upset by that cow. Don't you think we ought to warn her?'

'But you don't know for sure that Lisa's going to do it; it's probably all talk. In any case, what could you say to Fi? And if Lisa decides not to spill the beans you'll have stirred up Fi's suspicions unnecessarily. No, love, leave well alone.'

Julie drained the water from the saucepan and vigorously began mashing the potatoes. It wasn't

146

often that she and Geoff had differing perspectives on a situation. She could see the logic in his assertions, but her regard for Fiona, and her dislike of Lisa, fuelled as it had been by the telephone conversation, militated against the need for caution. She was aware that in any case Geoff's reluctance to become involved was also influenced by his distaste for anything connected with Mike's sex life.

'This is just about ready,' she said, dolloping the mash onto plates and reaching in the oven for the sausages. Despite their growing affluence Geoff retained his fondness for the good plain eating of his youth, and it was only in recent years that wine had replaced beer as an accompaniment to their meals.

'That looks grand, love,' said Geoff as he took his seat at the kitchen table. After a few mouthfuls he put down his fork. 'You do agree, don't you?' he said, 'You're not going to mention it to Fi, are you?'

Julie took an unnecessarily long time to chew and swallow her mouthful. 'I honestly don't know, babe. I'll sleep on it.'

***

Marcia spread the bulky envelopes over her kitchen table. She'd been taken aback at the size of the box containing voluminous stacks of A5 size brown envelopes presented to her by Adrian, and then had to listen while he began to explain that each envelope was unique to a particular student and contained separate reports written by each of the subject lecturers whose classes the student attended. Eventually she'd ushered him abruptly from her office and had immediately ordered Sylvia to find a caretaker to carry the box to her car.

She selected an envelope. Written on the front was *Melissa King, GCSE, Tutor A. Giddings*. She shook out the contents – six sheets of A4 paper, five headed with a subject designation, the sixth with *Personal Tutor*. On the latter, the personal tutor had added his name, 'Arthur Giddings', in neat, fussy, capital letters, but a quick glance at the other sheets revealed that most of the subject lecturers had entered comments without feeling the need to identify themselves. 'Sloppy, unprofessional bastards,' she thought.

She opened another envelope: an A-Level student this time, so only four reports. Again, no identification of the subject lecturers. A third envelope: the same. She blanched at the thought of the task ahead of her, until realising that each lecturer could be identified by his or her subject designation, though this might require reference to the staff lists, which she had stored on her lap-top. All she needed to do was to collect together a few reports for each subject and peruse the handwriting on them.

She set about opening more envelopes and piling their contents on the table, continuing with the task until she judged the pile to be big enough to contain samples of all the subjects offered in Adrian Havers' Programme Area. She bent to the task of arranging them, and soon there were 10 piles arranged on the table, representing the subjects from Humanities.

A drink now, perhaps? Yes, why not. In any case she needed to retrieve the offending memorandum from her briefcase, which she'd dumped in the hall on arrival. Returning to the kitchen she peered at the crumpled paper, at the same time pouring wine from the bottle she'd opened yesterday.

The handwriting on the memorandum was scrawled and wavery, as though written by one of advancing years, but perhaps executed with the paper on the writer's knee? The stains on the page looked suspiciously akin to beer, and she wouldn't mind betting that the deed had taken place in a pub, probably with an appreciative audience.

She decided to proceed on the basis of a process of elimination, and turned her attention to the reports. Spanish – of course, Giddings again. French – what dad would have called an 'educated' hand and signed by an E. Selby. History – unsigned; large, looped characters, written in green ink: might possibly degenerate into something like the offending scrawl if written in haste? Put them to one side for further examination. German – unsigned; childlike script, letters not joined, circles instead of dots over the *i*'s, quite a few spelling mistakes, and, oh God, a smiley emoticon at the bottom of each. English – unsigned, but a distinct possibility: scrawled, untidy, and the papers slightly creased; yes, of

149

course! It would have to be the English lecturer, why hadn't she thought of that before!

She gave a cursory glance over the remaining reports, rejecting them as being unworthy of further consideration, and returned to the prime suspect. She put the reports side by side with the memorandum and peered from one to the other. Yes, it had to be – the *m*'s were like *w*'s in both, the *r*'s were printed rather than looped. 'Gotcha!' she exclaimed out loud, and toasted herself with the wine. English, English: who was the English lecturer? A quick referral to her lap-top revealed it to be one Rhodri Evans.

Rhodri Evans. Of course. She'd picked him out at her very first staff meeting as being the scruffiest, dirtiest-looking individual in the room, and afterwards had asked Edgar Hickman to name him. At the time she'd made a mental note that he represented all that was wrong with the image of Further Education and that something would have to be done about it: indeed it was he who had been foremost in her mind when she'd written the paragraph about dress code in her memorandum.

She got up and paced the kitchen, glass of wine in hand. Though exulting in the success of her sleuthing, she now had the problem of deciding on an appropriate course of action. Such deliberation was best conducted from the comfort of her lounge, and she was moving towards it when her glance fell on the piles of paper and emptied envelopes littering the kitchen table. Ought she to go through the piles and restore each report to its rightful envelope? No, that was a secretary's job.

She retrieved the box and shovelled the documents into it. That would be a nice task with which to greet Sylvia in the morning.

***

Rhodri was engaged in a last-minute frantic tidying of his kitchen. Christine's overnight stay had not resulted in too much disturbance to the order that he'd managed to achieve after receiving Megan's letter, but she'd dallied over a substantial cooked breakfast and had not volunteered to wash up, saying that she had to get home and change before going to work. As he scoured the frying pan his thoughts alternated between the hassle that might result from his ill-advised fuck with a woman who seemed to ascribe to the event a much greater significance than he, and the pleasurable anticipation of Megan's imminent arrival. She hadn't stated a precise time but he hoped it would be early enough to take her for a drink, not to the *Woodman* of course, and then maybe to the *Bilash* for a curry afterwards. He was hoping that Mr Chowdery would relent and revoke his banning order once he saw that he was in the company of a young, well-dressed, well-spoken woman.

There was a knock at the door. Smiling broadly, he opened it, to be confronted by Christine. His smile vanished.

'Hello, Rhodri,' she said, and stared at him expectantly.

'Oh, it's you,' he said. 'Did you leave something here?'

151

'No, I thought we might get to know each other a bit more; have a drink in a quiet pub perhaps, then perhaps you'd like to come back to my place? Aren't you going to let me in?'

'Well, it's a bit inconvenient at the moment, you see -'

'You haven't got another woman in there, have you?' Her tone wavered between the coquettish and the accusatory.

'No, of course not.'

'Well, it's cold out here; you might at least invite me in to hear your explanation.'

No hint of coquettishness this time. Rhodri had a vision of Megan arriving to witness a doorstep confrontation.

'OK, just for a minute, then.'

She entered the kitchen. 'Oh my, we are tidy aren't we?' She sat on a stool. 'Well, Rhodri, what's so important that we can't spend some time together?

'Look, I've got a pile of preparation and marking to do. It's one of the drawbacks of the job. Much as I'd like to go out with you I couldn't relax knowing that all this work was here waiting for me.'

'Well, why don't I leave you to get on with it? Then after you've finished you can come round to my place.' She looked up at him from under her eyelashes. In the harsh light of the kitchen Rhodri began to reconsider his original appraisal of her as attractive; she was almost gaunt.

'Oh, I go on working till the small hours. I don't have a car, see. You wouldn't want to have to turn out to get me at two in the morning.'

She got up and moved close to him. 'What's wrong? Wasn't I any good? Don't go cool on me, please.'

Rhodri wondered what the hell he'd got himself into: in the long term there stretched before him five months of reproachful and accusatory glances in his evening class; perhaps even worse, barbed asides to her classmates. In the short term there was the prospect of an emotional scene to which Megan might be a witness; that, at all costs, must be avoided. He must get Christine out of the house.

'I'll see you tomorrow evening. It'll be much better when I'm relaxed.'

'Do you mean that, Rhodri? You're not just putting me off? Shall I come here?'

'No, let's meet in town.'

'Not the pub we went to last night, please.'

'OK. Do you know the *Falconer*?' She nodded.

'I'll see you in there at eight.'

'Are you sure? You won't stand me up, will you?'

Fucking hell, he thought; just go, woman, can't you?

'No, of course I won't.'

She lunged towards him, wrapped her arms round his neck and kissed him. 'Then you can come back to my place afterwards. I'll make it worth your while, you'll see.'

He released himself, and under the guise of an affectionate gesture put his hand on her lower back and gently ushered her to the door. 'Now I must get down to work. I'll see you tomorrow.'

She clung to him at the door and he was obliged to embrace her as a valedictory signal. When she finally walked to her car he continued to play his part by watching after her until she'd belted herself in; then, with a final wave (to which with horror he saw her respond by blowing him a kiss) he closed the door, entered the living room and sank into a chair with a sigh of relief.

He lit a cigarette and sat considering how he might manage to disentangle himself from Christine without provoking the sort of repercussions he feared might come from a woman who was so obviously a bag of neuroses. He could cope easily enough with the inevitable tears and tantrums consequent on his telling her, in effect, to piss off, but he feared for the conviviality of his evening class were it to contain a vengeful member set on disruption. Of course with luck she might leave in a fit of pique, but somehow he doubted it.

A tapping at his door jolted him out of his reverie. Springing to his feet, he stubbed out his cigarette and ran through the kitchen. He opened the door. There she was, fresh faced, wide-eyed, smiling the smile that had always melted him.

'Megan!' he exclaimed and held out his arms. She fell into them, and kissed him.

'Hello, dad!' she said.

***

'Fuckin' 'allo!' Carter called cheerily as he opened the front door, expecting Fiona's reply to come, as usual, from the kitchen. It didn't. She was sitting in the armchair, a glass of wine in her hand, smoking.

'Are you ok?' he asked, not looking at her as he threw down his duffle bag and divested himself of his coat.

'Why shouldn't I be?' Fiona's voice was level. She knew that he was always uneasy when faced with any departure from his ordered routine.

He turned to face her. 'Don't usually see you sitting here drinking before supper.'

'Didn't fancy cooking tonight.'

'Oh. What are we going to eat then?'

'Well, *you* could always cook a meal for once I suppose, but since I haven't shopped today it seems I'll be spared that pleasure. So it looks like we're off to the *Bilash* this evening, unless you'd rather go hungry of course.'

'That's fine by me. Shall we go for a drink first?'

'No. I don't like the *Woodman* early in the evening. Have a beer here if you want. I'm going to get a quick bath.' She rose and left the room without looking at him, taking her glass with her.

The walk to the *Bilash* was undertaken in silence. Mr Chowdrey, manager of the restaurant for over 30 years, greeted them cheerfully as they entered. Carter and his friends were welcome there, apart from Rhodri who was still barred from the premises following an occasion when he had expelled six pints of Bass over the floor of the gents. As Carter never tired of telling his various colleagues and partners over the years, he had seen several cohorts of waiters arrive from the sub-continent, slim, wavy-haired, fresh faced and deferential to the point of servility, only to depart after a few years, sturdier, greyer, and self-assured to the point of arrogance. Mr Chowdery, however, seemed settled for life; he had recently joined the local golf club, and Geoff had told Fiona that he was a member of the Chamber of Commerce.

Settled at their usual table by the window and having placed their order, Carter recounted the events of the NATFHE meeting, but Fiona's response was muted. As the lager and poppadoms were served he offered up the news he'd been saving.

'I've made an appointment to see Ski-slopes,' he announced, attempting unsuccessfully to break his poppadom into perfect quarters.

'Have you?' Fiona brushed the fragments away from her side of the table.

'Yeah. I decided as no-one else was prepared to take her on, I'd try to make her see reason. I'm ready for action. If I can get some concessions from her I reckon the whole college will be grateful.'

Fiona took a swallow of her lager and said nothing. Something that Rhodri had once said had made her aware that there was nothing Mike liked better than to receive accolades from his colleagues, to be the leader of the dissidents, the standard bearer of academic freedom. Rhodri had also hinted that Mike's charisma in such matters was in decline.

Carter pressed on. 'I thought you might give me some advice on how to handle it, my meeting with her, I mean.'

'Would you take my advice if I offered it?'

'Course I would. Look, what's the matter with you? I've hardly had a word out of you all evening, and now you're going all surly with me.'

'I had lunch with Stu today,' she blurted out.

'Stu? Lunch? What the fuck for?' His pint glass remained suspended in mid air.

'Oh for God's sake, it wasn't planned; he's the last person I'd make arrangements to see. I went to the *Waggoner* at lunchtime; thought I'd be by myself but bloody Stu was there.'

'What made you go to the *Waggoner*? You knew I wouldn't be there, I told you about the Union meeting.'

'I just fancied a drink and a sandwich, that's all: I am allowed in the place in your absence, I assume?'

Carter crammed the remains of the poppadom in his mouth and emptied his glass. 'Yeah, of course; was just surprised, that's all. Jesus, what did you and Markham find to talk about? You can't stand each other.'

Fiona's chewed while she considered her response. She didn't know *why* she was considering her response; she'd been thinking of little else all afternoon.

'He was telling me about last night in the *Woodman*.'

'What about it?'

'About you being with a girl.'

'Being with a girl?' Carter looked genuinely puzzled.

'Yes, with a girl, before you lost out to Rhod, apparently.'

Realisation appeared to dawn. He laughed. 'Fuckin' hell, I wasn't with that woman. Evans brought her in; she's one of his evening class students.'

'Then why did Stu say she was with you?'

'Jesus, I don't know. Oh, hang on, when Stu and Lisa came in I was chatting to her because Evans was playing pool with Geoff. What's with all this? You don't usually take any notice of anything Stu says.'

'When they left the pub, Rhod and this girl I mean, did you go after them?'

'Go after them? I *left* just after them, if that's what you mean.'

Fiona was silent. It all sounded very plausible; Mike wasn't protesting too much. She was saved from making an immediate response by the waiter removing their plates and taking their order for the main course. She was torn between letting the matter drop and investigating further. From what Mike had said it all seemed fairly innocent, but perhaps it was time to confront him with her nagging suspicions.

'Why does Stu hate you so much?' she asked.

'Don't think he dislikes me any more than he does anyone these days.'

'But why is he always making sly remarks about you? You know, sort of hinting that he knows more about you than he's prepared to say?'

'He probably makes the same remarks about everyone.'

'No, he doesn't.'

'You still haven't told me what's so significant about the time I left the pub.'

Go for it now, Fiona thought. 'Have you and Rhodri ever ... ever hunted together?'

He gazed at her evenly. 'What do you mean, hunted?'

'Christ, do I have to spell it out?'

'For fuck's sake woman, do you think I'd be able to score in the company of that ugly old sod?'

'Rhod's not without charm, you know. He knows how to talk to a woman, at least he does when he's not pissed.'

'So he's been trying to get into your knickers, has he?'

Fiona was not to be diverted.

'Stu implied that this girl was with both of you, and that you left the pub just after her and Rhodri because –'

'Shit!' Carter exploded. 'Listen. One, I'm in the pub with Geoff when Evans arrives with the girl. Two, Evans goes to play pool with Geoff so I'm left chatting to her. Three, Stu and Lisa arrive while I'm talking to her. Four, she gets so pissed off with them that she gets up and goes over to Evans, and they leave together. Five, I'm left talking to the bloody Markhams and they piss me off as well, so I leave. And six, I get home to you

159

by 9.30, had you forgotten? Oh, and point seven, Evans told me today that she stayed the night at his place.'

Carter's tirade was delivered in a crescendo that came to an abrupt halt when the waiter deposited the heating tray on the table and proceeded to light the candles. They watched the performance in silence. Carter waited till he'd returned to the kitchen before resuming, in a lower voice than before.

'So, does that satisfy you? Or perhaps you want to check out my story with Geoff? He was there all the time.'

'No. Sorry. It was just Stu that got to me. He always does.'

Even while saying this Fiona was aware that his response hadn't actually answered her original question, and that she'd once again squandered an opportunity to introduce the topic of their own relationship, to ask him what had been troubling him over recent months, to perhaps tell him of her arrangement to meet Simon in the hope that he would object to it

The waiter re-appeared, expertly balancing dishes and bowls along his forearms and was greeted with relief by both of them.

'Right then,' said Mike as he scooped rice onto his plate. 'How do you suggest I play it with Ski-slopes, then?'

Thursday morning

'Still having your fry-ups, then, dad,' Megan observed as Rhodri busied himself with eggs and sausages. 'I don't know how you manage to stay so skinny; in fact you're too thin. Wish I had that problem.'

'You've no need to worry, bach; you have a wonderful figure.'

'I have to work at it. D'you have any fruit juice, or fruit?'

'I think there's some juice in the cupboard up here – yes, here, orange, is that ok?'

'My God, dad, how old's this?' Megan peered at the carton.

'It's only been here for a few weeks,' Rhodri reassured her. 'How's your mother?'

The previous evening had been spent mainly catching up on Megan's news, and Rhiannon had not been mentioned. Since moving into Cardiff with her partner three years ago, Megan's contact with her mother had been limited. Theirs had never been an easy relationship. She had always been a daddy's girl, and the two had kept in contact after Rhodri's departure to the Midlands. When she entered adolescence, she'd begun staying with her father for week-long visits during the school holidays, Rhiannon by this time having re-married, and to a man whom Megan abhorred.

'Mum's all right, I suppose,' she said, tentatively sipping her orange juice. She took a seat at the kitchen table. 'I don't see that much of her since I've been in Cardiff. And you know I can't stand Graham – God knows what made her marry him. I took Griff to visit them once and *he* thought Graham was a prat, so it's not just me. She went for his money, I suppose. She needs it now – I reckon a boob-job will be on the cards any day. I think she's had Botox already'

Rhodri shovelled the contents of the frying pan onto a plate and joined her at the table.

'You don't want to be too hard on your mother; she had a rough time after we separated, bringing you up on her own. And you're not still blaming her for the break up, are you? You're a big girl now, Meg, you ought to know the score. These things happen. We both put it about a bit, you know.

'It's nothing to do with whose fault it was. It's just that I always got on better with you. Mum was all over me one minute, screaming at me the next. You were always the same. A bit too chilled out, at times perhaps, but always dependable.'

'Where did your generation get this 'chilled out' thing from?' Rhodri asked. 'It sounds the reverse of what I think it means. If you're chilled you must be cold, shivering even, and in that condition how can you be relaxed? 'Laid back' is far more onomatopoeic; why was that term discarded?'

'It's not been discarded, dad, you still hear it used on Radio 4, admittedly by boring old farts trying to show they're still cool, but used nevertheless. I don't suppose you have any proper coffee?'

'Only instant, as well you know. I'm too chilled out to bother with the hassle of cafeterias, or whatever you call them.'

Megan grinned. Over recent years her father had liked to play the old grouch when they were alone together. It didn't fool her. Although disquieted by his increasingly battered and unkempt appearance, she took comfort from the fact that he'd always seemed content with his lot. He seemed to have a wide circle of friends. Once she'd turned 17 her visits usually included a trip to whichever pub he was frequenting at the time where he was always surrounded by a crowd. She'd been intimidated by some of them at first, the college lecturers, but found they rarely engaged in intellectual discourse, although that guy Mike Carter sometimes tended to go on at great length about politics. She remembered first meeting Carter when she was a child, and she'd not taken to him because he ignored her totally. However, after she'd turned 14 it seemed he found it easier to chat to her, mainly about what sort of music she liked, but by that time she'd begun to be shy. Once she'd started accompanying her father to pub Carter began to single her out for his rather intense conversations, flattering at first, then rather boring, and eventually unwelcome. She'd taken to ensuring that she was never seated in a chair accessible to him, but it had taken more than that for him finally to get the message. Her dad hadn't seemed to notice anything had happened, and she'd never told him.

163

She rose to boil the kettle. 'D'you want some?' she asked, 'And where's your bread? I'll make myself some toast.'

'Please. The bread's in the wrapper in the drawer.'

'Oh, dad, not white sliced bread! This stuff'll taste like wet nappies. I'll get a proper loaf for you while you're at college.'

'There's no need, Meg, since you're not staying tonight. It's a good job I've got no lectures this afternoon otherwise I'd have seen nothing of you. Are you sure you have to go this evening?'

'Afraid so. I promised Ellen I'd be in London to stay the night. I haven't seen her for months, and I've only got a few days off. We don't all have teachers' holidays, you know.'

'OK, OK. What do you want to do this afternoon? I'll be finished by 12. We can meet in the pub for lunch and decide there.'

'Oh, I know exactly what we're going to do this afternoon, I've got it all planned out.'

'How's that, then?'

'Listen dad, I've got some news for you. Griff and I came up on the Premium Bonds last month – no, not the big one, but there's enough to be able to spend a bit of dosh without having to think about it. So we're going to do a bit of clothes shopping'

'Shopping, is it? I won't be very good company for you, Meg, I know nothing about women's clothes, see.'

'No, we're not going shopping for me, we're going for *you*. It's time I took you in hand. You look like an old tramp, d'you know? And why don't you get a decent haircut and your beard trimmed? Short hair would take years off you. And so would a pair of decent glasses. But we'll start by getting you some decent clothes.'

'No, Meg, can't let you do that.'

'Don't be so bloody stupid, dad.' Megan rarely swore, and Rhodri looked taken aback. 'I've got some money. I want to spend some on *you*, you're my father. Besides, it's getting like I'm ashamed to be with you, did you know that?'

She moved round the table, put her arm round his shoulder and her face against his cheek, despite the morsel of egg that clung to his beard. 'Come on, dad,' she implored, 'Do it for me.'

'I'll think about it,' he said. 'I've got to go now, I've got a ten o'clock. So you'll meet me in the *Waggoner* at about 12.30? No, on second thoughts, not the *Waggone*r: make it the *Swan.*'

'OK, but just for a sandwich and one drink. And that's on condition you come shopping with me. If you don't, I'll leave early for London; I mean it, dad.'

'I'll see you in the *Swan*, then,' he said. 'I'm not making any promises, mind.'

He got up and began to put on his donkey jacket.

'Aren't you going to clean your teeth?' Megan asked.

'Done them already.'

'But you've eaten since then, dad; besides, you've got egg in your beard.'

Sighing ostentatiously, he headed for the sink, then evidently remembering that she would prefer the activity to take place in the bathroom, grabbed his toothbrush and toothpaste and hurried upstairs. Emerging a few minutes later he ran down, kissed his daughter and walked out into the street.

Megan ate her toast. At least he hadn't given an outright 'no', she thought. She'd noticed that he'd been upset by her remarks, but this didn't surprise her. Even in her teens she had realised that her dad had a streak of sensitivity, try as he might to disguise it. His lack of concern for his appearance, a lovable eccentricity in his 40s, was now becoming one of his less attractive traits, not that this seemed to affect his ability to engage with women.

Megan knew little of her father's life in the town; he was evasive on the occasions when she'd tried to draw him out. In the pub his friends made occasional references to his capacity for drink, and hints about lechery, the latter hastily turned into a joke when they remembered his daughter was sitting with them. She assumed he had a sex life, but preferred not to think about it, distasteful as such a parental act always is to a child, but wondered why he was still evidently reluctant for her to meet any of his lovers. His house had never yielded up any evidence of female occupation, quite the reverse, given the increasing squalor in which he lived. The one room that he kept tidy and reasonably clean was the small spare bedroom which he said he used as a study: all it contained was a table, chair and a laptop computer. For some reason he'd sworn her to secrecy about the laptop and was unwilling to divulge the reason.

Whatever his social life, he needed taking in hand. He was in late middle-age. She had visions of him, once he retired, becoming a malodorous, tattered down-and-out, spending his teacher's pension on booze. And dope, of course. She'd never cared for the stuff herself, not liking the lethargy that it induced. It worried her that dope seemed such an integral part of her father's life: a hangover from his youth, she supposed. It seemed that quite a few of his circle indulged, particularly Mike Carter. She wished her dad would see less of Mike Carter.

She washed up the breakfast things, wondering how to spend the morning. He'd obviously made an effort to tidy the house in her honour; perhaps she might complete the process? He probably wouldn't even notice. Perhaps a quick going over with the hoover: she'd noticed that a superficial attempt had already been made, but the demarcation line between those parts of the carpets open to view and those half-hidden under desks and chairs was only too evident.

She pulled the ancient hoover from under the stairs and set about her task. She shifted the cardboard box that evidently served as a waste-paper basket from under her father's makeshift desk, registered that it was nearly full and made a mental note to empty it in the outside bin. But then she noticed, half hidden by screwed-up bits of paper, what was all too obviously an item of ladies

167

underwear. She lifted it out, holding it at arms length between her thumb and middle finger. A thong. A very small thong, a thong that would accommodate only very slim hips. Youthful hips. Very youthful hips. Hips even younger perhaps than hers.

Shaken, she sat down. She'd always assumed it her father's partners were women of his own age, well, slightly younger perhaps. Did women in their 40s and 50s wear thongs? Mum didn't; she needed all the support in the bum area that she could get. Some women of her age were trim, though. But somehow she had an inkling that this thong had adhered to youthful flesh. Was this why she'd never met any of dad's squeezes? The thought was disturbing. More than disturbing, upsetting. She found she was still holding the thong and threw it angrily back into the cardboard box.

***

'Just put it on the floor, Jim,' Marcia said to the caretaker, then, heartily, 'Good morning, Sylvia.'

Sylvia responded with less enthusiasm as Jim dumped the box by the side of her desk.

'Thanks, Jim. Now, Sylvia: after we've done the diary and dealt with the post I'm afraid I must ask you to put the reports in the box in their correct envelopes. It shouldn't take you too long if you get Joy or Kate in to help you.'

She swept into her inner office.

Sylvia investigated the contents of the box and swore under her breath. Trust Marcia to devise the

168

most demeaning task it was possible to ask without exceeding the list of duties on her job description. Not that a job description counted for much these days. Sylvia's, like all others in the college had been amended after Incorporation to include, at the end, the catch-all phrase *'To undertake such other reasonable duties that may from time to time be required.'* She considered Marcia's suggestion that she ask Joy or Kate to help her, but rejected the idea. She was a clever bitch, Marcia, in a cunning, streetwise sort of way. She knew that there was no way she, Sylvia, would reveal to her colleagues the demeaning nature of the task she'd been given.

The intercom buzzed. Marcia's voice crackled round the room. 'Time for coffee and the diary, if you wouldn't mind, Sylvia.'

Sylvia began the preparations for the meeting, wondering what had happened to make the cow so bloody cheerful.

Marcia was still rejoicing at the success of her detective work, but had decided not to rush into any decision about what action to take. She was due to have a meeting later that morning with a member of the local Chamber of Commerce: he was a recently appointed member of the Corporation, and had hinted that there might be a place for her in the Chamber given that the college could now claim to be operating as a business. This had excited her: quite apart from the networking opportunities that membership might bring, she had hopes for the opportunity to mix socially with managers in the private sector in whose company she might be less constrained by the dictates of political correctness and the need to demonstrate her academic credentials.

Sylvia entered with coffee, post and diary. The coffee was not to be shared today: Marcia was brisk with the post and Sylvia showed no inclination to engage in unnecessary conversation. The only addition to the diary, Sylvia advised, was a provisional appointment for a meeting with Michael Carter that afternoon.

'Michael Carter? Remind me, who is he? What does he want?'

'He's the history lecturer, in the Humanities Area. He wants to see you about your memorandum.'

Ah, the green-inked report-writer, thought Marcia. 'Does he indeed. Have I come across him before?'

'I don't know, do I?'

Marcia ignored the incivility. 'What does he look like? Please remember, Sylvia, that I've only been in post for five months: I can't be expected to have met all the staff individually.'

'Mike? Beard, glasses, collar length hair, going grey, usually wears jeans and brown leather jacket.'

Yes, of course, thought Marcia; she remembered him in the general staff meeting. Striking looking fellow despite the ageing-roué air.

'What can you tell me about him?'

'What do you mean?'

'How long has he been here? Does he have a history? Is there anything I should know?'

170

Sylvia coloured. 'He's been here for years. He's a good teacher, they say. His results are good.'

Marcia noticed the blush. Interesting. 'Well, perhaps you could get me his personal file. Set aside half an hour for the interview. Thank you, Sylvia, that will be all.'

Waiting for Sylvia to deliver the file, Marcia considered how she should handle the interview. Much would depend on what Carter had to say of course. Should she pre-empt any statement and let him know from the outset that there was to be no negotiation? She decided to adopt the reasonable approach, to listen first. She'd better have Edgar Hickman present if only as a silent witness; he was HR Director after all.

Sylvia entered and placed a folder in front of her. 'Mike Carter's file.'

'Thank you. Tell me, Sylvia, you've been here a long time; do you know Mr Carter personally?' Ah yes, another blush.

'What d'you mean, personally?' this said very defensively.

'I simply mean do you, and your husband of course, mix with Mr Carter socially? It's a small town; I imagine long-standing colleagues become friends and see each other outside work.'

Sylvia's laugh seemed a little forced. 'Absolutely not. Mike and Rhodri and that crowd aren't our sort at all; I mean, they're ok, but we don't have the same interests.'

'Rhodri?'

'Rhodri Evans. He and Mike have been friends for years. They knock about together a lot I believe, with some of the guys who used to work here, at least that's what I've been told.'

She's gabbling, thought Marcia.

'Thank you Sylvia, that's all I need trouble you with. Could you phone Edgar Hickman, let him know of my meeting with Carter and say I'd like him to be present? Oh, and I'll want coffee and biscuits, the best please, for my meeting with Mr Barnes from the Chamber of Commerce. He'll be here in about 15 minutes.'

Back in her outer office Sylvia made sure the door was closed, and keyed in the Humanities workroom. By chance, lucky chance, the phone was answered by Carter.

'Mike,' she spoke softly. 'Listen. Your meeting with Marcia's confirmed. She's got your personal file – no, hang on, don't worry. I've extracted the bit about... you know. Edgar Hickman's going to be present, though, and he knows... well, just keep your cool, won't you.'

Carter's appreciative response resulted in her third blush of the morning. She retrieved the extract from his personal file from under a pile of minutes and headed towards the shredder before realising that this task was best left until Marcia had vacated her office.

***

Lucas Harper made his usual crab-like entrance into the secretaries' office.

'Ah, Joy, how are we this morning, and you, Kate? Joy, I have a report here which needs to go to Paul, Edgar and Charles: there's no need for any amendments, just run off three copies and deliver them, it needs to get to them immediately. Return the top copy to me. It's highly confidential. Oh, and if you could bring me in a coffee.'

He sidled out.

'He's beyond,' said Kate. 'He doesn't even look you in the eye when he asks how you are. What's it all about, this report?'

'First I've heard about it,' said Joy. 'He always types his own stuff, I hardly get to see any of it except when I'm asked to duplicate it. It's always very badly laid out. They shouldn't let these managers loose on word processors.'

'Too right,' said Kate, 'but it's even worse when you have to make endless amendments to the stuff they've drafted. They know it's easy to make changes so they don't take the trouble to write properly in the first place. When it was a matter of us having to apply correcting fluid to Gestetner skins they made bloody certain their reports were well written, 'cos otherwise they had to wait an age for the corrected copies. You haven't the faintest idea what I'm talking about, have you?'

'Not really; what's a Gestetner thingy?'

'Oh, ancient history, never mind.'

Joy stood by the photocopier as it whirled into action, glancing idly at the pages as they spewed out. She picked one up to check. Her attention was caught by the word 'redundancy', and she began to read it properly.

'Hey, Kate, this looks a bit interesting. Have a look at this.'

Kate took the paper and skimmed it. 'Wow,' she said, 'looks like the wanker's got the bit between his teeth.' She rose from her chair, grabbed Joy by the waist and waltzed her round the room, singing 'There could be trouble ahead...'

Joy giggled. 'You're mental, you are. Hope I'm like you when I'm 50.'

***

As soon as he received the top copy of his report, Lucas hurried along the corridor with it, entering Sylvia's office even more obsequiously than he had Joy's, though his body language was belied by his pre-emptory demand to see the Principal if she was in. There followed a short altercation, Sylvia informing him of the imminent arrival of Mr Barnes, Lucas asserting that this matter would take only two minutes, Sylvia explaining that the Principal wished to be left undisturbed, Lucas responding that she would want to see a member of the SMT on an urgent matter. Sylvia eventually made a resigned telephone call through to Marcia. Lucas's servile posture was even more pronounced when he entered her office.

'Well, Lucas, what is it? I'm in a hurry.'

'I've finished my report on re-organisation. I thought you'd like to see it as soon as possible.'

174

'Is it the final report? Agreed with the others?

'Well, no, not yet, but I thought you'd like to have a glance at my thoughts before the others –'

'Lucas!' The voice was harsh. 'I thought I made it quite clear I want to see a draft report produced by the four of you. What's the point of me wasting my time by having to read two drafts? I've got more important things to do with my time. Go away.'

Lucas stood for a moment open mouthed. Marcia had never before spoken to him this way. Crestfallen, he turned and left.

'It must have been a very important matter, Mr Harper, given the length of the discussion in there,' Sylvia observed.

Lucas did not respond. He hurried back to his office, picked up the phone and told Joy that he expected to have had his coffee by now and what was she playing at, it was a simple enough request, and yes he *did* require the coffee before she delivered the copies of his report to the others.

***

Edgar Hickman was sifting through the Programme Leaders' reports on the progress of staff appraisals. Marcia had charged him with the task of undertaking a fundamental review of the creaking college system, with the instruction to 'pep it up, give it some balls', and to consider how the pay of staff could be linked to performance. Hence the job he was undertaking this morning, with no enthusiasm whatsoever.

175

His telephone rang. It was Sylvia: could he join the Principal at 2.30 for an interview with Michael Carter?

'Is that really a request, Sylvia? '

'You know better than that, Edgar.'

Sylvia briefed him on what the interview was about. It didn't surprise him; of all the staff in the college Mike Carter was the most likely to take issue with the Principal's proposals. The best of luck to him. Edgar had a sneaking regard for Mike, seeing in him the man that he would have liked to have been had he the guts to stand up for what he believed. It helped, of course, to be good looking, self-assured and charismatic; men with these advantages always seemed to come up smelling of roses regardless of the scrapes into which they might land, and Mike had certainly sailed close to the wind on several occasions. The last time it had come to a full disciplinary hearing. However, even Sparrow had not been immune to Mike's charm and powers of persuasion, and had imposed only a written warning, much to the anger of the aggrieved parent whose complaint had landed Mike in the dock. He wouldn't get away with it these days, thought Edgar

Sighing, he returned to the task in hand, only to be interrupted again by the entry of Joy. People tended not to knock before entering his office.

'Copy of a paper from Lucas Harper,' said Joy, placing it on his desk.

'Thanks. Hey, Joy, I'm a bit hassled at the moment: would you or Kate mind very much bringing me a cup of coffee?'

'Course not, Ed,' said Joy. 'It'll be with you as soon as I've delivered the rest of these.'

He glanced at Lucas's paper, then gave it his full attention on realising its content. He skim-read the executive summary, whistled, read it more carefully and exclaimed 'You cannot be serious!' He turned to the next section: page after page of figures, apparently an analysis of the financial implications of various options; then the conclusion, essentially a repeat of the executive summary.

For a brief moment he considered the possibility that the paper might be a joke: was Lucas engaged in some sort of self-mockery? No, the fellow was totally consumed with his own self-importance, and seemingly devoid of any sense of humour whatsoever. And also, it seemed, devoid of any sense of the educational needs of the college.

He sighed, anticipating Charles's justifiable but no doubt pompous response to the paper in the meeting to be held with Lucas the next day. Edgar was on Charles' side, of course, but wished that he would be less precious in debate: his message was always obscured by the way he chose to express it. In meetings his colleagues became irritated by the patronising tone he adopted. If only old Charles could be a bit more blokeish, Edgar thought.

On cue, Charles burst through the door. He ran his hand over his pate, a sure sign of agitation.

'Have you seen this?' he demanded, waving the offending paper. 'Harper's gone totally mad. I've never, in all my years in education, seen such

177

rubbish produced by a so-called manager. Do you know what he's proposing?'

'Yes, I've read it.'

'Listen to this. He's proposing, would you believe, a Faculty made up of Creative Arts, Hairdressing, Adult and Community, and Horticulture. And under whose leadership? Gregory Freeman! And that's not all –'

'I know, Charles; I've read it.'

'He can't be allowed to get away with it. The successful delivery of educational programmes requires the grouping together of practitioners with similar objectives, led by –'

'Hang on, hang on, mate. This isn't the final version to go to Marcia, is it? We're meeting with Lucas and Paul tomorrow to discuss it, aren't we?'

'Yes, yes. But we have to consider our tactics carefully. I've already considered this. I think our approach should be to propose a structure that has some educational validity. Lucas knows nothing about education: we should be able to persuade him to go along with what we suggest. And I think we should –'

'Just wait a minute, Charles. There might be another way.'

'What, for heaven's sake?'

Edgar considered the idea that had leapt out at him while Charles was talking. It might just possibly be worth following, even if the only benefit was to make Marcia look a fool.

Charles was impatiently drumming his fingers on the filing cabinet. 'Come on, Edgar; I've a lot to do.'

'OK Charles. You might think this is insane, but hear me out.'

Edgar gave a hurried outline of his plan, during which Charles' agitation became more pronounced. When Edgar had finished, he said 'But she'd make our lives a misery!'

'It couldn't be much more miserable than it already is,' said Edgar. 'Look, Charles, I'm 58. Two more years to do, and you've got three. What's the point of our continuing to battle away trying to restrain her when there's a simpler way of clipping her wings, and making her look an idiot at the same time?'

'But she'd try to get rid of us!'

'I doubt it. She needs us here for academic credibility.'

'I don't know. I'll have to give this some thought.' Charles looked at Edgar appraisingly. 'I didn't realise you could be so devious, Edgar.'

Edgar laughed. 'It's born of despair, mate.'

The door opened, and Joy entered with coffee.

'Oh, hi Charles,' she said. 'D'you want a coffee too?'

'Good heavens no. I have far more urgent things to do than sit around here drinking coffee.' He moved to go, but on reaching the door turned and said 'But thank you very much for the offer, Joy. It was most considerate of you.'

'What a pillock,' Joy said cheerfully as she handed Edgar his mug.

***

179

In the *Fox*, Fiona was seated at a stool by the bar. She'd decided that her best tactic was to arrive early, partly to gain the advantage secured by prior occupation of the territory, partly to calm herself with a stiff gin. She knew exactly what she had to say: she just needed to acquire the sangfroid to be able to say it clearly, concisely and firmly as early in the meeting as possible and then depart without having to endure a lunch in Simon's company.

The door opened and Simon entered. Yes, her mother was right; he had lost weight; his features were less boyish, more rumpled, but the suit, inevitably, was smart without being stylish. His sandy hair was thinning at the front and he'd soon have to dispense with the forelock.

He spotted her; a grin creased his face further; he advanced towards her eagerly.

'Fi! How good to see you! How are you darling? What can I get you?'

'Hello, Simon; I'm well, thank you: I'm ok for the moment.'

'Great, great: would you like to grab that table over there while I get a drink?'

She rapidly assessed the options: the table he'd indicated was in an alcove and threatened an unwanted degree of intimacy; on the other hand the bar staff would not be a welcome audience for the forthcoming conversation. She went over to the table and sat on a chair facing the window seat. She remembered to take deep breaths.

'Well, this is great, isn't it?' he said, placing his drink on the table. He hesitated before taking a seat opposite her. 'What do you want to eat?'

'Not yet, Simon. Let's get this conversation over with.'

Disappointment clouded his face for an instant.

'Ok, Fi. Well, how are things with you? I'm doing fine. The business has really taken off; things are going well, despite Blair. I've got staff to handle the day-to-day stuff now, treated myself to a Porsche, thinking of - '

'Yes, my mother told me all about it, and that's what I want to talk about, my mother, I mean.'

'Your ma? Why? She's ok isn't she? She seemed fine when I saw her the other day.'

'She's OK. Look, I can't stop you going to visit her if that's what you want to do, but I don't like you conspiring with her about me.'

'What d'you mean, conspiring? I always got on well with your ma, and –'

'You know what I mean. She'd like me to get back with you, and you're using her to try and put pressure on me. Simon, we're past history. It's over: it was over years ago. We ought to think about divorcing. I've got a new life and you ought to get one too. If ever I visit my mother and find you're there, I'll drive straight off again. I mean it. I'm not going to get into a nice cosy little three-way discussion.'

He toyed with his glass for a moment. 'So you're happy with your new life, are you?'

'Of course.'

'And it's all working out as you hoped, is it? Still studying are you? Thought you'd have qualified for University by now; that was the plan wasn't it? Your boyfriend helping you, is he?

181

Being the new man, doing the cooking and housework, and supporting you in all the ways you said I didn't?'

Fiona felt a deep, overwhelming urge for a cigarette. She had a pack in her bag, but daren't get them out. She hadn't smoked before meeting Mike. Simon had always hated it, though he wasn't averse to a cigar after a meal. It was her bloody mother, of course, that had told him about her abandoning her studies.

'How I live my life now is no concern of yours,' she snapped, 'I never asked any favours of you when we parted - ok, ok, I took the MG but that was the only thing, and anyway you insisted on it. I apologised enough for my behaviour at the time. I don't owe you anything, and you have no right to poke your nose into –'

A middle-aged couple sat down at the table adjacent to theirs and she became aware that her voice was raised. Simon had the hangdog demeanour that he always adopted when she'd gone on to the attack.

'Is that all then?' he said. 'Is that all you wanted to say to me?'

'Yes.'

'Well, in that case there's no point in our staying here. I suppose it's no good my offering you lunch.'

The middle-aged couple, who had not spoken to each other, exchanged raised eyebrows.

'No. I've said all I want to say. Just accept that there's no going back.' She swallowed the remains of her gin and stood up. 'Goodbye, Simon.'

She walked to the door.

Simon got to his feet and pushed his way between the two tables, ignoring the 'Well, *really*,' from the female half of the couple whose drink he'd spilled in his haste to extricate himself from the confines of the window seat. He followed Fiona out, catching her up as she reached her car.

'Fi, wait, please.'

'There's nothing more to discuss, Simon.'

'I know. I just want you to hear this.'

She opened the car door and made to get in. He grabbed her arm; she shook his hand away and sat in the driver's seat. 'You've got one minute, then.'

'I promise I won't pressure you any more. I'll even tell your ma to back off. I just want you to know this. If you should ever change your mind, no, listen, if you ever should, then I'll be there for you. It would be different. I'd let you lead your own life: you could study, go to University if you wanted. I wouldn't expect you to be the little housewife, I can afford a daily. You needn't have anything to do with my business associates if you didn't want. You could carry on seeing your new friends. Christ I wouldn't even expect you to sleep with me if you hate the idea so much. Think about it Fi, I can provide you with all the financial support you'd need, no strings attached.'

'Very altruistic of you,' said Fiona, turning on the ignition, 'and what would be in it for you?'

'Your company, of course. I miss you.'

She engaged the gear and drove off.

Thursday Afternoon

'Come on, dad,' said Megan.'My train goes at 5; we'll need a few hours to lick you into shape.'

Rhodri reluctantly drained his glass of the remainder of the one pint that he'd been allowed. He'd hoped that once he'd got his daughter into the *Swan* he'd be able to divert her from her objective, but no amount of chat about the college, her job or her mother had succeeded in distracting her.

Outside on the pavement, she stood back and looked at him thoughtfully.

'Right,' she said, 'I think the first thing is a visit to a hairdresser.'

'Why, for God's sake?' he asked. 'I thought this outing was to buy clothes.'

'You can't go into clothes shops looking like a down-and-out. I can imagine the sort of service we'll get from the assistants. I bet they can be a snooty lot in this town.'

'What sort of shops are you thinking of going to?' Rhodri was alarmed.

'Ones where we can buy something other than jeans and tee shirts. OK, where do usually get your hair cut, if you can remember that far back?'

Rhodri was at a loss. For the past fifteen years his hair had been trimmed, with varying degrees of expertise, by whichever young lady happened to be living with him at the time.

'Oh, I usually get a friend to give it a trim,' he said.

'Looks like you've been short of friends lately,' said Megan tartly. 'Come on, let's find a hairdresser.'

She set off down High Street, Rhodri following unhappily behind with her travelling bag. She turned into the new shopping precinct and stopped outside a premises from which music was blaring.

'Here you are dad; this should do.'

Rhodri peered through the darkened windows. 'But it's for women!' he protested, 'I'm not going in there.'

'It's unisex, dad. They all are these days.'

'Oh bloody hell.'

'Now listen, dad. I'm not going to embarrass you when you're in there. Go in, ask if it's necessary to make an appointment – shouldn't be, it's almost empty. When they ask you what you want, say a shampoo and trim - '

'A shampoo? What the hell for?'

'So they can blow-dry it of course.' She ignored Rhodri's groan and carried on. 'And when they come to cut it say you want it layered, about two centimetres long on top, not that you've got much on top, and tapered shorter to the neck and down the sides so it just touches the ears. Then if they ask you if you want it waxed - '

'Waxed? Waxed? That's what they used to do to moustaches!'

'It'll give body to your hair, so when they ask, say yes. Go on, go in.'

'What will you be doing?'

'Oh, I'll sit inside and read the magazines. Just to make sure you don't try and escape. Go on dad,

I'm sure you'll enjoy being attended to by a young lady.' She pushed him to the door.

They entered. Megan made straight for the armchairs by the widows and immersed herself in fashion magazines. Rhodri hovered uncertainly, bracing himself for all sorts of indignities.

Twenty minutes later, he'd begun to relax and enjoy himself. The process of having his hair washed and his scalp massaged by a young lady he found to be mildly arousing. Then, head wrapped in a towel, he'd been passed to another winsome girl to whom he gave the instructions that Megan had recommended. Her method of cutting hair seemed somewhat bizarre, but he soon surrendered to the moment. The girl seemed totally unconcerned that her breasts were pressing against his shoulders. He found himself responding to her chatter, learning that her name was Maxine, that she'd done her training at the College, that she had a steady boyfriend, that she loved her job and Gordon was a great boss, that he'd meet Gordon 'cos he'd be trimming his beard.

'Don't you do beards, then, Maxine?' he asked.

'No, I wasn't trained to do that; I used to do designer stubble but that's not so much in fashion now.'

'Pity,' he said. 'I like being seen to by you.'

A slight frown clouded her features and she didn't respond.

'I bet you do manicures, though, Maxine.'

'Manicures?' Her eyes widened. 'No, I don't, but Chantelle does. Do you want one?'

Rhodri grinned. 'No, don't worry, I was just reminded of *The Sting*.'

'*Sting*? D'you mean that old singer?'

'No, no: the film, you know, the one with Robert Redford?'

'Who's that then?'

'Oh, never mind.'

The conversation faltered and they lapsed into silence as she dried his hair, talk resuming only to discuss the business in hand – yes that's short enough for me, yes (as she held a mirror behind him) that's fine, yes, I would like a bit of wax.

'There you are then sir,' she said, 'If you'd like to wait a minute I'll see if Gordon's free to trim your beard.'

She moved rapidly away before he could thank her. He looked in the mirror, turning his head back and forth. He'd never paid much attention to his appearance, having surrendered to the ageing process when his hair had started to thin when in his 20s, a surrender that had come as something of a relief given that his early efforts to keep up with contemporary fashions had been risible in the extreme. However, he had to admit that the haircut had resulted in a distinct improvement.

A slim man, middle aged but with obvious aspirations to youth, appeared in the mirror in front of him.

'Hel-*lo*, sir, I'm Gordon. Beard trim is it? To follow the contours of your face?'

'I suppose so,' Rhodri grunted, 'I'll leave it to you.'

Gordon bent to his task, and began his own variety of customer-service chatter. When he learned that Rhodri taught English at the college he stopped and rested his hands on Rhodri's shoulders.

'Do you *really*?' he enthused, 'Well we *do* have a lot in common, Rhodri; you don't mind if I call you Rhodri, do you?'

'Suit yourself.' Rhodri shook his shoulders slightly. The action didn't have the desired effect.

'You see, I was a student at the college, oh aeons ago, that's where I learned my trade. I bet you know Mike Carter, don't you?'

'Oh yes, I know Mike Carter.'

'He taught us Liberal Studies. He was a *sweetie*, he really was.'

'I'm sure he'd be glad to know you thought that.'

'And of course I know his squeeze, the lovely Fiona; she's a regular here. Do you know Fiona?'

'Yes, I know Fiona.'

'Oh she's *so* gorgeous, so slim and sexy. If I was that way inclined I'd fancy her myself.' He giggled archly. 'I think Mike might have something to say about *that*, don't you?'

'I'm sure he would. Look, Gordon, if you don't mind, I'm in a bit of a hurry, see. Got things to do.'

'Of course, Rhodri.'

He rapidly completed operations on the beard, snipped at the eyebrows, and ran a small electric razor around the ears. Rhodri thanked him brusquely, struggled out of the gown, ignored the

188

proffered tissue paper, brushed himself down with his hand and hurried over to Megan.

'Dad, you look years younger already, you really do.'

'Right. Let's get out of here. I'll wait outside while you pay: I assume you're still insisting on paying?'

'My treat, dad, and it's worth every penny.'

Half an hour later, in *Next*, Megan had successfully persuaded him to try on and purchase a variety of crew-neck sweaters and cotton shirts, and a fleece, without incurring the protests that she was expecting. Disagreement began, however, when it came to trousers. Rhodri scrabbled amongst the piles of jeans, increasingly exasperated.

'Why are they all so baggy?' he asked. 'Where can I get a pair of Levis? They do still make them, I suppose?'

'It's called relaxed styling, dad. Everyone wears them like that now, well, men at least.'

'*This* man doesn't,' he grumped. 'I don't want to walk about with my crotch dangling between my knees. A man needs a bit of support.'

'You don't have to get them in that style – look, there are plenty here with a higher crotch. You're not going to get the sort of loin-hugging things that you've been wearing, not in here anyway. And in any case you ought to get a smart pair of chinos to go with the sweaters.'

'Why, for God's sake? I've been wearing jeans all my life.'

189

'Dad, older men look silly in tight jeans, yes, even thin men like you. When men get older something seems to happen to their waistlines – they get higher, their chests seem to disappear, so it looks like their belts are just under their armpits. Must be loss of muscle tone I suppose.'

'Well thanks very much.'

'And if your legs are thin, slim fitting jeans just serve to accentuate them. Look at Mike Carter.'

'Carter? Why do you mention him?'

'Because he's a prime example of a man clings to the dress of his youth. He doesn't realise how much better he would look if – well, I can't understand why that woman he lives with, Fiona is it? Why she doesn't take him in hand; she's a lovely looking girl and so well-dressed too, just the sort of person you'd think would influence the way he looks. I mean, he's still quite good looking, you'd have thought –'

'You seem to have given a lot of thought to Carter,' Rhodri interrupted, 'Fancy him, do you?'

'As if! Dad, give me credit for a bit of nous.'

'Need any help?' The assistant had been observing the effect that Rhodri's rummaging was having on the neatly folded stacks of jeans.

'No.' Rhodri was dismissive.

'Hang on, dad,' Megan intervened. 'Yes, perhaps you could help us. We want jeans that aren't too loose fitting and which also have a low waist. Waist 32 inches, leg 33.'

The young man eyed her appreciatively, then selected three pairs from the disordered pile. 'I think these might be to dad's liking.' There was a

190

smirk on his face to accompany the slight emphasis that he placed on the word 'dad'.

'Go and try these on then,' said Megan hurriedly, fearful of her father's response. She thrust the jeans into his hands and pushed him towards the changing room curtain. After a few moments muffled curses could be heard as Rhodri experienced the sweaty claustrophobia of robing and disrobing in a tropical temperature in a confined space. Megan dismissed the assistant, and then picked two pairs of chinos from the rail.

Rhodri emerged from the cubicle, red in the face.

'Found a pair you like?' she asked brightly.

'I've found a pair that will do,' he replied grudgingly.

'You did put your shoes back on to check whether the length was ok, I hope?'

'Oh, for God's sake!

'OK, OK. But you'll need to check the length with these.' She proffered the chinos.

'Oh, no!'

'Oh yes, dad. Come on, just for me?'

As he re-entered the cubicle she reminded him to try them with his shoes on and asked him to let her see them when they were on. A few more muffled curses later he emerged sheepishly, wearing the blue pair. Unfortunately his emergence coincided with the reappearance of the assistant, who turned to Megan and said, 'Dad looks really cool in those, doesn't he?'

'Now you look here, sonny –' Rhodri began, only to be interrupted by Megan. 'They're fine. If the stone-coloured ones are the same size we'll take both. Get 'em off, dad, while I pay.'

Muttering to himself, Rhodri made a further foray into the cubicle. Megan passed the assistant her credit card and ignored his attempts at conversation. She turned back to the cubicle, and as her father made his final exit, hissed at him, 'Save what you're going to say to him until he's finished wrapping your chinos.'

The process complete, the assistant handed the bags to Rhodri, expressing the hope that he was satisfied with his purchases. Rhodri replied mildly that the purchases were ok which was more than could be said for the vendor who was basically an over-opinionated under-educated patronising little prat who'd be advised to cross the street if ever he saw him, Rhodri, coming towards him. As the young man stood open-mouthed Megan added that he'd be advised to attend to his acne and halitosis if he wished to progress beyond his current menial position in the retail trade.

Outside, they grinned at each other.

'That wasn't so bad, was it? said Megan.

'Could do with a coffee and a fag,' Rhodri replied. 'We've got an hour before your coach; let's relax, bach.'

'Oh, I was thinking that we might look at shoes, and then –'

'No! That's it! I've done enough. Positively no more.'

Megan looked at him, and nodded. 'OK, you've done pretty well I suppose. Promise me you'll think about getting yourself some shoes though;

those dirty old suedes will look terrible with your new chinos.'

'What's good enough for Ken Clarke is good enough for me,' said Rhodri. 'Come on, let's get a coffee.'

There was another disagreement about what sort of coffee shop they should visit, Megan favouring one of the new establishments that offered selection of caffeinated beverages, her father preferring the old caff near the coach station where the only choice was instant but where it was still permitted to smoke. In the end Megan relented. She sat precariously on the edge of a grubby bench and watched her father as he walked to the serving area, nodding affably to members of the rag-bag clientele - chattering elderly women swathed in shapeless brown overcoats; silent, sad-looking old men sitting alone and staring blankly into space, and a few unkempt youths guffawing raucously in the way that unkempt youths always had. She was uncertain whether her father took a perverse pleasure in mingling with low life or whether he was genuinely unaware of his surroundings, merely seeking out that with which he was most familiar from his childhood and adolescence in the Valleys. If this was the company he chose to keep she wondered how he ever got to meet the sort of girl with the sort of figure that could wear the sort of thong that had found its way into his waste-paper basket.

He returned to the table and deposited on it two over-full mugs of a weak milky beverage before taking his seat with an old man's grunt and fishing for his cigarettes.

'So,' he said, 'I hope you're satisfied with the results of all your efforts. Hope you think it was worth all the money you've spent.'

'Yes to both. Come on now, don't pretend you're not pleased with the outcome. When are you going to start wearing your new clothes? Your young lady friends will be well impressed.'

He glanced at her sharply.

'I have friends of all ages, Meg. I don't discriminate.'

'Why do I never get to meet your lady friends, dad? I don't mean the ones in the pub, I mean the ones who shack up with you – oh yes, I know you must have some live-in partners sometimes. What is it about them you're ashamed of? Are they younger than me by any chance?'

He looked at her levelly. 'Let's just say, Meg, that the age difference between me and the few women who have chosen to keep me company is not much more than that between you and Griff.'

Megan decided it would be unwise to pursue this topic; without him ever having said as much, dad had made it obvious that Griff was not to his liking.

'So when are you going to give your new gear an outing, then? How about in the pub tonight – you are going to the pub tonight as usual, I suppose? I'd like to see the look on Mike Carter's face when he sees you.'

'There you go again; you seem to regard Carter as some sort of yardstick by which you judge my appearance. What is it with him?'

'I told you, dad. He fancies himself something rotten, but he doesn't do himself any favours by the way he dresses.'

'But you admitted he was good looking: are you sure you don't fancy him?'

'No! If you must know I don't like him, and I wish you didn't spend so much time with him.'

'Why's that then?'

'Because you always smoke dope when you're together, and it's not good –'

'No, why don't you *like* him? I know he couldn't relate to you when you were a kid, but since you grew up he's been friendly enough whenever you've seen him, hasn't he?'

'Oh, he's certainly been friendly.'

'What do you mean?'

'Corny chat up-lines, dad. It started when I was about 15. He tried to make out he was so, like, *today*, talking about music, but he had no idea what sort of stuff I liked; it was pathetic, really. Then when I started my A-Levels he tried a different tack – bloody politics! He kept going on about how he was a Marxist; I didn't know what a Marxist was and I didn't care, so he said I needed educating and that he was the man to do it.'

Rhodri snorted. 'Marxist! Carter's no more a Marxist than Tony Blair. Marxist! It's just an image he likes to portray. It probably impressed his students in the 70s, but if that was the best chat-up line he could think of then I'm not surprised he turned you off.'

Megan was silent for a moment. She'd never revealed the extent of Carter's approaches at the time: it wasn't the sort of thing a teenager broached with a father. But now, in her thirties, past embarrassment, those events might possibly be revealed; the confidence would perhaps be a means of cementing their relationship, given that both her father's current love-life and her relationship with Griff were taboo topics. She decided to risk it.

'It wasn't music or Marx that was the turn-off. He started coming on to me.'

Rhodri stared at her. 'What d'you mean? How?'

'Oh, the usual come-ons, you know, compliments about my figure, risqué remarks, brushing against my thigh –'

'Where did all this happen?'

'In the pub, of course. It was at the times when you were playing pool.'

'The bastard! How old were you when this happened?'

'Oh, about 16 or 17 I suppose.'

Rhodri did a rapid calculation – this would have been the late 1980s. Yes, Carter was a free agent then; Christ, the bastard was shagging everything that moved. The shock produced by Megan's revelation briefly erased the memory that he'd been engaged in the same pursuit himself. Megan was his daughter for God's sake, and Carter was supposed to be his friend, no, more his partner in the pursuit of pleasure. He broke into a slight sweat when he remembered that their joint endeavours had often involved girls the same age as his daughter – why had this not occurred to him at the time? Or had he been aware, but unconcerned?

'He didn't try anything, I hope?'

'He followed me out to the toilets once and tried a quick grope but I just laughed at him. Then there was one time…' She hesitated.

'Go on.' Rhodri felt a sensation of nausea. Why had she never told him this before?

'Well, it was a few months later, when we were round at his place after the pub. You went out to get some cigarettes. He tried it on again and… well, when I started fighting him off, he hit me round the face. Not hard, but enough to scare me.'

Rhodri stared at her, mouth agape.

'He apologised, of course. I think he may even have frightened himself. But ever since then he's ignored me. Haven't you noticed?'

'But… why didn't you tell me about it as soon as I got back to his place?'

'I was embarrassed, dad. And anyway you were drunk. Don't worry. It was a long time ago. I'm a big girl now.'

Rhodri was overwhelmed by self-disgust. It had never occurred to him to consider Mike's attitude to Megan, or vice-versa. And for him never to have noticed what had been going on the pub all those years ago! As Megan said, he was probably always too pissed. Then, suddenly, vying with his shame came the feeling of utter loathing for Carter.

197

He stood up. He needed to be active.

'Come on Meg, you don't want to miss your coach. You carry my shopping, I'll take your bag.'

On the way to the coach stop Megan chattered about her forthcoming long weekend in London. Rhodri's responses were monosyllabic, his thoughts elsewhere. Carter! That fucking bastard Carter!

Once at the stop she turned to him. 'Don't wait, dad; I hate protracted goodbyes.' She kissed him. 'Look after yourself. Go easy on the booze.'

He hugged her. 'Thanks for everything, Meg. Don't make it so long before you come again.'

Her farewell remark was to advise him to get a mobile phone so they could text each other.

***

Carter, in preparation for his meeting with the Principal, had not visited the *Waggoner* that lunchtime. Instead he'd remained in the staff workroom and had treated Arthur, Elizabeth, Heidi and Kelvin to a résumé of the various tactics that he could adopt, ranging from a head-on assault on her fascist tendencies to a gentle reasoned response to any opening gambit that she might deliver.

'Well, what do you lot think?' he asked eventually.

Heidi said he should play it cool, Kelvin concurred with Heidi, and Arthur listed all the options open but reached no conclusion. Elizabeth said nothing, and continued to prepare for her next lecture with studied concentration.

'What about you, then, Liz?' said Carter.

She affected surprise at being addressed. 'I beg your pardon?'

'I've got a meeting with Martell in 15 minutes, to discuss her memorandum,' he said slowly and deliberately, 'and I'm sure you're aware of that as you've been present throughout this discussion. I'd value your opinion on how I should approach the meeting, if you can possibly divert your attention from your preparation.'

Elizabeth placed her pen on her desk, slowly arranged her papers in a neat pile and turned to face him.

'It will surely be no surprise to you to learn that I hold no opinions on how you should conduct yourself in your meeting. This, as you well know, is because I concur with everything the Principal proposes in her memorandum. As your objective is, I believe, to attempt to dissuade her from pursuing this policy then it would not be in my interest, nor that of the college, to advise you in this matter. I'm sure that in any case you would not pay the slightest attention to such advice were it to be given.'

'Probably not, Liz,' said Carter mildly, 'I was asking out of purely academic interest.'

'Were you to seek my advice on how to conduct yourself *generally* I would be more than happy to oblige, though again I'm sure you'd pay no heed.'

'Try me, Liz, try me.'

'On second thoughts I believe I'd be wasting my time. The cliché about old dogs and new tricks comes to mind, though in your case perhaps old goats would be more appropriate.'

'Now you're paying me compliments, and as I have the wisdom that comes with my years, I'd like to offer *you* some advice; you're not obliged to follow it of course.'

'I doubt very much that any advice you have to give would be worth my considering, so please don't bother.' She turned back to her papers.

'It's no bother. I have a sure-fire cure for your malaise, and your malaise, in case you didn't know, is that you are a sour, embittered, uptight killjoy. I don't know what it was in your past that made you that way –'

'Now hang on a minute, Michael,' Arthur interjected, 'Let's stick to the matter under discussion, shall we? Elizabeth has every right not to –'

'This *is* the matter under discussion, now,' said Carter, 'She gives us all grief with her prissy put-downs, and she's probably after your job, Arthur.'

Elizabeth rose from her seat and began stuffing her papers in her briefcase. Kelvin looked as though he wished he were elsewhere. Heidi glanced from Carter to Elizabeth and back again with ill-disguised excitement. Arthur stood opening and closing his mouth.

Carter moved to stand between Elizabeth and the door.

'You're quite an attractive woman, Liz: you've got a good body on you. Why don't you go and get laid? You'd feel a lot better for it.'

Kelvin gasped. Heidi's eyes widened. Arthur put his hand to his face.

Elizabeth flushed deeply and there was a tremor in her voice. 'You are *disgusting*. You're not fit to be in the profession, and I hope the Principal realises it. I have nothing more to say to you. I wish to leave now; please let me pass.'

'I'm serious, Liz. I bet if you were given a good seeing to all your neuroses would disappear. And I bet you'd be good at it, too, once you've been taught a few tricks. And you'd be doing us all a favour if you were less uptight. So how about it? Oh, don't worry, I'm not offering my services.'

The expected haughty response did not materialise. Instead there was a sob. Elizabeth lowered her head, pushed past Carter and blundered towards the door, weeping as she went.

'Shit, Mike,' said Heidi, 'She's well upset; think I'd better go after her and calm her down.' She hurried out, bumping into Barbara who was extinguishing her cigarette at the door.

'What's going on?' she asked, 'I've been nearly knocked over twice, first by Miss Iceberg who looked as though she was crying, then by Heidi. What have I missed?'

'Kelv and Arthur'll tell you,' said Carter. 'I've got a date with Ski-slopes. Wish me luck.'

***

Marcia had changed her mind about having Edgar Hickman present. He couldn't be totally relied on to play by the rules of cabinet solidarity. Much

201

better to confront Carter alone, and call Hickman in at a later stage should he be needed to assist with the formalities of disciplinary procedures. Sylvia had been detailed to inform him that his presence would no longer be required.

How she handled Carter depended, of course, on what his approach would be. What sort of man was he anyway? His personal file had told her nothing. The pre-Incorporation documents had been the usual bland summary – previous posts, starting salary, one promotion to Lecturer Grade 2 back in 1977. After Incorporation – just one appraisal document, an expression of mutual appreciation between him and Havers. He'd been at the college for over 30 years – if he were that good a teacher why hadn't he moved on? OK, he'd achieved senior practitioner status, but that came to everyone in the end so long as they'd not had their hands in the till or bedded the students.

Her phone rang. 'Mike Carter's here,' Sylvia informed her.

'Tell him to wait just a minute.'

She pulled a mirror from her draw, checked her make-up and hair, placed a straight-backed chair in front of her desk, pulled her own leather executive version to the side of the desk (a compromise to ensure that she was in a position to revert to a full demonstration of her status should the meeting require it), sat in it, crossed her legs, reached for the phone and asked Sylvia to tell Carter to enter.

She remained seated as he entered; greeted him with a 'Good afternoon Mr Carter' and waved him to the chair. He sat. There was silence as they held

202

each other's gaze. She noticed for the first time the penetrating blue eyes behind his glasses. Then he gave a quick glance at her legs. She congratulated herself on scoring the first point.

'Well, Mr Carter,' she said evenly, 'you sought this meeting. I'm assuming this is in response to my memorandum. What is it that you wish to say?'

'I'd like you to clarify your proposals. The name's Mike, by the way.'

'I don't think there's anything to clarify, Mr Carter. And they're not proposals, they're a statement of policy. I assume from your presence here that you feel you are unable to comply with some or all of the new regulations.'

Carter pushed back his chair and angled it so he was facing her, stretched out his legs and folded his arms. Long legs, Marcia noticed. Tight denims. She still liked tight denims on a man, so long as he had slim hips – but not to be worn at work of course.

'Are you saying that your proposed regulations are non-negotiable?' Carter made the enquiry mildly, no hint of challenge.

'Certainly.'

'Then why bother inviting staff to come and see you if they have objections?'

'Simply so that I can point out the probable consequences of non-compliance.'

Carter stroked his beard. Marcia crossed her legs.

'Can I put something to you?' he asked.

'If you wish.'

'Would you agree that the process of education is enhanced when students respect their lecturers and can relate to them as mentors?'

'That seems reasonable.'

'My students respect me. They can relate to me. I do a good job; you've only got to look at my results. I've dressed casually for the last 30 years here. It doesn't affect my performance. I don't come into contact with anyone who'd be offended by the way I dress. At parents' evenings most of the parents dress casually themselves. If I were teaching businessmen, or out touting for custom, or even working in one of the vocational areas, I might concede that your proposals would have a certain validity. But I don't. I'm a classroom teacher, an academic. If I'm made to feel uncomfortable, and if the students feel uncomfortable with me, then it will affect my performance adversely.'

His peroration was delivered slowly and calmly.

'Do you have any more to say?' asked Marcia. She was irritated at his describing himself as an academic, discomforted by his calm mode of delivery, and uncertain what tone to adopt in response.

'I was hoping this would be a conversation, not a set-piece debate,' said Carter, and he smiled at her. White teeth, rather cruel mouth, Marcia observed.

'I thought you'd like to get everything off your chest first,' said Marcia, then, realising she'd delivered a cliché, unwittingly gave a nervous smile and passed her tongue over her lips.

Carter returned the smile.

'OK, then, I'll put my case.' He then, concisely and cogently, listed all the reasons for his disagreement with her position.

Marcia had answers to all his assertions but was still undecided how she should express them. He was an articulate man; he had charisma, no doubt he had allies. While she had no doubts about her policy, and would have no compunction in going down the road of disciplinary procedures were he to prove recalcitrant, nevertheless she would prefer to try to win him over. No compromises, of course. Why was the bastard so attractive? Play for time.

'Would you like some coffee, Michael?' She was surprised to hear herself thus addressing him.

'Please.'

She buzzed Sylvia. How to occupy the minutes it would take for the coffee to be delivered? She didn't want the substantive discussion to be interrupted by Sylvia's entry.

'I suggest we go and sit at the table,' she said. 'It's easier to handle coffee there.'

They stood up simultaneously; she caught a waft of patchouli oil. They sat at the corner of the table at right angles to each other. He briefly cast his eyes round the room, then looked at her intently.

'I believe you've been at the college for over 30 years,' said Marcia. 'No doubt you'll have seen some changes.'

'Sure have, and not all of them for the better.'

They began a halting conversation concerning the various educational initiatives to which colleges had been subjected over the years. Marcia was finding the hint of patchouli oil unnerving; there was little so evocative of the pleasures of the past as a long-forgotten scent. She was relieved when Sylvia entered with the coffee.

'Thank you, Sylvia. Have you finished re-filing those student reports?'

'Yes. I worked all through lunch.'

Marcia saw an opportunity to reach a rapprochement with her secretary while at the same time demonstrating her humanity to Carter.

'I'm sorry to have had to burden you with such a task. If you're up to date with things, why don't you take the rest of the day off?'

'Really?'

'Yes, really. Go on, you get off. The cleaners will deal with the coffee things.'

'Well, OK, thanks.' Sylvia again raised her eyebrows at Carter, and left hurriedly lest Marcia change her mind. Her munificence had come at an opportune time: Sylvia had friends coming round that evening and she'd not had the chance to visit Tesco.

'To business,' said Marcia, as she poured the coffee. 'I've heard what you've said, Mr Carter. I'm not an unreasonable woman, but I'm constrained by the need to bring professionalism to this institution. Appearances count for a lot in these competitive times. Much as I would like to seek a compromise with you, I'm unable to do so. There are others in this college, less committed than you I'm sure, who would take advantage if I was to give an inch.'

'If you *were* to give an inch.'

'I beg your pardon?'

'Oh, forget it. So you're saying I've got to comply? What happens if I don't?' Carter's tone was suddenly far more confrontational.

'I would have to take disciplinary action. But Mr Carter, think for a moment. You have only two years before retirement. Do you really wish to end your career fighting a battle you can't win? To leave on a sour note? All for the sake of having to dress more smartly?'

'It's much more than that as I've tried to explain, but you obviously weren't listening. There are matters of principle at stake –'

'Principle! Your right to smoke, to use bad language, to hob-nob with teenagers?' A sudden surge of anger at the man's effrontery swamped the fascination that he'd begun to exert. Her voice became strident. 'I can't believe I'm having this discussion with a man of your age. Isn't it about time you grew up?'

'I'm talking about academic freedom –'

'Nonsense!' The word *academic*, uttered again by Carter, infuriated her. 'You're talking about your so-called freedom to behave exactly as you wish regardless of the consequences for the institution. We can do very well without that sort of licence. No!' as Carter tried to interrupt, 'I've heard enough of this rubbish. You're an elitist, aren't you? You think because you've got some academic degree that you're somehow superior, don't you? You wouldn't survive a minute in a job outside the classroom.'

Carter stood up, tight lipped. Marcia stood as well, face stony, eyes shuttered.

'This discussion is ended, Mr Carter. You have until Monday to decide your course of action. See me then, 3pm. You will be aware of the consequences for you should you choose to maintain your ridiculous stance.'

They glared at each other. The coffee cups, still full, rested on the table between them, mute testimony to the failure of rapprochement.

'OK, then.' said Carter, almost casually. 'It's a date. I assume you'll have no objection to my being chaperoned by my Union representative? After all, I don't want to be taken advantage of, do I?'

With some effort Marcia managed to keep her voice low and calm. 'Quite frankly it's immaterial to me who you bring with you. The result of the meeting will depend on the decision only you can make. Good afternoon, Mr Carter.'

Carter left the room with a 'Seeya, Marcia'

She sat for a moment, recovering her poise and swallowed her cooling coffee. Then she picked up Carter's file from her desk and entered Sylvia's office. Good job she'd given her the afternoon off: the soundproofing between their rooms was not all that it might be, and she didn't relish the idea of Sylvia having heard her raised voice. On the other hand the room had not been left in its usual immaculate state: her secretary had obviously been in a hurry to leave.

She opened the cabinet containing the staff files and inserted Carter's into its correct position. Tuning, she brushed against a pile of paper balanced precariously on Sylvia's desk; it teetered for a second before collapsing onto the floor. Swearing under her breath, she stooped to recover the papers, and in replacing them on the desk top was alerted by a single page which had Carter's name in the heading. She snatched it up and read: *Michael Carter: notes on a meeting with the Principal, 13/02/1978*

She skim-read the paper, then re-read it, slowly, then punched the air with a 'Yes!' Suddenly, Monday's meeting with Carter was a prospect to be relished. And, she realised with glee, she had her secretary over a barrel. All this and Rhodri Evans too! Total victory seemed to be hers.

***

Carter entered the staff workroom looking pleased with himself. Arthur, Heidi and Barbara looked up expectantly as he entered. He sat at his desk, saying nothing. Barbara knew his game: he was one of those who knew that self-revelation was the antithesis of charisma: mystery enhanced attraction.

'Well?' Heidi was the first to break, 'Howd'ya get on, then?'

'Not too bad at all,' he said, 'I'm still here; think I won the first round: battle resumes on Monday.'

'Good on yer, Mike,' said Barbara. Arthur, unusually, kept his counsel.

'Think you were a bit hard on Liz, though,' said Heidi, 'She was well upset. Never seen her like that before. She's asked me round to her place this evening.'

'Are you going?'

'Yeah, well, like I think she's lonely. I've got nothing else on.'

'Don't get involved,' Carter advised. 'Her sort are like bloody leeches. Why don't you go instead, Arthur? Do her a favour; I reckon a solid, mature type like you is just what she needs. You might even score.'

Arthur pursed his lips. Heidi giggled. Barbara gave a rasping chuckle, which degenerated into a phlegmy smoker's cough.

***

Fiona, back in the house after her brief meeting with Simon, paced the room, unable to settle, and was aware that there was nothing to settle to. She felt she was drifting; where was she headed? Simon had reminded her of her former ambition to go to university, and had implied that the freedom she'd sought by leaving him had not been won. Was he right?

When she first met Mike and his friends she'd felt liberated by the prospect of new horizons, new challenges, which, through the doors that Mike had opened, might lead eventually perhaps to a higher education and then a career that might define her, identify her. She knew she was intelligent, and bitterly regretted not having gone to university when 18 – if only her parents had been less wealthy, if only she'd not become enmeshed in the County Set while a teenager. She'd been defined by her good looks, but also, she now realised, imprisoned by them; they had made her doubly privileged. Why had she settled for safe, secure, Simon? It was expediency, of course: when young, one opts for a partner who seems right at a particular point in time.

But was she now any more fulfilled, any more free, any happier? The intellectual stimulation with which Mike had seduced her when attending his evening class was now less in evidence. He still treated her to tutorials, but these were now more often tedious commentaries on the nature of college affairs than the enlightening expositions on history, politics, music, landscape, that he'd given early in their relationship.

Then there was sex, of course. Mike's mastery of bedroom techniques had reawakened her libido that had lain dormant throughout the years of Simon's unimaginative and respectful advances. Now he seemed to have a problem. At first she'd wondered whether he'd found a diversion elsewhere, but this was unlikely – he was either at work, in the pub, or sitting at home listening to music, always with the headphones on, which made her feel excluded.

The doorbell rang. She started, not being used to daytime callers. Opening the door, she was surprised and pleased to find it was Julie. Of all

Mike's circle it was Julie, only eight years her senior, cheerful, uncomplicated, native of the area, intelligent if relatively untutored, with whom she had most in common and with whom she was most likely to engage in conversation in the pub. She'd often thought of inviting her round for coffee, but Julie had her own circle of daytime girl friends, their friendship cemented by the shared experience of parenthood. Occasionally Fiona had to shake off a spasm of self-pity at having been denied the raft of experiences acquired by those who had raised children, comforting herself by the thought that she'd been spared the expense and hassle, and had the compensation of a lithe body.

Julie, who could most kindly be described as voluptuous, accepted Fiona's offer of coffee and began to chatter about Jimmy's latest squeeze who was a nice girl, and how Jimmy seemed to be really keen on her, and how it was great to see him making a go of a relationship and how she was hoping it might come to something. While talking she happily munched through the plate of chocolate biscuits that Fiona had put in front of her. Fiona was in the middle of enquiring about the health of Julie's father when she was interrupted by Julie blurting out, 'Has Lisa phoned you by any chance?'

'Lisa?' Fiona was amazed by the question. 'God no, why should she? She can't bring herself to speak to me even when we're both in a crowd. She made it quite clear ages ago that she hates my guts.'

'Oh, Lisa's like that with everyone; she's a cow, a sad cow really. Don't take it personally.'

'But why should she want to phone me?'

Julie hesitated.

'Come on, Julie, what's all this about?'

Julie toyed with her empty coffee mug.

'Well, the thing is, Lisa phoned *me* last night. She was going on about Tuesday evening in the *Woodman.*'

Fiona fast backtracked to yesterday's conversations with Stu in the *Waggoner* and with Mike in the *Bilash.* 'What about it? What *was* going on?'

Julie gave a breathy, hesitant account of the events in the *Woodman*, followed by a rather more cogent description of Lisa's phone call and how the bitch was out to make trouble, ending with a plea that she hoped Fiona didn't think she was interfering, but that she didn't want Fiona to be upset which was why she'd come round just in case Lisa might call to spread her poison.

Fiona heard her out in silence. She was relieved to hear third party confirmation of Mike's story, angered by Lisa's malice, and touched by Julie's concern for her welfare.

'I don't think you're interfering at all, Julie,' she said. 'Thanks for the warning about Lisa. In fact I already knew exactly what happened that evening because Mike told me. Fancy another coffee?'

Julie accepted the offer with alacrity. When Fiona returned from the kitchen with refilled mugs Julie began a gossipy vilification of Lisa followed by an equally censorious attack on Stu, saying that the two thoroughly deserved each other.

'Don't they just?' agreed Fiona, 'What exactly is their problem? Why are they so vindictive? Julie, you've known them all a lot longer than I have: what is it that Stu's got against Mike? I've asked Mike, but he says it's just the way Stu is.'

'Oh, it probably goes back to that time when Mike and Hilary –' Julie stopped in mid sentence.

'When Mike and Hilary what?'

'Nothing really; it was all along time ago.'

'Look, Julie, I know about this Hilary: she was a part-time lecturer at the college and Mike lived with her for a few years in the 70s, didn't he? He says very little about his past but he did tell me about her. So what has she and Mike got to do with Stu?'

'Yes, Mike lived with Hilary for a while. That was after she'd left Geoff, of course.'

'Geoff? *Geoff?*' Fiona's voice expressed total amazement. 'Hilary was with *Geoff*? Mike never told me that.'

'Oh, didn't he?' Julie said lamely. 'I don't suppose he thought it was important.'

'I bet he didn't. Come on, Julie, you've let one cat out of the bag; you've got to tell me about this Mike Hilary Stu thing. Anything that affects the way all you lot relate to each other I have a right to know about, surely? I'm part of your circle now, aren't I? Look, I fancy a proper drink – how about you?

Julie, not usually a daytime imbiber, suddenly wanted a drink very much. There was no escape from the situation into which she'd blundered. To refuse Fiona's demands would seem churlish and in any case, Julie had begun to feel sorry for this woman who, for all her vivacious attractiveness, seemed to be subject to the same indifference that was the eventual fate of all women unfortunate enough to have been seduced by Mike Carter. She could do better for herself than this, she thought, glancing round the poky room with its shabby furniture.

Fiona returned from the kitchen with glasses, a bottle of gin, half full, and a large plastic bottle of tonic. She poured them both a generous measure.

'I don't make a habit of this,' she said, 'but I think I might need it. So might you.' She sat down next to Julie on the settee. 'Come on, then, tell me all.'

'Are you sure, Fi?'

'Yes. Certain.'

'Well, I got quite friendly with Hilary before she left; you know, once I'd got together with Geoff. It was her that told me most of what happened. It all began when ...'

Thursday evening

Heidi, sitting at Elizabeth's dining table, was still a little ill at ease, despite having drunk four large glasses of wine. The pristine cleanliness and tidiness of the flat, the formality of the meal, and Elizabeth's insistence on talking incessantly about literature, art and the theatre had reduced her to giving monosyllabic responses.

She'd accepted Elizabeth's invitation, following the tearful confrontation with Carter that afternoon, in the expectation that her colleague would at last open up and reveal a little of herself. But she seemed unable to shed the armour of her professional reserve. She was even dressed formally, a tailored blouse and long black skirt. Heidi was wearing a thin low-cut top and jeans that exposed her midriff and the top of her thong.

She'd brought with her a bottle of cheap plonk, forgetting that Elizabeth didn't drink. She didn't even possess wine glasses and had, with some reluctance, provided a tumbler from which Heidi had been gulping throughout the meal. She took a large swallow and decided to take the conversational initiative in the hope that Elizabeth might eventually start chatting rather than lecturing.

'Hey, Liz,' she said, 'They're a funny lot in our workroom, aren't they? I mean, Arthur's an old woman, Kelv's a real geek, Graham's an old fart. Old Barbara's quite a laugh though, and Derek's ok when he's not going on about NATFHE, and Rhod can be a real –'

'They are certainly an eclectic collection,' said Elizabeth. 'I sometimes have a certain sympathy for Adrian Havers, though of course he's totally ineffectual as a manager.'

'Do you enjoy being at the College, Mon?'

'I quite enjoy some of the teaching –'

'No, I don't mean the teaching, I mean do you like being there, I mean, you know, being with the other lecturers.'

'I have to say that for an educational institution there's not the sort of intellectual discourse that I'd hoped I'd find.'

'I don't mean intellectual thingies. Look, a lot of the staff go out together in the evening; don't you ever fancy doing that?'

'I'm not really a social animal. And I don't think I'd find their company to my taste.'

Heidi poured herself another glass of wine. Shit, she's clamming up on me, she thought. Try another tack.

'Have you got a guy, Liz?'

Elizabeth coloured. 'No.'

'But you're quite fit, Liz. Surely you must have had plenty of offers? What about when you were at Uni?'

'I'll go and get the cheese,' said Elizabeth hastily, rising and collecting up the plates.

Left at the dining table, Heidi was seized by a suspicion about Elizabeth's possible sexual orientation. This possibility had not occurred to her before: indeed, with the self-absorption of the

217

young she'd not given Elizabeth's predilections more than a passing thought. But now, after her host's reaction to the casual question to which any young woman might reasonably be expected to give an answer, things began to fall into place – her dislike of Mike's sexual innuendos, her disparagement of male managers, her evident distaste for the mixed camaraderie of the pub, her admiration for the Principal, and perhaps, she realised with a start, the assiduous preparation that had gone into the preparation of a candlelit supper for two. The evening suddenly had possibilities, for what she didn't know, but at least it might be interesting, something to add to her store of experiences. Heidi was heterosexual to the core of her being, but was quite prepared to give Liz a bit encouragement if that was what it would take for her to unbutton and reveal something of herself. It might make a good story to tell: something else to shock Kelvin with.

'Help yourself to grapes and cheese,' said the re-emergent Elizabeth, 'We'll have coffee afterwards, shall we?'

'OK by me,' said Heidi. 'I've got me wine to finish, anyway.' She poured herself another glass.

'I was wondering,' said Elizabeth, 'whether you might consider accompanying me to London one weekend? There's so much I'd like to show you.'

'What sort of things?'

'Well, I've been telling you about all the art galleries. I'd love to take you round: it would be a pleasure for me as well. These things are much better enjoyed with a companion, and perhaps we could go to a concert at the Barbican in the evening. I'm sure you'd enjoy it, Heidi. Do say you'll come.'

'Where would we stay, then?'

'In a hotel, of course.'

'Bit expensive, wouldn't it be?'

'Oh, I'll pay, and we can share a room; if that's all right with you, of course.'

'Cool.' Heidi slipped off her shoe, extended her leg under the table, made contact with Elizabeth's ankle, and let her foot rest there. No reaction.

'Oh, I'm so pleased. Is there anything else you'd like to do while we're there?'

'Like what, Liz?' She very gently, almost imperceptibly, rubbed her toe against Elizabeth's ankle. Still no reaction.

'Well, things that interest you; maybe see some of the sights. Have you been on the Eye?'

'Done that. No, after we've done the galleries and things I'd like a meal and then we can chill out in the hotel with a bottle of wine and maybe watch the telly: they have some interesting stuff on the telly in some hotels. D'you fancy that, Liz?'

Her toe began a slow ascent of the front of Elizabeth's calf. At last a response: Elizabeth coloured and looked away; her leg twitched, but remained in situ.

'Oh, I don't know.' Her voice shook slightly, then she said more firmly, 'I'll make some coffee, won't you go and sit in the lounge?' She rose and hurried to the kitchen.

Heidi remained at the table for a moment, trying to unscramble the mixed messages that her

219

companion had delivered. She sat, tipsily mulling over the various scenarios that presented themselves, her natural inclination to explore every new avenue vying with an inner voice which warned her not to get involved with someone who was, well, a bit peculiar.

The silence from the kitchen, no clattering of coffee cups nor gurgling of a percolator, roused her. She eased off her remaining shoe and padded silently to the door, which was ajar. Peering through the gap she saw Elizabeth standing stock still, eyes closed, shoulders hunched, apparently engaged in deep-breathing exercises.

'Are you all right?' she asked.

Elizabeth started and opened her eyes: on seeing Heidi her face crumpled.

'Oh, Heidi, I'm sorry, I'm so sorry.'

'What for? What's the matter?' She put her hand on Elizabeth's arm. To her consternation, for the second time that day, Elizabeth began to weep. She did what anyone would do in the circumstances; put a comforting arm round her shoulder, but Elizabeth jerked away.

'No! No, I can't.'

'Can't what, Liz?'

'I'm not – I'm not that way. I'm sorry if I gave that impression.'

'You mean you're not gay?'

'Of course not.' Evident indignation quelled her tears. 'And I had no idea that you, that you were that way - '

'Me? *I'm* not gay, Liz; what gave you that idea?'

220

'But you were …. you were …. your foot, under the table …. I thought –'

'Oh, I was just being friendly. It's no big deal; forget it, Liz.'

Elizabeth took a deep breath and held herself erect.

'Heidi, my suggestion that we visit London together was a gesture of friendship, nothing more. We're two young women still new to the college and to Streetbridge, both as yet without a circle of friends; you must find the weekends a little tedious, as I do. I thought it would be amusing to get away for a while. As I said, galleries and museums are much better visited with a companion. My offer is of course still open, now we've cleared up our little misunderstanding. I do hope you still feel able to join me. Now, shall we have that coffee?'

Oh God, thought Heidi, the poor cow is just lonely, not only lonely but needy – how the hell do I get out of this without offending her?

'I don't think I want coffee, thanks,' she said, 'I've got a nine o'clock tomorrow and I haven't prepared it. Think I'd better go.'

Elizabeth's face was momentarily stricken before she adopted an expression of extreme hauteur. 'Very well, if that's what you wish. You might at least have the courtesy to respond to my offer of a visit to London, even if it is, as I imagine, in the negative.'

Suddenly a solution to Heidi's dilemma presented itself.

'Okay, I'll come with you, so long as you do me a favour first.'

'And what might that be?'

'Come to the *Woodman* with me tomorrow night. The crowd that go there are all, like, oldies. Come and keep me company. I'll ask Kelvin to come as well. You don't have to drink, you know, I mean you can have fruit juice and stuff.'

'Who are the crowd?'

'Oh, I think Barbara, and sometimes Derek with his wife, and some other guys who used to work at the college, with their wives, and Rhod of course, and Mike, but Mike will be with his girlfriend so you needn't worry about him.'

The anticipated prompt emphatic rejection did not materialise.

'I'll think about it, Heidi,' Elizabeth said eventually, 'I'm not used to pubs; if I agree to come, will you accompany me into the bar?'

'Yeah, okay. Look, I'd better go now. Thanks for an awesome meal; I'll see you later.'

'Later? Tonight, you mean?'

Heidi was puzzled. 'No, like tomorrow, at work.'

***

'Hello, Marcia?' Fred's voice boomed down the line.

'Yes, Chairman?' Marcia carried the phone over to the dining room table where she'd been trying to commit to paper the various courses of

222

action that she might take following the day's events.

'Thought you might like to know. I've had a word with old Waldren, and he doesn't see any problems.'

'Waldren?' Fred was one of those who always started a conversation seeming to assume a prior telepathic communication with the listener.

'Johnny Waldren, you know, chairman of the Chamber of Commerce.'

'Yes, of course; sorry to be so obtuse, Fred. You mean he thinks my membership will be approved?'

'Absolutely. He appreciates that colleges are commercial enterprises these days. Some of the backwoodsmen might still object, but he's sure that when it comes to the vote he'll get it through. There are a lot of youngsters in the Chamber these days.'

'That's good news, Fred. Thanks again for all your lobbying.'

'A pleasure, my dear. All well with you?'

'Yes, very well, Fred. I'll bring you up to speed when we meet to discuss the next Corporation meeting.'

'I'll look forward to that. Goodnight.'

'Goodnight, Chairman.'

Marcia returned the phone to its stand, giving thanks that the Chairman's telephone manner was as terse as his business lunches were protracted, as though he'd never properly got to grips with communication through that new-fangled instrument.

She decided to treat herself to a celebratory glass of wine. Membership of the Chamber of Commerce would bring benefits to the college, of course. But more than that she relished the thought of mixing with like-minded entrepreneurs, and the social possibilities that such contact might bring. By 'youngsters' Fred probably meant men of her own age. After six months of self-imposed purdah in her new post it was time to spread her wings a little.

Things were going well. She had Mike Carter over a barrel, and Sylvia too. Also to come was the confrontation with Rhodri Evans. All had committed offences which warranted disciplinary action, and in the case of the first two, probable dismissal. She'd have to be careful, however. While most staff valued a quiet life, too much management pugnacity might result in pushing them towards industrial action, which, though inevitably unsuccessful, would bring adverse publicity to the college at a time when it needed to be marketed as a modern, forward-thinking centre of excellence.

It was time that she should start giving thought to the agenda for the next Corporation meeting. She swallowed the last dregs of wine, moved purposefully into her study and switched on her laptop. Faced with the blank screen, she sat for a few minutes marshalling her thoughts, then applied herself to the keyboard with gusto, thoughts of Carter and Sylvia and Evans almost, but not entirely, extinguished.

***

After Julie's apologetic and slightly drunken departure, very late in the afternoon, Fiona had busied herself around the house and then set to work in the kitchen to start the preparation of an evening meal for one. She felt surprisingly calm. Calm, but betrayed, and very angry that she should have been made to look such a fool. The vague uneasiness and angst of the past weeks had been replaced by a steely resolve. Things could no longer continue like this: there would have to be a confrontation. In a perverse way she was looking forward to Mike's arrival: while not relishing the showdown, she was impatient for the calmer waters that must surely follow the catharsis.

She knew she wasn't Mike's intellectual equal, but over the years had learned that in debate on domestic or personal issues she could more than hold her own. In such situations she became her mother's daughter and adopted the haughty froideur that Mrs Smythe utilised with members of the lower orders who failed to know their place. Mike had little defence against this, except to accuse her of being an upper class bitch, and the fact that he had to resort to such crude invective was a tacit admission that he'd been worsened. Such disputes had hitherto been confined to the minutiae of domestic life, but Fiona, self-confidence growing alongside her anger, knew that to adopt her mother's style would be useful in the conflict to come.

And if she were to act the part, by God she'd dress for it. She abandoned meal preparation, ran upstairs, tore off her jeans and tee-shirt, changed into a black velvet skirt and a white, loose fitting blouse, brushed her hair, applied discreet make-up and perfume, then walked slowly down the stairs on kitten heels, straight-backed, head erect in the manner she'd learned in her childhood deportment classes. Sitting down on the arm chair, legs neatly crossed at the knee as befitted her dress, she appraised the room and decided it was poky, shabby, old-fashioned, lacking any style, *lower-middle-class*, and what was more, she could think these thoughts without any twinge of conscience assailing her. She'd made too many compromises in this ménage. Things were going to change.

Carter's key turned in the lock.

'Hey, Fi,' he said, almost before he'd closed the door, 'My meeting with Ski-slopes went well, I think; she put herself at a disadvantage by – hey, what are you scrubbed up for? Are we going out?'

'No, we're not going out, at least I'm not.'

Carter dropped his duffle bag on the floor, to be followed immediately by his leather jacket. Fiona rose, picked them up, consigned them to the cupboard under the stairs, then resumed her seat.

'What's with you?' demanded Carter.

'I just thought we might try to adopt a more civilised way of living for a change.'

'Civilised? What's brought this on? Have you been visiting your mother?'

'No. I've been entertaining here as it happens.'

'Entertaining? Who?'

226

'Julie. Sit down, Mike, I want to talk to you.'

He sank onto a cushion opposite her. She tugged her skirt down over her knees.

'Julie was here all afternoon. Nice girl, Julie. I've never really spoken to her alone before. She was most enlightening.'

'What d'you mean?'

'She told me things I ought to have been told years ago. Told by you.'

'What the fuck are you going on about?'

'Come off it, Mike. Why did you never tell me that your Hilary woman was once Geoff's partner, when Geoff first came to the college?'

Carter got up and went to the cupboard under the stairs, where he retrieved a pack of cigarettes from his jacket. He lit one before he resumed his seat. Fiona noticed that all the time he avoided eye-contact with her.

'Didn't think it was important,' he said, after exhaling expansively. 'It was a long time ago.'

'It was the way in which you got together with Hilary that I found interesting,' said Fiona. She was gasping for a cigarette herself, but was determined to appear calm. 'Not very gentlemanly, was it, to screw a part-time lecturer who was the partner of a colleague? And doing the deed in the flat you shared with a compliant little shop assistant?'

'She worked in a book-shop for God's sake, and — '

'I'm not interested in her, poor put-upon little girl that she probably was. Let's pursue your time with Hilary, shall we? Didn't last long, did it? Two

227

years, Julie told me. And she told me how it ended. Lisa, apparently, took great delight in informing all and sundry what happened.'

'I don't have to listen to all this shit,' said Carter, still avoiding eye contact.

'But it's not shit, is it Mike? Are you going to deny what everyone in Streetbridge except me seems to know? That cosy little exchange at Stu's place a few months after he and Lisa had arrived here? You seducing Lisa, Hilary seducing Stu ? What a charming couple you and Hilary must have been. Pity you didn't stay together. It would have done all of us a favour.'

Fiona continued to stare fixedly at Carter throughout her speech. When she finished he ground out his cigarette, and, for the first time, looked at her.

'Jesus, Fi, all that was yonks ago; Christ, you must have been just a schoolkid at the time. I've never made any secret of the fact I've put it about a bit. I didn't think you'd want to know the details.'

His hand shook slightly as he lit another cigarette.

'You don't get it, do you? Don't you understand how humiliated I feel? I've been sitting in the pub with you and Geoff and Julie and Lisa and Stu practically every Friday evening for five years, and all of them knew about this, and no doubt Rhod does as well, and you didn't once think that I had a right to know. Why? Trying to protect me, were you? The poor little rich girl, not blessed with a university education, not an academic, not capable of understanding the avant-garde ways of intellectuals?'

'Julie's not an academic –'

'No, thank God, which is probably why she finally had the decency to tell me. And common decency isn't something you know much about, is it? I'm no prude, for heaven's sake, and I know I was seeing you on the side while I was still living with Simon, but to seduce a colleague's partner in the flat you shared with your girlfriend! And to seduce Lisa in her own house, practically in front of Stu –'

'Hang on Fi, Julie hasn't told you the whole story: it wasn't me that did the seducing, Hilary and Lisa came on to *me*, and then Stu got his revenge by - '

'Oh, come on! Don't make out you were the innocent party; give me credit for a bit of intelligence, please.'

Carter stood up. 'OK, OK! Whatever you say! If that's what you want to believe. But it's not important is it? It's ancient history. I don't ask you about details of your past, do I? And what made bloody Julie decide to go into the confessional after all this time?'

'She had her reasons, and believe it or not, it was partly to protect me from Lisa's vicious tongue, but I'm not prepared to go into that now. There are more important things to discuss.'

'Like what? Can't we have something to eat first? I'm bloody starving.'

Fiona stood up, confident that she looked her best. She noted that even in his discomfort Mike's

229

eyes travelled up and down her body. He was 58, and beginning to look it; his options were running out. She was 35, in her prime; time was on her side. The relationship could still be salvaged, but it would have to be on her terms.

'Let's sit at the kitchen table – no, not to eat. In any case I've only prepared a snack for myself. Come on, I've still things to say to you, and I'd prefer to say them across a table.'

She moved to the kitchen and sat down. Carter reluctantly joined her. She indicated that he should take the chair opposite, and was gratified, though not a little surprised, to see that he sat immediately.

'Fuckin' hell, what is this, a formal negotiation?'

'Oh, there's nothing to negotiate, Mike, believe me. I'm going to give you my conditions for staying with you. Most of them are domestic: things like sharing the housework and cooking and shopping, oh, and decorating this place and getting some decent furniture. Some of them are social: I'd like us to develop mutual interests outside the *Woodman.* I don't mind going there once in a while, but not twice a week. We never go to the cinema, or the theatre, or to concerts, or even just out for a meal, except for your bloody curries. And I'd like you to start giving me support and encouragement in continuing my education, like you said you would when we first got together.'

'Bloody hell,' he said.

'I still think we can make a go of things, Mike, but it's got to be a partnership. And I want an assurance from you.'

'Want quite a lot, don't you?'

'No more than is my right. I want you to promise me that there aren't any more sordid little secrets that the others all know about which you've kept from me. If you can't give me that assurance, I want you to tell me about them, now.'

'Blimey, do you want me to provide a list of every woman I've shagged over the past 35 years?'

'No. Straight sex I can understand, so long, of course, that you've not been unfaithful to me. It's the sordid partner-swapping I find so objectionable, particularly if it involves people who I know. So, can you give me that assurance?'

'Yeah, you know it all now. Nothing else happened involving the others.'

'And since we've been together you've not been having bits on the side?'

'No, of course not.'

'You'd better be telling the truth, Mike.'

'Yeah, it's the truth. Can we eat now?'

'Well, *I* can. If *you* want anything you'll have to prepare it yourself.'

She found it hard to disguise her smile at seeing his crestfallen features, and decided to relent a little.

'After you've eaten and washed up you can tell me all about your meeting with the Principal,' she said in a warmer tone than she'd used all evening.

He was silent for a moment, then – 'How about us buying a dishwasher?'

231

***

Half-way through serving vegetables to her guests, Sylvia suddenly dropped the spoon, scattering sauté potatoes over the table.

'Are you all right, Sylv?' said her husband, 'You've gone really pale.'

'Yes, yes, just an accident; you know me, always clumsy. I'll go and get some kitchen towel.'

She scuttled from the room. How could she be so stupid, so forgetful, so unprofessional as to leave confidential documents strewn over her office? She broke into a sweat: Marcia must surely have seen the extract from Mike's file, or were they pushed under other papers? There was a chance that she might have left everything undisturbed. An adrenaline rush half propelled her to the door with the idea of returning to the college even at this late hour to file everything away. But what excuse could she make to her guests? How could she later explain it to her husband? It was hopeless. Her only hope was to get into work so early tomorrow that there'd be no chance of Marcia preceding her. Always assuming that she hadn't discovered the file this evening, of course.

She re-entered the lounge, resigned to a night of torment.

***

Rhodri, still smarting from Megan's revelations, was in no mood for his meeting with Christine. He fancied an evening by himself at home, deciding whether he should confront Carter. Now he was faced with the task of dumping the distinctly unappealing Christine in such a manner that would not provoke a public scene. Most women would quickly get such a message before it had to be made explicit, and would seek to extricate themselves from such a situation with affronted dignity. Christine, however, was the sort to look for offence and seize on it hysterically.

He groaned, stood up, and approached his kitchen mirror with a view to smoothing down his thinning strands of hair before venturing out, but was taken aback by his reflection. Christ! He'd forgotten about the close crop he'd been given. He found himself studying his features with interest. Megan was right; it had taken years off him. He remembered his purchases, still in the carrier bags that he'd tossed carelessly on the settee when he'd come in. Well, the new clothes would have to be worn sometime, he supposed, and tonight's visit to the *Falconer*, a rather decorous pub, provided an excuse to break them in. He extracted the new pair of jeans, ripped off the labels and pulled them on. They felt ok, not too baggy. May as well go for the full Monty; he decided on the turtleneck sweater and the fleece. He grabbed his wallet and cigarettes and made a purposeful exit.

He'd only once before visited the *Falconer*, about 15 years ago when he'd first arrived in Streetbridge. It was almost unchanged. Polished wooden tables with wheelback chairs occupied the centre of the lounge, upholstered benches behind lower tables lined the horse-brass festooned walls, the lighting was low and there were no electronic games and no music. He approached the bar, which was traditional, with bottles, tankards and spirit measures on the rear wall and hand pumps and ashtrays on the counter, behind which stood a stout middle-aged tweed-jacketed moustached man with pronounced bags under his eyes, in desultory conversation with three customers of similar age and appearance who were perched precariously on bar-stools.

He took his pint of Bass, which had been served cheerfully and politely, over to one of the low tables close to the door. He studied the room, sparsely occupied with clientele all of a certain age, and wondered how the pub had managed to withstand all the fashionable assaults of the late 20th century and still remain in business. It had been in something of a time warp even at the time of his first visit. He remembered that Geoff had said that the Chamber of Commerce used one of its upstairs rooms as a meeting place, and looking again at the drinkers at the bar it seemed they did have all the attributes of the remnants of the town's petit-bourgeoisie. He found himself enjoying the quiet and comfort, marked the place down as a future solitary refuge, and resolved not to tell his colleagues of his discovery.

The door swung open and Christine entered. She stood uncertainly, peering round the room. The passage of twenty-four hours had done nothing to enhance her appeal. Her gaze swept over him once, then again, and with a smile of recognition she approached.

'Hello,' she said, irritatingly emphasising the second syllable. 'You've had your hair cut! Oh, Rhodri, it really suits you.' She sat on the bench seat next to him, squeezed his arm and put her face close to his.

'What do you want?' Rhodri asked brusquely. 'The Bass is good.'

'Yes please, just a half.'

He made his way to the bar, suddenly conscious of his new clothes and realising with dismay that he was wearing them in the company of someone who was self-centred enough to believe that his transformation had been undertaken with her approbation in mind. On his return with her half pint he sat on the chair opposite her.

'Rhodri, I really like that sweater, and the fleece; are they new?'

'My daughter bought them for me.'

'Oh, do you have a daughter? How old is she? I didn't know you were married. You *are* a dark horse, aren't you? I like men with a bit of mystery about them.'

'No mystery. I'm divorced. Megan's 31. She lives in Wales. Don't see her very often.'

'I expect you miss her. Still, you can't cling on to your children, can you? Why don't you come and sit next to me? It's not very cosy like this. It's a nice pub, isn't it? Much nicer than that place you took me to on Tuesday. It was a good idea to meet here, we don't want to run into any of your

235

colleagues, do we? Come on, come and sit here.'
She took breath to sip delicately at her beer.

Rhodri took refuge in the manipulation of cigarette and lighter.

'Look, Christine, bach –'

'Oh I do like it when you use that word. Is it Welsh for darling?'

'Not really. Listen, I think I need to put you straight on a few things –'

'Oh, serious is it?' she smiled archly.

'Possibly. Look, I think you might have the wrong idea about where we're going. The point is, we're not going anywhere, see? Tuesday was a mistake; it shouldn't have happened, and it's not going to happen again.'

She stared at him, glass still half raised to her lips.

'But why? Didn't you enjoy it? Wasn't I any good?'

'It's not that. I think you want what you'd probably call a relationship. I don't. I'm not cut out for it. I'm a weirdo, a boozer, a philanderer, see? And I'm old enough to be your father. And –'

'I don't care how old you are. I thought you liked me. Is it because I'm one of your students? I'm 29, it's not against the law, is it?' Her voice was reaching a pitch where it was audible at the bar. The three old boys on the stools each gave her a sideways glance.

'Keep your voice down. It's nothing to do with what you are. I'm trying to explain. Look, would you really be content just to be my casual screw?'

'If that's what you want, then yes, I would. I wouldn't make any demands, just as long as I can see you now and again, perhaps after the evening class. Yes, that's an idea, isn't it? We can be together every Tuesday evening; oh, not every Tuesday if you don't want, but sometimes, just now and again if you like. That's all I want, Rhodri, honestly.' She grabbed his hand across the table and held on to it.

Rhodri jerked his hand away. He'd anticipated outrage, not compliance. The woman was unhinged; would nothing serve to make her shrink from him? In desperation he tried another tack.

'It wouldn't just be a casual liaison. My tastes are far more unorthodox than that. I don't think you'd like what I'm really into. I've got a sordid past. It's all part of the circle I move in.'

'What do you mean?'

'Well, how would you like me to share you with, let's say Mike Carter, for example?'

'Share? I don't understand. And what's Mike Carter got to do with us?

'Nothing, yet. But he's had a lot to do with *me*. If you can manage to sit there for a few minutes without interrupting I'll tell you about our history. Then you'd see what you'd be letting yourself in for. Are you sure you want to hear this?'

She nodded. Rhodri took a swallow from his mug and began.

Fifteen minutes later Rhodri made his way to the bar to refresh his glass, relieved that Christine's reaction to his story had been one of horrified

237

silence; no tears, no tantrums. In fact towards the end her expression had been blank, and she'd risen and left the pub without a word. He was, it seemed, free of her.

'Another pint, please,' he said, pushing his glass towards the landlord.

'Bass, is it?'

Rhodri nodded.

'I think you're well out of it with that one, my friend,' said the landlord as he pulled at the pump.

'Know her, do you?' said Rhodri.

'Only by reputation. She's poison, pure poison. A bit unbalanced if you ask me.'

He took his pint back to the table and sat, savouring his solitude. Telling Christine his history had been a masterstroke. And as Carter had been so much a part of his past, it was entirely appropriate that his role in it should have been included.

Friday daytime

Sylvia had to force herself not to run as she hurried along the corridor to her office. She'd had little sleep that night. Joe had of course noticed that something was wrong during supper. She'd tossed and turned into the small hours, her mind racing as she envisaged the various scenarios, none of them pleasant, that might face her when she arrived at the college the next morning. Finally she'd got up to make a cup of tea, and sat nursing it in the kitchen, rehearsing various explanations that she might provide for the excision of part of Mike's file. The best she'd come up with was that the documents must have fallen out when she'd extracted the file from the cabinet, but she couldn't see Marcia swallowing that. From fevered apprehension of the following day's events her mind had turned to the humiliating further consequences of her action – disciplinary procedures, dismissal. How could she explain that to Joe? 'Dismissal?' she could hear his astonished reaction. 'Just for forgetting to file something?' It would all be bound come out, of course; her marriage would collapse, she'd be left without a job, without a husband, without a house. After an age, groggy with worry and exhaustion, she'd returned to bed, there to toss and turn again until finally falling into a restless sleep an hour before it was time to get up.

Marcia's BMW hadn't been in the car park. A stay of execution; there might still be a chance. She reached her office, fumbled with her keys,

dropped them, fumbled again, opened the door –
Oh thank God! Thank God! The piles of paper
were strewn over her desk, just where she'd left
them. She scrabbled amongst them – yes! The
offending extract! She picked it up gingerly as
though it might burn. The grinding of the shredder
as it consumed the pages was sweet music. She
slumped into her chair, relief flooding over her.
She'd been stupid, of course; Marcia was not the
sort to demean herself by tidying up after her
secretary. The thought spurred her into action –
better shift the rest of the documents before she
arrived.

'Good morning, Sylvia,' said Marcia as she
entered. 'Ah, clearing up yesterday's mess, I see.
Most unlike you to leave your office disordered.
You must have been in a hurry to get away.
Nothing confidential amongst those documents I
hope; don't forget the cleaners have keys to all
offices.' Her tone was coldly neutral rather than
accusatory.

'No, nothing confidential. Sorry to leave a
mess. I had to go shopping. We had people to
supper.'

'How fortunate for you, then, that I decided to
let you leave early.'

'Yes, thanks, Marcia. I'll bring the post in as
soon as I've cleared this.'

'No. Immediately, please.' She swept into her
office.

Was this just her normal haughty manner,
Sylvia wondered, or was there a hint of additional

iciness? No, she was being paranoid. She set about opening the post.

In her office, Marcia permitted herself a smile of satisfaction. Tempting as it was to confront Sylvia with her crime, it would have to wait until Carter had been dealt with. In fact a delay would provide an opportunity to demean her PA with menial tasks before she wielded the axe. She would freeze her out of her confidence; keep her guessing about her appointments, reduce her to a mere shorthand-typist. In any case, she was no longer to be trusted. If she could meddle with a staff file, of what other disloyalties might she be capable?

She reached in the desk drawer for the papers for the afternoon's Principals' meeting and began to read, annotating the documents as she did.

Sylvia entered with the post and coffee, sat down though unbidden, and received terse instructions regarding Marcia's responses to the mail. 'What about your diary?' she asked, as Marcia signalled that their meeting was over by turning towards her PC.

'You know that I'm at the Midlands' Principals' meeting this morning. I'll be back at about two. Keep this afternoon clear.'

'No other appointments?'

'None that need concern you. I want you to draw up a revised list of staff telephone extension numbers and workrooms. The one we're using is at least six months out of date.'

'But Human Resources usually do that.'

241

'Not any more. It's your responsibility now. Please take my cup away, I've finished my coffee.'

Satisfied with the puzzled expression on Sylvia's face as she departed, Marcia picked up the phone.

'Adrian. Principal here. Is your Mr Evans in college yet?'

'Oh, well, probably not, he doesn't teach till eleven.'

'When he deigns to arrive, tell him I wish to see him at 3 this afternoon. Give him this information privately, and tell him it would be in his interest not to divulge to his colleagues that he has this appointment.'

A moment's silence. 'Oh: right.' Another pause. 'Has he done something wrong? Should I be there also?'

'Your presence won't be necessary Adrian. Just make sure he's here on time.'

She rang off. Keep the bastards guessing, she thought, and don't trust anyone.

***

Lucas was waiting for the arrival of his colleagues. The spreadsheet summary of his restructuring proposals was, he thought, beautiful in its simplicity and the financial gains breathtaking in their scope, but Charles Jay wouldn't see it like that of course. He was bound to raise objections based on some sort of spurious educational philosophy. And Edgar Hickman was as bad, far too sentimental about the staff. It was Human

242

Resources he was supposed to be in charge of, after all: why couldn't he see that the staff were just that – resources; resources to be utilised in the most cost-effective way?

He was secure in the knowledge that Marcia's desire for restructuring was driven by a financial imperative, and that she was confident in his ability to deliver the sort of plan she wanted. Paul Tasker could be relied upon to support him, but Paul was a lightweight: the ultimate responsibility rested on his, Lucas's, shoulders. Jay and Hickman would have to be persuaded that their role in drafting the document was simply to provide an emollient commentary.

He checked his watch: five minutes to go. Was there something he'd forgotten? Remembering, he picked up the phone.

'Kate? Lucas Harper. Could you remind Joy that I need coffee for my meeting at ten?'

'I was just about to ring you. Joy's not in today.'

'Why?'

'Off sick. Her usual problem.'

'Oh, yes,' blushing as he remembered Joy's menstrual sufferings, 'well, you'll make us coffee then, won't you, Kate?'

Taking Kate's silence for assent, he resumed his wait, wishing that his office were larger. It didn't lend itself to meetings of more than three people: any more than that and he was obliged to emerge from behind his desk, push it back, and sit with the others in a democratic circle in front of it. He could use the Board Room, he supposed, but this would rob him of the advantage of being on home territory. In any case it was quite amusing to watch Charles, who suffered from back problems, attempting to disguise his discomfort as he fidgeted on one of the narrow upright chairs.

His three colleagues, led by Charles, entered without knocking, he noted with irritation. They did not exchange greetings.

'Perhaps we could get down to business,' he said. 'I assume you agree that as it's my paper we're discussing, I should take the chair?'

'By all means, if you wish to be so formal,' said Charles.

'OK by me,' said Edgar.

Paul nodded and took a swig of water from the bottle he always carried with him.

'I assume you've all read my paper,' Lucas began. 'It is, of course, a résumé of the financial advantage to be gained by my proposals and the staffing implications of their implementation. Our task is first to discuss and, I hope, agree my proposals, and then to draft a fuller document, which will go into the whys and wherefores. Do you agree this is how we should proceed?'

Paul nodded.

'Oh, absolutely,' said Charles.

'Yup, but are we going to have some coffee?' said Edgar.

'It will be here soon. Now, if we could make a start. My spreadsheet summarises what I propose. No doubt you have some questions.'

'None whatsoever,' said Charles.

'Nor me,' said Edgar.

Paul made as if to speak, then shook his head.

Lucas was taken aback, then suspicious. What game were they playing?

'Surely you must have some observations?'

'Certainly I have an observation,' said Charles. 'You asked if we had any questions. I don't. Your paper is abundantly clear.'

'A model of clarity,' said Edgar.

Lucas was foundering, and was rescued by the arrival of Kate with the coffee.

'Only instant, I'm afraid,' she said. 'With Joy off I've got my work cut out.'

Lucas was about to protest but was pre-empted by Charles's effusive thanks and by Edgar saying that was fine by him. He was further annoyed by noticing that Edgar and Kate exchanged a wink.

'Perhaps you'd let me have your observations, then,' he said, once Kate had left.

'A masterly proposal,' said Charles. 'The savings you've achieved are mind-boggling.'

'Yes, breathtaking,' said Edgar. 'I'd never have been able to come up with something like that.'

'I agree,' said Paul.

Lucas felt the lurching sensation that comes from half-falling through a door that one expects to be locked. 'Are you saying you agree with all the proposals? Even the new Faculty structure?'

'But of course,' said Charles. 'The structure is driven by the financial imperative, isn't it? Alter the structure and you'd fail to achieve your savings, yes? And that grouping of Hairdressing, Creative Arts, Adult Education and Secretarial Studies is truly remarkable.'

'Remarkable indeed, and with Gregory Freeman as Head, as well. A masterstroke,' said Edgar. 'What name would you give to that Faculty?'

'I hadn't considered the titles,' conceded Lucas.

'No matter,' said Charles. 'A mere detail.'

Lucas began to relax. It was going better than he'd ever dreamed, but then, on reflection, Jay and Hickman had at last probably begun to realise their limitations when it came to finance. He smiled; a rare occurrence.

'Well, I'm glad to have your agreement. Now we come to where I need your expertise. I think the spreadsheet says it all, but Marcia would like a narrative report. You're better with words than me, so can you cobble something together in time for it to be typed this afternoon? I'd like Marcia to get a copy before our Monday meeting.'

'That's a simple matter,' said Charles. 'All you need do is to list the staff in your new faculties, along with their roles, and then as an appendix list all those who are to be made redundant. Then refer to your spreadsheet for the details of the savings. You don't need our input for that, surely?'

'But don't you think the Principal would like something a bit more, well, a bit more wordy?'

'Good God no,' said Edgar. 'You know how she always bangs on about me and Charles being long-winded. Keep it concise: she'll love it.'

'Well, if you're sure. You won't have any objections to me putting your names to it? It is supposed to be a team proposal, after all.'

'We'd be honoured,' said Charles. 'Now, if you don't mind, my back's giving me trouble; I need to walk about a bit.'

'And I've got a pile of work to do,' said Edgar. 'We'll leave it in your capable hands, Lucas.'

In the corridor, Charles and Edgar waited until Paul had wandered off, then exchanged grins.

'Do you think he swallowed that?' said Edgar.

'Of course he did. He wouldn't know irony if it reared up and bit him. I must say it's a bit of luck Joy being absent: there's a fair chance Kate won't be able to type out the report today, which means Marcia won't get it until just before the meeting.'

'Yes, it is a bit of luck, isn't it?' said Edgar.

***

'No, let's go into my classroom,' said Carter. 'It's nearly break; don't want all the other buggers to hear.'

Sighing, Derek followed Carter out of the workroom. 'I hope this isn't going to take long,' he grumbled. 'I was hoping to get on with organising the ballot on the pay claim.'

'Won't take five minutes.' Carter shut the classroom door. 'I've got an appointment with Ski-slopes on Monday. I need you to be present as my union rep.'

Derek groaned. 'What have you done now?'

Carter gave an account of his last meeting with the Principal and said that he thought the bitch might be wavering, and that if he could have

Derek's support he reckoned she might be prepared to compromise over the matter of dress, and maybe on some other of her crazy ideas.

'Well I reckon you're on a loser,' said Derek. 'If it turns into a formal disciplinary hearing then she'll have your file in front of her, and we both know what's in that, don't we? She'll seize on your warning and you'll be for the high jump, Mike. And there won't be much I can do to save you.'

Carter smiled knowingly. 'Ah, well, she may well have the file in front of her, but it won't be complete. The record of that warning won't be there.'

'What? How the hell d'you know that?'

'I have my sources. So, if she has no record of past misdemeanours I reckon we've got everything to play for. I suggest you weigh in on the academic freedom issue, while I re-state the inconsistencies in her other proposals, and then –'

'Hold it there. There's only one way your file could have been tampered with. You've got Sylvia to do your dirty work, haven't you?' Derek began to massage his chin in agitation.

'It was her idea, not mine. Sylv and I have an understanding.'

'I know all about your so-called understandings!' Derek's voice was raised. 'You're a sexual predator, you bastard. God knows what it is that women see in you, but you just use them, Carter; you get them in your clutches and then get them to do your bidding. Sylvia must be out of her head to do a thing like that. What did

248

you do, threaten that you'd tell her husband about your little understanding? I wouldn't put it past you to go in for a spot of blackmail, you shit.'

'What sort of person do you think I am? It was her idea, I tell you.'

'I've already said what sort of person I think you are. Do you really think I'm going to go along with this? You've made me party to information that's an instant dismissal offence.'

'But fuckin' hell, Derek, it's the NATFHE Rep's job to support his members. Remember I'm making a stand for all the staff and –'

'Don't you lecture me on what my job is! I'm not a barrister in a court of law. If a union member breaches the college code of conduct then he's on his own. The union doesn't defend the indefensible; we do have *some* principles, but that's not something I'd expect you to understand.' Puce with anger, Derek stood up and walked to the door.

Carter scrambled to his feet. 'But, hang on, Derek, are you saying you won't be representing me at the meeting? As far as Ski-slopes is concerned it's just about non-compliance with her edict, nothing to do with screwing students or doctoring files. So you won't be going against your principles by being there.'

Derek turned to face him. 'I'll be there, though God knows I've got more important things to do with my time. But support you I will not. That means I won't be arguing on your behalf about the rights and wrongs of the Principal's memo. I'll be there to see that the hearing is conducted in accordance with agreed procedures, and to make sure you get a fair hearing, that's all. Now, I'm going to try and get a coffee in what remains of the break.'

He slammed the door behind him. Alone in the classroom, Carter stood stock still for a moment, then viciously kicked the metal waste-paper basket across the room.

***

As she entered the workroom, Elizabeth was surprised to see Heidi sitting on Kelvin's desk, swinging her legs. 'C'mon, Kelv,' she was saying, 'Just give it a go; like it's Friday night, surely you don't prepare lectures on a Friday?'

'Well, no, but –'

'We'll all be there,' said Heidi. 'Even Liz is going to come, aren't you, Liz?'

'Come? Where?'

'To the pub, tonight. Don't make like you've forgotten.'

'Oh, yes, of course.'

Barbara looked up. 'Bugger me, Liz, we are honoured. Never thought we'd see you at the Friday night piss-up. Hear that, Arthur? Elizabeth's coming to the *Woodman*. Why don't you break the habit of a lifetime and join us as well?'

'Oh, I don't think so,' said Arthur, assiduously arranging the papers, files and books on his desk into their proper order. 'I think I'll leave that sort of carousing to you young ones. Thanks very much for the invitation, though, Barbara: it's much appreciated.'

'Blimey; thanks for the compliment, Arthur: it's yonks since I've been called one of the young ones.' She winked at Heidi. 'How about you, Graham? Looks like it's going to be a bit of a do if these two are going to come.'

'Sorry?' Graham was immersed in sticking coloured tabs on his lecture notes.

'Oh, never mind.'

Graham's inability to go anywhere by himself without first obtaining the permission of his wife was well known, as well as the fact that such permission was rarely forthcoming.

'Are you coming to the staff lounge then, Heidi?' asked Elizabeth.

'No, I fancy staying here for once. Besides, the coffee in the lounge is crap. Kelv's gonna make me a cup of instant, aren't you Kelv?'

Blushing, Kelvin sprang to his feet and advanced on the kettle standing on the soiled table in the corner. Elizabeth fought to contain the unwelcome feelings of hurt and disappointment: was she being punished in some way for last night? She looked at Heidi, still perched on Kelvin's desk, her skirt at mid thigh. How did she manage to have such brown legs in the middle of January?

'Can I get you a coffee as well, Elizabeth?' said Kelvin.

'Oh. Well, yes, thank you.'

Arthur looked up. 'Well, Elizabeth, since you're staying here for coffee, perhaps we could discuss

251

some thoughts I've had about how to get the part-time lecturers to submit syllabuses. If you'd like to have a look at what I've drafted out…'

Elizabeth reluctantly moved over to his desk and began to lend half an ear to his monologue. Kelvin delivered the coffees and resumed his seat, half hoping that Heidi would get off his desk but half pleased when she didn't. Barbara read her book. Graham remained immersed in the decoration of his notes. No-one turned when the door opened, and Rhodri was half way towards the kettle before Barbara glanced up.

'Bugger me! Evans! What's with all this?'

All eyes turned to Rhodri as he busied himself with kettle, coffee jar and mug.

'Hey, Rhod,' said Heidi. 'You look almost cool!'

'Oh God,' moaned Barbara. 'I know what this is all about; he's on the pull again, I bet.'

'I have to say, Rhodri, that it's a distinct improvement,' said Arthur. 'I suppose we have the Principal's memorandum to thank for this transformation. Very wise of you, if I may say so.'

Rhodri carried his coffee to his desk and sat down. He took a swallow from his mug, and, each in turn, looked his colleagues in the eye.

'Sorry to disappoint you all, but it's got nothing to do with Ski-slopes' memo, and no, Barb, I'm not on the pull. If you must know, this is Megan's doing. There comes a time when it's wise to humour one's daughter, and to tell the truth I just couldn't be arsed to put up with any more nagging.'

252

'Daughter?' Elizabeth was incredulous. 'You have a daughter?'

'Why does that surprise you, Liz?' said Rhodri mildly. 'Don't you think I've got lead in my pencil?'

Barbara chortled.

Elizabeth was too taken aback to notice the indelicacy. 'It's just that, well, I didn't have you down as a family man. When... I mean how old were you ...'

'Megan's older than you, if that's what you're getting at.'

'And she's a credit to him,' said Barbara, 'and she's got good taste as well: nice chinos, Rhod, and the fleece suits you. And I like the haircut; takes years of you, Christ, you're almost fanciable.'

'Reeling in the years, are you, Barb?'

'If it gives you a Steely Dan, then yes, mate.'

They grinned at each other. Their colleagues looked mystified.

Derek entered; brows furrowed. He marched straight to the coffee jar intent on refreshment in the five minutes remaining before his next lecture.

'Hey, Derek, what do you reckon to our Rhodri, then?' said Barbara.

Derek glanced up, registered Rhodri's transformation, and said that he was pleased that someone was showing a bit of sense and why couldn't Rhod knock some of it into his mate Carter. He'd reached his desk and was shuffling around his NATFHE correspondence when Carter entered. The room hushed in anticipation.

253

Carter hadn't even reached his desk when he noticed. His double-take was genuine.

'Jesus Christ, Evans, what the fuck's happened to you?'

Elizabeth put down her coffee cup and told Arthur she was sorry, but she'd have to go where the company was a little more congenial. She gave a look of appeal to Heidi as she walked to the door, but Heidi's gaze was swivelling between Carter and Rhodri.

'Isn't it obvious?' said Rhodri, staring challengingly at Carter. 'I've bought some new gear and had my hair cut. Have a problem with that, do you?'

'You've sold out, haven't you? You bastard! You told me you were with me on this. Who's been getting at you? Am I the only person in this place who's prepared to make a stand?' He stood menacingly over Rhodri, who'd continued to sip at his coffee during the tirade.

'No-one's been getting at me, you histrionic twat. I make my own decisions. And it has nothing to do with Ski-slopes' edict. I decided it was time for a change. But you don't believe in change, do you?'

'Time for a change! Bullshit! You've been a dirty scruffy git ever since you've been here, and now, just at the time when Ski-slopes applies the screws, you decide it's time for a change. Expect me to believe that, do you?'

'Don't be an arsehole, Mike,' Barbara interjected. 'It was Megan who persuaded him to scrub up, and she's done him a favour, I reckon.'

254

'Oh, it's Megan is it?' Carter renewed his assault. 'How convenient to have a darling daughter to defer to! Help you choose your fancy gear, did she? Held daddy's hand throughout the process, did she?'

Rhodri rose to his feet, slowly, and stood in front of Carter, close to him. The room had to strain to hear his soft, deliberate response. 'Just a word of advice, Carter. You'll not mention Megan's name in any context again, see? If you do, I'll take great pleasure in pushing your teeth right down your throat.'

Rhodri's colleagues were used to his occasional foul language, accustomed to his sexual references, tolerant of his sarcasms, but never before had he shown any aggressive tendencies. They were enthralled, not just by the invective, but that it should have been directed at his friend. Carter, just as surprised, was evidently groping for a response. The two stood facing each other, a high noon parody.

The door opened. It was Adrian Havers. The tension in the room was palpable. He glanced at the tableau in front of him, was immediately aware of confrontation, and asked Rhodri, even before registering his metamorphosis, if he could spare a minute in private.

As Rhodri left with Adrian the room relaxed, though not Carter, who remained standing as though primed for fight or flight. Heidi swung herself from Kelvin's desk and approached him. Her eyes were shining with excitement.

'Will all you lot be in the *Woodman* tonight, Mike?'

'What? Oh, yeah, of course; why?'

'Don't want to miss any action, do I?'

***

Fiona hummed to herself as she put away the shopping, leaving in the lounge the pile of reference books that she'd obtained from the library. She'd look at those when things were tidied away, when she could settle with a cup of coffee and one of her strictly rationed cigarettes. She felt happier than she'd been for weeks, months possibly.

It had been so easy to resolve, once the method had come to her. Last night she'd evidently reawakened in Mike the fascination he'd felt for her when first they'd met. Mike had listened in silence to her ultimatum, had conceded that he might have been at fault, had agreed to take his share of household chores, had promised to support her in her revived ambition to further her education. The evening had ended with their cuddling in bed, but only a cuddle: he'd seemed not to wish to go further, and this had come as some relief. After Julie's revelations she wasn't ready to celebrate with sex. Plenty of time for that.

She left the chicken breasts to thaw on the drainer; Mike would be cooking them tonight, no doubt ham-fistedly and probably with inedible results, but it would be a great leap for mankind. She found herself quite looking forward to the evening *Woodman* session, relaxed as she would be in her new-found confidence. She certainly wouldn't stand for any more shit from Stu and Lisa.

She made her coffee and carried it into the living room, relishing the prospect of the coming cigarette and studying the university prospectuses that she'd obtained from the library. 'You're half way there, having studied in a sixth form,' Mike had said. 'Just join our Access course; then it'll be a piece of piss.' She hadn't mentioned that she wasn't inclined to study history: exposure to Rhod in his more serious moments had revived her interest in English literature. Warwick University was the obvious choice, of course: she could commute there.

She rifled through the pile of prospectuses, searching for Warwick's, then settled down to read it, lighting the longed-for cigarette. The telephone rang. *Shit.*

'Hello?'

'Is that the residence of Michael Carter?' Female voice, faint Birmingham accent.

'Residence? I suppose you could call it that. Who's speaking?'

'Is that Fiona Smythe?'

'Lewis. Smythe was my maiden name. Who's speaking please?'

'Ah, Fiona; you probably don't remember me: I'm Christine Fitzroy. We were at school together.'

'Were we? Sorry, don't think I remember you.'

'I was lower down the school when you were a prefect. I certainly remember you.'

257

'How did you know I was on this number?'

'Oh, I know a few people at the college. Someone mentioned that you lived with Mike Carter.'

Alarm bells. 'So?'

'I'd like very much to meet you again. It's about the school, you see –'

'I'm sorry; I've had nothing to do with the school since I left. Now if you don't mind –'

'Oh, but Fiona, I'm sure you'd be interested in what I have to tell you; it concerns you directly.'

'Look, I'm busy. Just say what you have to say, please.'

'It's not something we can talk about on the phone, Fiona, we need to meet. I'm not working today: would you like to meet for lunch? I live on the Tedrington Road, there's a nice pub there, the *Bell*; d'you know it?'

The voice was insistent. Despite herself, Fiona was curious, and not a little apprehensive: the mention of Mike's name was responsible for that. Christine Fitzroy? The name was vaguely familiar, but she couldn't put a face to it.

'Who is it you know at the college?'

'Oh, quite a few of the lecturers. I'm an evening class student. I'll tell you all about myself when we meet; there's a lot to catch up on. Please say you'll come.'

Fiona's sense of well-being had evaporated. She knew that to ignore the invitation wasn't an option; she'd be nagged by not knowing what she probably didn't want to know. She'd have to accept.

'OK, I can spare you half an hour. I hope you're not wasting my time. I'll be at the *Bell* by one. How do I recognise you?'

'I'm sure I'll recognise *you.*'

'Right. Goodbye.'

***

Christine had found a table by the window, and was sitting in a state of anticipation which nevertheless was still tinged with the bitterness and anger that had been with her since last night's meeting with Rhodri. Over the phone, Fiona's snooty, self-confident bray, unchanged since school, had strengthened her resolve. Stuck-up cow deserved all that was coming to her. The sixth-form sex-goddess, they'd called her, those whose first-form pashes had been acknowledged with quiet tolerance. But Christine's gifts of sweets, proffered each day after hours hanging around outside the prefects' room, had been rejected with ever increasing scorn, until the day she'd been told she was a ghastly little girl and that she should piss off. And she was given a detention.

Through the widow she saw an MG swing into the car park. A slim blonde woman got out, locked the doors and walked purposefully towards to entrance. Yes, that was her; she'd know that walk anywhere. How old would she be, 35? The cow didn't seem to have aged at all; all the pampering that money could buy, no doubt. That suede jacket must have cost a fortune.

She stood and waved as Fiona pushed through the door. 'Yes, I recognised you immediately,' she said. 'Fiona Smythe, after all these years. What would you like to drink?'

'No, I'll get my own,' said Fiona.

Standing waiting to be served, Fiona searched her memory. No, don't think I know the woman from Adam, she thought. Not unattractive, but the face was somehow pinched, the speech over-effusive, and she ought to do something with that hair.

'Right,' she said, sitting down with her fruit juice. 'Would you please tell me what all this is about? Something to do with the Grammar School, you said?'

'Yes. I remember you so well from those days. You were a prefect, and I was just a little first-former. I don't suppose you even noticed me.'

'Probably not, unless you were one of the naughty ones.'

'No, I was as good as gold. Do you remember Miss Humphries, the Physics teacher? She was an old bat, wasn't she?'

Fiona conceded that yes, she remembered Miss Humphries, and was then enjoined to recall Miss Samuels, and Mrs Bancroft, and then found herself reluctantly joining in the remembrance game as her companion chattered on about staff and pupils and the icy changing rooms and the communal showers and the horrible navy-blue knickers they had to wear, until she found she'd finished her

260

fruit juice and that she was still no wiser as to why she'd been asked here.

'Is this all about some school fundraising appeal?' she interrupted the flow, 'because if so, I'm not interested.'

'Oh, nothing like that,' Christine smirked: there was no other word to describe it. 'What did you do after you left school, Fiona? I seem to remember hearing you married one of the local toffs. What happened; are you divorced?

Fiona, though tempted to tell her to mind her own business, remained silent.

'So you're living with Mike Carter. I met him earlier this week, in the *Woodman*. I was in there with Rhodri. I'm in Rhodri's evening class; we're good friends.'

So *this* was the woman that Stu had been referring to, the woman that Julie had told her about. Surely that issue had been resolved?

'So?'

'Your Mike and Rhodri seem to have been friends for a long time. You know Rhodri well, I bet?'

'Obviously. Now look, you'd better get to the point, otherwise I'm going to leave.'

'Quite a party, is it, when you three get together?'

Fiona started to get up, but Christine clutched her arm. 'Oh, come on; don't make out you don't know what I'm talking about. You'd better sit down unless you want the whole pub to hear what I'm going to say.' The voice had become harsh, the Brummie nasal whine more pronounced.

261

Fiona resumed her seat. Feelings of distaste for this appalling woman were mixed with foreboding about what it was that she might know. She felt slightly nauseous.

'You are obviously a very sad and rather disturbed individual'. It took a supreme effort to prevent her voice trembling. 'So sad, in fact, that I'll humour you. I'm giving you five minutes to say what you have to say. After that you can scream the pub down for all I care.'

'*I'm* sad? You poor bitch. Aren't you included in their little threesomes then? Too posh for that, are you? Not like some of the women at the college.'

'What women?' Fiona blurted out the question, a Pavlovian reaction.

'Oh, I don't know all their names, but it was the one who teaches Economics, Barbara is it? that got them started. You mean to say your Mike hasn't told you? Can't be a very close relationship you've got. Hang on, I haven't finished yet –'

Fiona had got up and was hurrying to the door.

'Yeah, you'd better go and check up on what he's doing now. I would, if I was living with a man like that!' The pub fell silent as Christine's shriek reached a crescendo, and all eyes turned to her.

'What are you lot looking at?' she yelled, then, suddenly, burst into tears.

***

Marcia was late back. She hadn't enjoyed the meeting with her fellow Principals. The monthly gatherings, which rotated around the colleges in the county, were a hangover from the days when the Local Authority had determined the provision in each institution. After Incorporation the meetings had continued, the stated objective being to investigate co-operative ventures. Marcia had so far witnessed little evidence of co-operation. Some of the old guard were matey enough, but the newer ones seemed more concerned to score points off each other. It was Buchanan, the Principal of Midshires College, who worried her the most. His was by far the largest institution in the area, situated far too close to Streetbridge for comfort, and his aggressive marketing was proving damaging to her college's enrolments. Marcia was used to cut-throat competition in private industry, but there one could maximise income through one's own endeavours rather than being subject to the whim of the government's arcane funding formula. All the more important, therefore, that expenditure be cut to the bone so as to free resources for marketing and more profitable provision: why couldn't Hickman and Jay appreciate this?

And now she had Evans to deal with in the next ten minutes. Was she spending too much time on internal disciplinary matters? Shouldn't she be devoting her energies to the broad sweep of strategy? For a moment she was tempted to postpone or even cancel Evans's interview, but no; the confrontation, in which she held the trump card, would be enjoyable, would provide instant gratification. Besides, it was all part of the game plan, the emasculation of the dissidents, the softening-up process necessary to ensure staff compliance with her drive for efficiency.

She swept into the outer office. Sylvia was hunched over her keyboard and did not greet her.

'Have you finished revising the staff lists?' she said.

'Not yet. I hadn't got the database on my computer, remember, so I had to import it from Human Resources and it got mangled in the process, so –'

'Spare me the details, please, Sylvia; just so long as it's finished today.' She entered her inner office and closed the door.

Sylvia gave the door a two-fingered gesture. Sod the woman. She was tempted to make a hash of the staff lists just for spite, but was prevented by her innate professionalism and the knowledge that in her present mood Marcia would seize on any evidence of incompetence as an excuse for further retribution.

There was a knock at the door. 'Come in!' she shouted, and immediately joined the long line of those who that day had looked twice at the born-again Rhodri.

'Bloody hell, Rhod, what's happened to you?'

'Just fancied a change.'

'Well, it's a change for the better. What brings you up here, anyway?'

'Got a meeting with the boss.'

'Have you? When?'

'Now.'

'I haven't got you in the diary – oh, hang on, you aren't her three o'clock appointment, are you?'

'Yes.'

Baffled about what the reason could be for such an unlikely meeting, Sylvia phoned through to announce Rhodri's arrival and, bemused, gazed at him as he entered the bunker. As ever, his expression and demeanour had given nothing away. Rhod never explained or apologised, his manner was always mild; behind those granny glasses his shrewd eyes revealed no emotion, nothing but an observer's detachment. He was, she suddenly realised, effortlessly cool, a word once inappropriate for one so unkempt, but now, with the close-cropped hair and the smart casualness of his dress, revealed as entirely apt.

She felt a sudden need to gossip. It could be a solitary existence, trapped in her office, constrained by the dictates of confidentiality. She sometimes visited the staff lounge for coffee, but it was never a relaxing break; many of the junior members of staff evidently regarded her as a lackey of the management and responded guardedly to her friendly overtures. But she needed to talk to someone about what might have prompted Rhod's transformation and his unlikely meeting with Marcia: Karen in refectory was the obvious confidante. Three o'clock; yes, Karen would be taking a tea break in her cubby hole in the kitchen.

As she walked through the crowded refectory she spotted Mike. The table at which he was sitting was festooned with students, but he was not part of their guffawing and giggling assembly. He rose to greet her.

'Hey, Sylvie, thanks for what you did; you're a star. I won't forget it.' He touched her arm briefly.

Sylvia had no wish to be reminded of the hasty action that had caused her sleepless night. 'No, forget it ever happened, please Mike. And don't ever tell anyone.' She was desperate to change the subject. 'What about Rhod then? Have you seen the new look?'

Carter grimaced. 'Yeah. Never thought he'd kow-tow to Skislopes's dictat.'

'Oh, d'you think that's why he did it? Doesn't sound like Rhod. You might be right, though; he's with her now.'

'What? Evans? With Martell?'

'Oh God Mike, I shouldn't have told you that. Her diary's confidential.'

'Did *he* ask to see *her*? Or was it the other way about?

'I don't know. I didn't arrange the meeting. Look, Mike, please forget I told you about it.'

Carter was obviously somewhere else.

'Mike? Please?'

He turned to face her. 'What?'

'Forget I told you about their meeting.'

'Yeah. Right.' He walked off, face stony.

Sylvia, as troubled as she'd ever been, made her way to the refuge of Karen's cubby-hole.

***

266

'Sit down, Mr Evans.' Marcia, remembering her occasional sightings of him at staff meetings, was no less surprised than any of his other colleagues at his metamorphosis, but her expression remained neutral. The man was almost smart, she thought, and it then occurred to her that this might be in deference to her memorandum. *He's on the run!* She hugged herself. Not that he'd gone anywhere near far enough: smart-casual was not an option. However, a first and final written warning for gross insubordination might encourage the purchase of a collar, tie and jacket.

She sat staring at him across her desk, unspeaking, for a full 30 seconds. He seemed not discomforted in the slightest; he returned her gaze, with occasional breaks to glance at her breasts. Arrogant bastard.

'I'd like you to have a look at this.' She extracted the tattered memorandum from the file in front of her and pushed it across the desk. He picked it up, held it in front of him and began to peruse it, head back, eyes cast down in the fashion of those with bi-focal spectacles. Normally such a posture spoke of merely of age: with Evans however it served to remind her of those patronising polytechnic lecturers who had demolished her essays during tutorials.

He returned the memo to the desk, and looked across at her.

'Well?' she said. 'What's your response to that?'

'To your memorandum or to the annotations thereon? If you're asking me about the former, I'd

267

need an hour to give a considered response. If you refer to the latter, I'd say that the comments, though apposite, are somewhat discourteous.'

Was he being sarcastic? The lilt of his Welsh accent disguised his intentions. What the hell does *apposite* mean, anyway? She took another paper from the file and pushed it across to him.

'What's this?'

'I suggest you look at it.'

'It's one of my student report forms. Sorry, I'm not with you.'

'I'll come to the point. The scrawlings on the memorandum are in your handwriting.'

He examined the two papers. 'There's certainly a similarity, I'll grant you. That must have taken a lot of detective work: how many report forms did you have to examine to come up with this? I'm surprised you have the time. Or did Adrian Havers do it for you? If that's the sort of thing a Programme Area Head has to do I'm glad I'm just a humble lecturer.'

Marcia was momentarily shamed by the memory of her deviousness in obtaining the student reports and the time that went into examining them. She felt herself colouring slightly. Stay on the offensive, she told herself.

'Mr Evans, do you deny that the handwriting on the memorandum is yours?'

'I won't deny that it's similar to mine, but I imagine you'd have to get a handwriting expert in to confirm it, should you wish to go to those lengths of course. But do I seem the sort of person who'd resort to such condemnatory banalities? I'm an English lecturer, see. When I correct scripts my comments are always constructive.'

'Mr Evans, I'm not interested in your marking methods –'

'Excuse me, could I just pursue something with you?' He gave no time for a response. 'I don't know anything about running a college, or anything about leadership, but I imagine it must demand qualities that few of us have or even know about. It must, I'm sure, also be about having confidence in the expertise of your colleagues, and the ability to utilise their expertise. You have a Finance colleague to deliver the budget, don't you? And a computer whiz-kid to deliver IT? And Charles Jay deals with the curriculum, and Edgar Hickman with personnel matters?'

'We're here to establish whether you defaced my –'

'Forgive me, but I imagine you're not ashamed of not being an expert in IT or the curriculum or personnel?'

'Of *course* I'm not,' Marcia was so taken aback by the effrontery of the question that she found herself answering it.

'Then why should you be ashamed of not being an expert in the use of English? There's no reason why you should be. You have more important things to think about. So why don't you think of using an English specialist to help you with communication?'

'Enough!' Marcia found herself standing up. 'I did not ask you here to discuss how I run the college. I suggest you go away and think carefully

269

about the position you're in. I shall continue to pursue this matter. You'll be having another interview with me next week.'

Rhodri rose. 'I'm sorry if I've offended you; it wasn't my intention, I assure you. I was simply trying to be helpful. I'll see you next week, then.'

Marcia sank back in her chair as he left the room. How could she possibly have handled that so badly? Why had she allowed him to take the initiative? It was his bloody English lecturer fluency of course, enhanced by that Welsh lilt. How could she rescue the situation? What could she say next time to bring him to heel? She hadn't even got him to deny that he was culpable; had he done so, she would have at least now be feeling a moral superiority. Worse, she couldn't deny the logic of his argument about utilising the expertise of others. Casting around for solace, the only comfort she could draw from the encounter was that he seemed to have taken some notice of her dress edict.

Friday evening

In the *Woodman*, Rita occupied her usual place at the bar, gin in her left hand, cigarette in her right, waiting for the Friday night revelries to begin. The only others present were Todger and his mates, occupied at the pool table, their first pints only half drained, their profanities subdued. It would be some time before the College crowd drifted in. Rita liked them; they chatted to her when they came to the bar, and added a bit of class to the place. Not that they were stuck up: some of them could match her oath for oath, and it was amusing to listen to their conversation, not that she could understand much of it.

The door swung open and three strangers entered, a lad and two girls. Rita stared at them: it wasn't often that newcomers braved the *Woodman*. They couldn't be tourists, not at this time of year; anyway they were too young. They stood around uncertainly for a few moments. Todger and his mates rested on their cues, appraising the two girls, especially the brunette with the miniskirt. You don't stand a chance with that one, Todger me old mate. Far too classy.

The brunette led the other two to the bar. 'What d'ya want, Liz? What about you, Kelv?'

They elected respectively for a mineral water and a half of lager.

'Oh, come on, chill, you two, like it's Friday night, let's get wasted.'

'Heidi, you know I don't drink.' said the other female. By Christ she had a posh accent, thought

271

Rita; don't think she'll last long in here. Auburn haired, about the same age as the brunette, but dressed far less youthfully. No make up, either.

'I think I'll start slowly,' the lad said. He looked no more than a schoolboy, and distinctly ill at ease; oddly dressed as well. Did his mum knit him that sweater, Rita wondered?

The brunette peered round the bar.

'George is down in the cellar,' Rita informed her. 'George? *George!*' she yelled. 'You've got customers!'

George came grunting up the cellar steps and the brunette placed the order. 'No, just give me the bottle, please,' she said as George made to pour her lager into a glass.

'What about you, young man?' he said. 'D'you want it in the bottle?'

'He'll have a glass, won't you Kelv?' said the brunette, and the lad nodded assent.

Rita watched as the three carried their drinks over to the table beside the door. They made an oddly assorted trio and they didn't seem very relaxed with each other. The brunette remained standing until the other two sat, then pulled a chair round so that she could seat herself beside the lad. Rita, who had developed the observational acuity of the lonely, noticed the disappointment that flickered over the other girl's face. *Interesting.*

'Got some young customers at last then, George. You'll soon have to start stocking alcopops.'

George humphed. 'They'll have to take me as they find me. If they don't like what I serve they know what they can do.'

The door opened; ah, the first of the college crowd. It was Barbara; Rita liked Barbara; she sometimes brought her drink over to the bar to chat. To her surprise, she acknowledged the three youngsters with a wave. 'You made it here then, Liz,' she heard her say. 'Good on yer.'

'Friends of yours, are they, Barb?' Rita asked as Barbara reached the bar.

'Well, colleagues, Rita.'

'Bugger me, they're not teachers are they? That lad looks like he ought to be in school himself.'

'I know. Makes you sick, doesn't it.'

Barbara took her pint and carried it over to the trio.

'Hey, George, did yer hear that? Those three are teachers at the college. Bloody hell, old Barb looks old enough to be their mother.'

'Strange woman, that one, never seen her with a man,' said George. 'D'you reckon she's one of those?'

Rita cackled. 'Nah, but I reckon that posh one over there might be. See the way she keeps looking at the brunette, the one with the skirt just below sea-level? No, Barb's got a fella, she told me. She lives with him in Levington. He don't like her college mates, that's why he never comes here.'

'Can't say I blame him. Funny load o' buggers, that lot. Fancy 'emselves, don't they? One of these days old Todger's going to land one on that Carter bloke.'

'That'll be fun,' said Rita. 'Give us another gin, George.'

Elizabeth was giving distracted responses to Barbara's attempts to converse. What a ghastly place this was; cheaply furnished, dirty, smoky, smelling of stale tobacco, and of something else whenever the door to the gentlemen's toilet was opened. Gentlemen! Not a word that accurately described the clientele; those men playing billiards or snooker or whatever it's called. Low life! Just the sort of people she took pains to avoid. And that terrible old woman sitting by the bar! She glanced at her watch: only seven-thirty; heaven knows what the place would be like when it began to fill up.

Why had Heidi suggested coming here? Surely this wasn't her usual haunt? Elizabeth watched her chatting to Kelvin. She seemed happy enough, which was more than could be said for Kelvin; the lad was wearing his frightened-rabbit expression and he kept glancing over his shoulder at the oiks playing billiards.

This was a terrible price she was having to pay to secure Heidi's companionship on a visit to London. Perhaps Heidi had deliberately chosen this place hoping that she'd leave in disgust? Was this Heidi's way of attempting to free herself from her obligation? Surely not; the girl was so open, so outspoken; if she'd not wished to go to London she would have made her position clear. Or was it all some sort of game? Elizabeth had never indulged in game-playing; she didn't know the rules.

A well of unhappiness rose to submerge her underlying unease. She forced herself to pay attention to Barbara who was asking her what had finally persuaded her to join her colleagues socially.

'Well, it was Heidi who persuaded me to come along. I think she wanted some company in order to brave a place like this.' She noticed that Barbara raised her eyebrows at this suggestion, and hastily added, 'I mean she wanted me to help stiffen Kelvin's resolve; the poor lad doesn't get out much, you see.'

'I don't think it's his resolve that needs stiffening, Mon, and I reckon Heidi's more than capable of doing that by herself.' Barbara grinned and took a swallow from her pint glass.

Elizabeth recoiled. After five months at the college she had still to analyse her attitude to Barbara. At one level the woman was the female equivalent of Carter and Evans, capable of the same foul language and sordid innuendo – and a heavy smoker as well; she was smoking now. But there had been several occasions when she'd pulled them up sharply when their so-called wit had crossed the boundary into crude misogynistic bombast. She could also, on occasions, demonstrate kindness and understanding for the feelings of others: even now, though smoking, she was being careful to hold the cigarette below the table and to turn aside when exhaling.

'Anyway, Liz,' she was saying, 'for what it's worth I think you were right to join us. For one thing it'll help you mend your fences with Mike after that row you two had on Thursday.'

Elizabeth bridled. 'I can assure you that was not my intention in coming here.'

Barbara eyed her quizzically. 'If you don't mind me saying, Liz, you don't do yourself any favours with Mike, or with Rhod come to that. Oh, I know they can be a crude couple of buggers, but you shouldn't rise to the bait, it just serves to egg them on. And they're not so bad when you get to know them. Rhod's very kind underneath all that gruffness, and Mike's not nearly so self-assured as he likes to make out. I'm very fond of them, but then I've known them for years.'

'They are of a generation that I can't begin to understand.'

'Oh come on, it's not a generational thing, is it? They're about the same age as old Albert, and Derek, and Graham, and you get on ok with them. I'm not that much younger myself. I can't believe you're hung up about age. Anyway, what about young Heidi; she can share a joke with them, can't she?'

Elizabeth felt the first stirrings of anger. 'You think so? So why does Heidi elect to come to the staff common room with me rather than sit in the work room in the coffee break with them? Had you considered that?'

Barbara's eyes narrowed. 'She goes there to avoid Albert; don't fool yourself mate.'

'What are you implying?' Apprehension battled with Elizabeth's rising ire.

'Don't get your knickers in a twist, Liz, I'm not implying anything. Look, you and Heidi might be the same age and both new to teaching, but let's face it, that's all you have in common. She's a bright lively kid, but she's not exactly an intellectual, is she? Not really a potential soul-mate for you. You've got far more in common with Mike and Rhod, if you did but know it. It *is* possible to have an intelligent conversation with them if you take them as you find them. And they're both bloody good teachers, especially Rhod. I'm empty; d'you want another drink?'

Elizabeth shook her head. Barbara made her way to the bar. The pub had began to fill up with a varied assortment of low-life during their conversation, but Elizabeth was more concerned with what Barbara had said about Heidi, and the way she had said it. Did she think that she, Elizabeth, viewed Heidi as anything more than a friend? What arrant nonsense. What, other than a warped mind, could even consider such a possibility? She must enlighten Barbara, make her aware that her interest in Heidi was that of a mentor.

'Well, bugger me, it's Liz; never thought to see you in here, bach.'

She started. Deep in thought, she hadn't registered Rhodri's entry. He was accompanied by a middle aged couple, the male boyish of face with a moustache and thick black curly hair, unfashionably long; the female plump, blonde and pretty in a faded sort of way.

'Oh, well, I thought it would make a change,' she said lamely.

'Well, it's good to see you here.' He touched her briefly on the shoulder and sat down opposite her.

Elizabeth recoiled at his touch. 'That's Barbara's seat.'

'Don't think she'll mind. Hey, Geoff, Julie, this is Liz. She's the new French lecturer. And those two over there are Kelvin and Heidi.'

Hellos! and *His!* were exchanged, though Elizabeth said 'Pleased to meet you.' Geoff went to the bar, returning with Barbara and a tray full of drinks. Tables were pushed together, chairs re-arranged, and Elizabeth found herself opposite Julie, who immediately began to talk to her.

She seems a pleasant enough woman, thought Elizabeth, not too much between the ears perhaps, but with an acceptable accent and speech mercifully devoid of oaths and vulgarities. Neither did she lack social graces. It was evident, Elizabeth realised, that she was trying to make her feel at home, asking questions about her interests, and recounting her own. She reluctantly surrendered to an exchange of trivia with her, longing for the evening to end.

Heidi was getting restless. The price of avoiding an intense conversation with Liz had been to chat with Kelvin, but oh-my-god he was hard work. Barbara would have been more fun, but she was chatting to Liz. She thought things might get livelier when Rhod came in, but he'd started talking to Barb and Liz. The couple who came in with him looked ok, the guy wasn't bad looking for a wrinkly; he might have been nice to chat up, but after he got the round in he'd sat opposite Kelvin and started talking about Geography! Course, that's just the sort of thing to turn Kelv on; what a saddo!

She was seated on the edge of the group, not a position she was used to: she liked to be in the middle, exchanging snappy asides with those surrounding her, but everyone else was talking in pairs – even Liz. That Julie woman who was chatting to her must have been quite a looker when she was young – she's not bad now, needs to lose some weight though. Liz keeps glancing at me: oh-my-god, I was well mental to ask her here, never thought she'd come. Is she that way, or isn't she? She probably doesn't know herself.

She surveyed the room, now in its way to being full. What a place to spend Friday evening, she thought; I must be the only one here under 40, apart from Kelv and Liz of course. Some of the seedy old buggers can't take their eyes of my legs, dirty old wankers, especially that greasy biker by the pool table. Why aren't I in the *Eagle*? Reckon I might escape there in a bit if Mike doesn't show. What has he done to rattle Rhod's cage? Was hoping to find out tonight. Would be ok to see Mike outside work again; he's got something about him; perhaps we could give it another shot.

'So you teach German at the college then?' The blonde was addressing her.

'Sorry? Oh, yeah, that's right.'

279

'Geoff, my old man over there, he used to teach there, ages ago that was. He's in business now.'

'Yeah, I know, he taught Geography, like Kelvin. Like, how long ago was it when he was there?'

'Oh, he left in '81. He'd been there for about seven years.'

'So Mike Carter would have been there when he was?'

The blonde raised her eyebrows. 'Too right; Mike's a fixture.'

'Where is he tonight? Thought he always came here on a Friday.'

'Yes. He's usually here by now, with Fiona, his lady.'

Heidi noticed that the blonde looked a bit worried as she imparted this news. Something's been going on, wonder how *she's* involved?

Her thoughts were interrupted by the arrival of another couple. More casual introductions; Stu and Lisa apparently; wonder if they ever had anything to do with the college? They look really gross, especially Lisa, all tarted up in that ancient hippie dress with make-up plastered over her face; wow, she's staggering, looks like she's on the way to being wasted already. Hope she doesn't start talking to me. What a crowd of sad old nutters.

Julie was not her usual relaxed self. Where are Fiona and Mike she wondered? Oh God, please let their absence not be anything to do with what I told Fi yesterday afternoon. I shouldn't have spilled the beans; I didn't intend to; all I wanted to do was forewarn her about Lisa. That bloody woman, she always manages to cause trouble.

She sipped at her half of cider and looked round the group. Stu, with his habitual sneering expression, was listening to Rhod's bawdy conversation with Barbara and interjecting the occasional remark. Lisa, already far gone (she must have been at the wine long before she arrived), was staring vacantly round the room: it wouldn't be long before the onset of either raucous shrieking or tearful sulks. It was the same scene that Julie had witnessed week after week for more years than she cared to remember, but without the redeeming presence of Fiona or the slight frisson engendered by Mike. Geoff would normally have escaped to the pool table by now, but he seemed to be trapped in earnest conversation with that young man. Of the three young newcomers the lad at least seemed to be connecting with the regulars, which was more than could be said for the two girls. They seemed most ill-matched. Heidi looked as though she'd be more at home clubbing it somewhere, while the other one, Elizabeth was it? seemed to be on the verge of tears.

She asked herself again why Geoff maintained his links with this crowd, now that he'd started developing contacts in the town's business community. She'd found that she preferred the rather more genteel company of its social evenings in the *Falconer*; she certainly seemed now to have more in common with the Streetbridge business wives than with Lisa or Barbara. She glanced round the smoky room with its rag-bag collection of male artisans, brassy women spilling out of their too-tight clothes, grungy drop-outs, ageing hippies, motor-cycling yobs and, seated around her, what passed for the town's intelligentsia. For the first time she saw it as though the eyes of her *Windmill* acquaintances. She'd had enough of it. Geoff only came for reasons of sentiment; he was an old softie. She was sure he could be persuaded to sever the links, well, at least to make his attendance less regular; hadn't he said that the billiard table in the Conservative Club was so much better to play on than the clapped-out old table here? And he wouldn't have to put up with Todger and his mates and their ill-disguised contempt for the college crowd.

The door opened. It was Carter.

He walked straight to the bar without acknowledging anyone. Julie's apprehension deepened when it became apparent that Fiona wasn't with him. Most of the others had also registered her absence: 'Where's Lady Fiona tonight?' from Lisa. 'Where's Fi?' from Barbara. Rhod said nothing but appeared puzzled. Heidi detached herself from the edge of the conversation with Geoff and the lad, and looked alert. Elizabeth visibly tensed.

Mike turned and approached them with his pint. My God, what's the matter with him? He looked ghastly, pallid under the sallow complexion; his hair, usually so carefully coiffured, was awry, his expression grim. There was no cheerful 'Fuckin' 'allo'. He pulled a vacant chair from a nearby table and dragged it to the far end of the group, next to

Geoff and the young lad. The group fell silent. It was left to Barbara to ask the question again.

'Where's Fiona tonight, then, Mike?'

'Dunno.' was grunted. Tobacco and cigarette papers made their appearance. Barbara and Rhod were silent. Even Stu and Lisa were temporarily mute.

Julie had to know what had happened.

'Is she coming on later, then, Mike?'

'How the hell should I know?'

Julie was taken aback by the aggression in his response; he was usually so cool, so measured, except when he was talking politics of course.

'If it makes you lot of gossiping old women happy,' he said to the group at large, 'I don't know where the fuck she is. She wasn't in when I got home. And she'd left the place in a mess.'

He dragged on his roll-up, than ground it, only half smoked, in the ashtray. His hand was shaking.

'What d'you mean? What sort of mess?' Julie asked.

'All my gear scattered all over the place. Looks like she's taken some of her stuff. She hasn't even bothered to close the drawers.'

'Mike,' Julie leaned towards him and whispered. 'Did she tell you about my visit yesterday? Was it something to do with that? I didn't mean to land you in it, I mean –'

'Yeah, she told me what you'd told her. If it eases your conscience, we got all that sorted; least I thought we had. I dunno what the fuck's got into her. Hey, young Kelvin, you finally made it here then?'

283

He obviously didn't want to talk more about it. Julie's relief that Fiona's disappearance seemed not to be a direct result of their Thursday tete-a-tete was tempered by concern for her welfare.

Conversation amongst the group gradually resumed, stutteringly at first, then increasing in volume and tempo as Carter, a silent figure listening to the exchanges between Geoff and Kelvin, gradually became forgotten, though not by Julie. She even found herself feeling sorry for him.

The evening was winding itself up to the usual Friday night crescendo. Shrieks and guffaws punctuated the shouted exchanges between the various tables, shots on the pool table were missed with increasing frequency and obscene curses, whisky chasers had begun to accompany the pints, hands were placed openly on thighs and more surreptitiously on backsides in anticipation of evening pleasures to come, George and his weekend bar staff sweated and slipped on the beer-spilled floor, the ancient extractor fans fought a losing battle with the onslaught from Marlboro Lites, and the college crowd had fully regained its animation, though Carter and Elizabeth were set apart both from the badinage and from each other.

It was Rita, perched ever more precariously on her stool and peering glassy-eyed around the room, who first registered the entry of Fiona. She saw her standing for a moment at the door as if this were her first visit to the pub, then she straightened her back and walked briskly to the tables where the others were sitting, there to stop and stare fixedly at Carter. She was, as usual, casually but immaculately dressed in designer jeans and top, her hair shone as though just washed, her minimal make-up had been carefully and discreetly applied.

One by one her friends noticed her arrival and greeted her. She ignored them, and remained standing. They looked at her anew; where was the usual broad grin, the toss of the hair, the 'Hi you guys' delivered in the clear county cadence? She appeared, to those who were sufficiently sober to notice, strained; her expression determined. It was only Julie who registered the same slight tremor in her hands that had earlier afflicted her partner.

It was Carter who broke the silence. 'Where the hell were you? And what's with all the mess in the house?'

She continued to stare at him, silent, as though waiting to ensure she had the attention of all present.

'You *shit*,' she said eventually. She didn't have to shout, blessed as she was with the commanding voice of her class. 'You absolute shit. You lied to me. You said you'd told me everything, that there were no more sordid secrets. But there are, aren't there? Horrid, filthy secrets. You disgust me. You're low life, you belong in the gutter.'

Carter looked at her open mouthed. It was Lisa, by now in her shrill phase, who chose to speak. 'Wassa matter Fi? Didn't you know what a dirty sod he was when you shacked up with him? Thought it was that that turned you on.' She hiccupped, then giggled.

285

Fiona turned to face her. 'You *pathetic* woman. Take a look at yourself. You're a drunk, a lush, an alcoholic. That by itself would be disgusting enough, but the thought of you and Carter together, with the full acquiescence of your husband, and practically in his presence, turns my stomach. Not that you aren't ideally suited to each other.'

'You fucking stuck up cow!' Lisa shrieked, 'Think you're superior to us, don't you? We've all got degrees. What have you got, you ignorant rich-bitch?'

The pub fell silent, all eyes turned to the group. Rita, still observant through her gin haze, noted the alert, excited expression on the face of the mini-skirted girl and the aghast faces of her two young companions. Barbara stood up and placed her hand on Fiona's arm, but Fiona shook it off and rounded on her.

'Don't you touch me. Don't you *dare* touch me. You're worse than Lisa. You're nothing but a whore, an old whore.'

Barbara stood her ground. 'What's got into you, Fi? What are you on about?'

'Is Alzheimer's setting in? Well, I suppose you're almost old enough. Let's try and jog your memory, shall we? You? Evans? Carter? All together? Tell me, how does that work? I'm not sure I can work out the mechanics, but no doubt you've had a lot of practice'

Barbara slumped back on her chair. Rhodri and Carter, at opposite ends of the table, were mute statues. A smile began to spread over Stu's face.

Julie rose and moved to sit next to Geoff; he put his arm round her shoulders protectively.

Fiona turned to them: Julie blanched in anticipation of the onslaught to come.

'Julie, don't worry, this isn't the result of what you said. All that was a vicarage tea-party compared to what I've learned came after. You and Geoff are the only people here with a scrap of decency. I can understand why you left FE, Geoff; you're far too enterprising and gentlemanly to be mixing with this lot. And if you three' (she addressed Heidi, Kelvin and Elizabeth) 'are at the college I'd advise you to get out before you're totally corrupted, unless you have been already of course.'

'I can assure you –' began Elizabeth, but she was interrupted by Carter.

'Cool it, Fi, for Christ's sake. All that shit was years ago –'

'I don't care when it was. You promised me that you'd told me everything, and you hadn't. If you lied about that, you could be lying about everything. You're totally untrustworthy. How do I know you're still not carrying on with your sordid little adventures even while I'm living with you?'

Heidi didn't pause to think before she spoke. The wisecrack was out of her mouth in an instant. 'No, I don't think he is. Like, he can't get it up, can he? I should know.'

It took a few moments for the implications of Heidi's remark to sink into the collective

287

consciousness. All sat frozen in a cartoon-like tableau. Elizabeth was the first to react; ashen faced, she stood, forced her way between the two tables, spilling Kelvin's lager in the process, and groped her way towards the door. Kelvin scuttled after her.

For the first time since her entrance, Fiona's composure slipped; her lower lip trembled. She ran her hand through her hair, swallowed and half turned away.

'Fi, wait,' Carter said.

She turned back to face him. 'I'm going back to mummy's.' (*'Mummy's!* Stu sniggered.) 'I'd be grateful if you could arrange to be out tomorrow morning, I still have a few of my things to collect and I don't wish to see you. When I've finished I'll post my key through your letter box. Goodbye. Julie, I'd like to keep in touch; I'll phone you.'

Her long legs took her to the door in four strides.

'What are you about, you cow!' screamed Lisa at Julie, 'What gave you the right to tell my private business to that bitch? You're just as stuck up as she is; two Streetbridge posh-totties together.'

'Shut it you stupid woman.' This from Stu. And at the same time, from Barbara to Rhodri; 'It must have been *you* that told her about all that. What the hell were you thinking of?'

'What do you take me for? For God's sake, Barb, give me credit for a bit of discretion.'

Carter interjected: 'Who else could have told her, you bastard?'

288

Barbara resumed her interrogation. 'It *must* have been you, Evans, who else knew?'

Rhodri gestured towards Carter.

'Oh for fuck's sake you Welsh tosser. You're not suggesting I told her? What would be in it for me?'

'Don't ask me to analyse your motives, Carter. When it comes to trying to make it with fresh tottie you're capable of anything. Though come to think of it, if you're after young Heidi here, you'll need Fi out of the way won't you? You need lots of time to rise to the occasion, it seems. Have you ever been honest with your women, Carter?'

'I know what's eating you, Evans,' Carter grimaced. 'Your precious daughter's been here hasn't she? Finally got round to telling you about our little gropes, has she?'

The hubbub of competing questions, accusations and denials was silenced by Carter's final remark. Rhodri stood up, then resumed his seat and began to roll a cigarette. The eyes of the others swivelled expectantly between the two of them, the hush in the room broken only by Rita's chesty cough, instantly suppressed.

'Carter,' Rhodri said finally, 'I can't be bothered to respond to that. You're a lightweight, a poseur, a chameleon. You have no convictions. You're guided by your vanity and your need to project the image in which you've chosen to cast yourself. You have no depth, no inner resource, no ontological security. Your so-called Marxism is a charade. You profess an adherence to an ideology that has no relevance to contemporary society

289

simply as a means to impress the impressionable. You don't realise the amusement that this generates amongst we who know you for what you are.'

He paused to light a cigarette.

'Have you finished?' said Carter, 'because –'

'No, I haven't finished. You also make claims to be a hedonist, a free spirit keeping the flame of the 1960s alive. You're no hedonist, Carter, and you never were. I've watched you, over the years. Dope, booze, women – it's all carefully cultivated isn't it? All part of the image. You bask in the reputation that you think you have. You're too self-aware to be a true hedonist. Lurking in the recesses of your psyche is a lower-middle class conformist. You affect disdain for the well-off and the successful. But it's envy, isn't it? You'd like to be up there with them. You claim you could have been, had you chosen to take up Jefferson's offer of promotion – how many times have we had to listen to that story? Too late now; you're an old man. Look at the people in power; they're all young. The torch has long passed from you baby boomers. But you wouldn't have made it in any case; you lack the self-confidence.'

Carter's knuckles were white as he grasped his beer glass. 'What the fuck do you know about it? Just because you've sold out with your new gear and your cropped hair. And I'm a war-baby, you arsehole, not a baby-boomer. Let me tell you –'

Rhodri held up his arm. 'Wait, Carter, you'll have your chance when I've finished. I'm sorry for you, in some respects. But not as sorry as I am for

290

those girls who've been fucked up by your pathetic attempts to reconcile your inner conflicts. And when you realised that your pulling days were coming to an end, what did you do? You shacked up with a toff, one of those whom you profess to despise. You seduced her with promises to assist her liberation and enlightenment, then tried to turn her into a compliant little housewife. Is that your way of waging class war? Looks like you've failed, comrade; she was always more than a match for you, was Fiona, I knew that soon after I first met her. And now, it seems from what Heidi's told us, you probably aren't even able to satisfy her physically. You're screwed, Carter; impotent in every conceivable respect.'

Carter's mouth had been working as Rhodri warmed to his theme. He suddenly jerked to his feet and advanced on him, arms flailing. Lisa screamed; Barbara shouted for Carter to stop; Stu lumbered round the table and tried to grab Carter's arms from behind.

'Rumble!' yelled a delighted Todger, and advanced on the group, pool-cue in hand, followed by his leather-jacketed acolytes. The pub erupted into a general melee as the regulars seized their long-awaited chance to give those poncy college twats a good pasting. From behind the bar George nodded at his mates, the group of five heavies who habitually sat quietly in the far corner, and it took only two minutes for them to rid the pub of the combatants.

Rita asked for another gin and tonic.

Outside, Geoff and Julie ran towards their Mondeo parked at the street corner, followed closely behind by Barbara, Stu and a staggering Lisa. Geoff urged them all into the car and drove off.

'What about the others?' panted Julie.

'They'll have to look after themselves. Where are you parked, Barb?'

'In High Street.'

'OK. I'll drop you there, and you two as well, you can walk home from there.'

'Can't you give us a lift, Geoff?' wheedled Lisa.

'No. I'm not a taxi service.'

'Bastard,' said Stu.

Rhodri and Heidi avoided harm by the simple expedient of standing motionless outside the pub door while potential assailants chased after Carter, their prime target. When they'd all disappeared round the corner, Heidi turned to Rhodri, eyes shining.

'Hey, that was well exciting! Where shall we go now? It's only ten.'

'I'm going home to listen to Mahler. He'll be a good antidote to tonight.'

'Oh.' There was a pause, then – 'Are you going to walk me home first, Rhod?'

'No, bach. I've had quite enough excitement for one night.'

The Weekend

Rhodri was not at ease with himself.

The Friday night confrontation with Carter hadn't disturbed him unduly; he'd known in any case that the road they'd travelled together was coming to its end. It was Barbara's conviction that he'd broken a confidence that he'd found upsetting, and he'd spent most of Saturday puzzling over how Fiona could have found out. There had been something niggling deep in his memory concerning Fiona's history that seemed to be of relevance to this problem, but, like the faint trace of a dream that remains on waking, it was stubbornly irretrievable.

It had not been until Saturday evening that the truth revealed itself. After a day spent shopping for goods that a fortnight before he would never have envisaged buying, and unsuccessfully trying make progress with his novel, he desperately needed a drink but realised that he was, along with the rest of them, probably *persona non grata* at the *Woodman*. Not wishing to drink alone, and wanting at all costs to avoid an encounter with Carter, he'd phoned Geoff to ask what he was doing that evening, to be informed that he and Julie were going for a drink in the *Falconer* and that they had no objection to his joining them so long as he was not accompanied by Carter.

He'd walked into the *Falconer* to find Geoff and Julie occupying the same table at which he'd sat with Christine on Thursday, and with a jolt the trapdoors over his memory sprang open – of course! Christine! He'd told Christine of his adventures with Carter, and to add verisimilitude had been gratuitously explicit and had named names. And – another door opened - hadn't Christine said she'd known Fiona at school? And had disliked her? As the muddied waters cleared he was horrified by the realisation that he *had* in fact broken a confidence, and that his attempt to rid himself of Christine while at the same time besmirching Carter had resulted in distress for two friends, Fiona and Barbara. Geoff and Julie had found him a strangely muted companion for the remainder of the evening.

Sunday had passed in a haze of indecision and inactivity. Should he contact Fiona to tell her that it was he, not Carter, who was the instigator that long-ago night that they'd spent with Barbara? What good would it do? In any case, he didn't know how to contact Fiona now she'd walked out on Carter. And Barbara – should he ring her to attempt an explanation and an apology? She'd probably slam down the phone on hearing his voice. He'd made a further attempt at his novel, but found that his whole perspective on the human condition had changed over the previous 24 hours, and he was unable to write with his usual voice. The physical release that might have been obtained from a thorough cleaning of his house had been denied him; Megan's efforts had pre-empted that.

Now, in the evening, he was trying to take refuge in marihuana, Mahler and *Middlemarch*. But they were failing to provide the usual solace.

Monday

Adrian Havers had decided to broach his ideas directly with his staff before issuing a memo about it. Experience had taught him that it was wise to gauge reaction to any proposal for change before committing himself to paper. They were a strangely conservative lot, resistant to any change, particularly the older ones, and the self-proclaimed radicals, Carter, Evans, Sidelski and Deakin, were the worst.

So he'd had to brace himself for his visit to the staff work-room during the morning break and for the outpourings that would doubtless result from his suggestions. If he arrived early enough he'd be able to catch most of the staff present before Elizabeth and Heidi adjourned to the common room: Elizabeth could be relied upon to be sensible and voice her support. Without her, the only voice raised in his favour would be Arthur's, and God save us from our allies.

He pushed open the door, ready to shout 'Good Morning' sufficiently loudly to attract attention, but found the room surprisingly hushed. Graham was of course immersed in his preparation, but Arthur was not giving his usual lecture to Barbara: she was bent over her work with the air of one who must not be disturbed and Arthur had evidently taken the hint; no, it would have taken more than a hint to deter him. Barbara must have engaged in plain speaking. Derek was sorting ballot papers into two piles on his desk and shaking his head sorrowfully in the process. Mike Carter, whose desk faced the wall, was, for once, not sitting sideways in his chair haranguing his colleagues, but was hunched silently over his work, back to the room. Even young Heidi seemed constrained; no provocative display of thigh today: her legs were tucked decorously under her desk and she was sucking her pen, apparently lost in thought. No sign of Elizabeth and Kelvin, nor Rhodri, but then he was bound to be late.

'Morning, folks,' he said heartily. Arthur and Graham responded courteously, Derek waved an abstracted hand, Heidi gave a casual *Hi*, Barbara grunted, Mike seemed not to have registered his presence at all.

'Thought I ought to let you know that I'm thinking of changing the way we timetable our mock A-Levels,' he said, trying to make his tone casual. Arthur smoothed his Jackie Charlton strands down across his pate and sat back expectantly, Graham placed a finger at a vital point in his notes and looked up, Heidi removed the pen from her mouth and stared at him vacantly. From the others there was no discernable response.

'Yes, well, I've been a bit concerned for some time about the loss of teaching time resulting from the mock A-Levels being extended over a fortnight. I'd like to see them being completed more quickly, in a week if possible. I'm going to send you a memo outlining how I think it might be done, but I thought it fair to let you know in advance.'

Arthur folded his hands over his ample stomach and said that while he agreed that too much valuable teaching time was taken up by the present arrangements, he did have some doubts about whether it could be managed in a week. He assured Adrian that he'd give his paper careful consideration, and that any comments he might have on it would be constructive.

'Thank you, Arthur. What about the rest of you? Graham? Derek?'

'I've got more pressing problems at the moment, Adrian,' said Derek. 'I'll wait till I see your paper.'

'I'd be worried about being able to fit in all my preparation in that week,' said Graham. 'I'd like to think about it.'

'Barbara? What about you?'

Barbara turned to face him. Bloody hell, she looked terrible, as though she'd had no sleep over the whole weekend. She often did look a bit rough on Monday mornings, but this was something else.

'You'll do whatever you want to do in the end, won't you?' she said, her voice thick with catarrh. 'Can't be bothered to argue the toss, Adrian.' She got up and walked towards the kettle.

'What about you, Mike?' Adrian addressed the back of Carter's head. 'I imagine you've got something to say about it?'

Carter turned stiffly, his hand shielding his eyes. My God, thought Adrian, what's he been up to? A graze all down one cheek, and is that a black eye he's trying to hide? He looks ill, the beardless bits pallid under his sallow complexion. His hair's greasy as well – he's usually so proud of his hair, washes it every day, someone told me.

'Mike, what on earth's happened to you? Are you all right?'

'Yeah.'

'What's happened to your face?'

'Got thumped by some heavies in town. I'm ok.'

'Well, you don't look it. Have you had that eye looked at? It might - '

'I'm ok, I tell you. And as far as your mock exam proposal's concerned, I think it's shit.' He turned back to face his desk.

A predictable reaction, thought Adrian, though expressed more succinctly than was usual. He turned to Heidi.

'What do you think, Heidi?'

'Whatever.'

Adrian fought back a welling tide of irritation. Of all the Programme Areas in the college the staff in his must be the most difficult to handle, but today they seemed more obstructive than he'd ever known them.

'Have Kelvin and Elizabeth been in?' He broadcast the question to the room in general in the hope of eliciting a civil response from one of them.

'They're in the common room,' said Rhodri as he entered. On seeing him, Carter rose suddenly, knocking over his chair in the process, and scrambled to the door, arm still shielding his face.

'In a hurry, our Carter,' said Rhodri. 'Get me a coffee if you're making one, could you Barb?'

'Fuck off,' said Barbara.

Adrian had had enough. 'Perhaps one of you could let Rhodri know my proposals for mock exams. I've got to go.' And he went; hurriedly.

'Well, Rhodri,' said Arthur as the door closed, 'the proposals are quite reasonable, to my mind; you see - '

'No doubt he's going to issue a memo about them?'

'Yes, of course, but - '

'Then I'll wait for that, if you don't mind, Arthur. I've got a few things to think about, see.'

***

'Good morning, Sylvia,' Marcia's voice was cheerful, even friendly, as she entered the office.

What had been bugging her last week? thought Sylvia. Whatever it was seems to have blown over. Perhaps she's had a good seeing to over the weekend. Or perhaps she *is* on the change? It would explain her mood swings; hell, she's difficult enough to cope with as it is; not sure I can put up with menopausal unpredictability.

'If you could come in with the post as soon as you're ready; oh, and bring any papers submitted for the SMT meeting. Coffee can wait, I've a lot to deal with this morning.'

Sylvia, relieved that she'd not been given more menial tasks to perform said that she'd be with her in five minutes. Marcia said that this was fine. Sylvia said that it was no problem. Marcia said that this was good. The exchange of polite banalities was on the way to becoming oriental.

Seated at her desk waiting for Sylvia, Marcia relished the prospect of the day ahead; it was to be filled with just the right combination of managerial and personal gratification. The first steps along the road to college reorganisation would be taken, Carter would be confronted, humiliated and suspended, and Sylvia; well, she hadn't yet decided how to deal with Sylvia, but revenge would be best served cold. Only the niggling worry over the predatory ambitions of the Principal of Midshires College cast a slight pall over the future, but once reorganisation had taken place she would have the financial resources to meet his challenge. And there was the unresolved matter of Evans, of course, but for some reason this issue seemed less important than it had; no, it *was* important, but less urgent. It could be kept on the back burner.

'What have we got, then?' she asked as Sylvia entered with the post.

'Nothing of much importance, but there's a letter here from the Chamber of Commerce you'll be pleased to read.'

Marcia resisted the temptation to grab the letter and waited until Sylvia had deposited the pile in front of her. She waded through the dross and eventually came to it – yes! It was from the Hon. Sec. of the Chamber, a Mr Chowdrey, and it formally invited her to take up her membership. That hadn't taken long; good old Fred! She grinned. The day was getting even better.

'Could you reply to Mr Chowdrey saying I am delighted to accept.'

Sylvia took the letter. 'That must be old Mr Chowdrey from the Bilash; I didn't realise he was so high up in the town's business community.'

'The Bilash?'

'Yes, it's an Indian restaurant in town, it's been there for at least 30 years.'

'Right. Do you have the papers for the SMT meeting?'

'No. I haven't had anything.'

'Are you sure? There should be a paper from Lucas – well, from all four of them in fact; concerning reorganisation.'

'No, nothing.'

Marcia jabbed at her phone pad. Her loudspeaker was turned on and Lucas Harper's disembodied voice confirmed his presence.

'Lucas. Where's your paper? The SMT meeting's only 30 minutes away. I was expecting to read it beforehand.'

'Yes, I'm very sorry, Marcia, but Joy's away again and Kate is having to word-process it and she's being a bit slow.'

'For God's sake! What's *wrong* with your secretary? She was off last Friday, wasn't she? What's she got?'

A hesitation. 'Um, women's problems, I think.'

'Really! Just make sure I have sight of that paper before the meeting.'

'I'll do my best, Marcia.'

'Let's hope that's good enough.' She slammed down the receiver.

'Lot of it about,' commented Sylvia.

'What d'you mean? Lot of what?'

'Women's problems.'

Marcia looked sharply at her secretary; was she being insolent again? She received an open smile in return. Perhaps not. Nevertheless, this might be an opportune moment to turn the screw a little.

'Only one item for the diary today, apart from the usual Monday meetings. Three o'clock, meeting with Michael Carter. Edgar Hickman will also be present, and probably Carter's Union representative. It shouldn't last more than 15 minutes.' Yes! A slight widening of the eyes.

'So if I could have Carter's file, please: I'd like to familiarise myself with that gentleman's record, and I'll do that now, before the SMT meeting.'

Sylvia complied with the request. As soon as she was out of the door, Marcia unlocked a desk drawer, extracted a single sheet of paper and inserted it in Carter's file. Then she sat back, impatiently waiting the delivery of Lucas Harper's paper.

Thirty minutes later she was still waiting. Charles, Edgar and Paul had arrived and were sitting round the boardroom table. She was in no mood to participate in their pre-meeting small talk; they were irritating her; Charles and Edgar were exchanging flippant remarks about George Bush, and at one point dissolved into what could only be described as giggles.

At last, three minutes late, Lucas hurried in, breathless and flustered.

302

'Marcia, I'm so sorry, Kate's only just finished our paper; I had to stand over her to make sure she gave it her undivided attention. She's not very quick on the keyboard, is she?' he said to Edgar.

'We never have any problems with her, do we Charles?' said Edgar.

'No. And in my experience the thing that secretaries can't abide is being stood over when they're trying to concentrate.'

'We're not here to discuss the likes and dislikes of secretaries,' snapped Marcia. 'If that's your paper that you're clutching, Lucas, please distribute it. You'll all have to sit here while I digest it. I hope it's concise and to the point.'

'Oh, yes, it is. My apologies again, Marcia.'

The papers were handed round. Marcia began reading intently. Edgar and Charles looked neither at her nor at each other and resorted to staring out the window at the melee of students making their way to classes. Lucas re-read his paper. Only Paul was witness to the pursing of Marcia's lips, the meeting of her eyebrows, the slow flush spreading from her neck up to her cheeks.

She slammed the papers down on the table.

'Is this some sort of joke?' she demanded, staring at Lucas.

Evidently nonplussed, he began stuttering.

Her eyes swivelled between Edgar, Charles and Paul. 'Are you three party to this nonsense?'

Charles cleared his throat. 'If you're asking whether the paper was agreed by the four of us, then yes, it was, but I fail to see why you should describe it as nonsense. The plan delivers just the sort of savings you said you required.'

Marcia's glare was turned again on Lucas. 'You produced the first draft of the proposals, didn't you?'

'Well, yes, Marcia; you asked me to chair the working party, so naturally - '

'And you other three met to discuss Lucas's draft? What sort of input did you make? Did you suggest any changes?'

Charles nodded at Edgar, who replied – 'No, we didn't make any substantive changes; we didn't think we were qualified to do so. We're not finance experts, not like Lucas here.'

'But you must know that the structure you propose is unworkable!' Marcia's voice was almost a screech. 'Any idiot can see it's rubbish: I'd be a laughing stock if I presented this to the Academic Board. Even the Corporation would look askance. What the hell were you thinking about? You two' (she addressed Charles and Edgar) 'call yourselves educationalists, you must know that this is total cr- totally unworkable. What's got into you? Is this deliberate sabotage?

Charles puffed out his chest. 'I resent that remark, Principal. You are impugning our professionalism. Had you asked us to propose a structure for the college with the purpose of enhancing curriculum delivery then of course we would have done so. But you made it quite clear to Lucas that the main objective was to be the maximisation of savings. That is what Lucas has done, brilliantly in my opinion. As Edgar says, we are not qualified to make judgements in the arcane world of finance and budgets. Had we altered Lucas's proposed structure, you would have lost the savings. I would appreciate an apology for your suggestion about sabotage.'

Marcia seethed silently. She had no intention of apologising. The bastards, the disloyal, conniving bastards. It was obviously an attempt to wrong-foot her. How could Lucas be so naïve as to be taken in? What should she do now; ask them to go back and submit fresh proposals? Or do it all herself? Either way the timetable for implementation had been scuppered.

Her gorge rose further. She stood up.

'This meeting is closed. And the Programme Leaders' meeting is cancelled. I may wish to see you all individually at a later date. I assume you all have work to do.'

She moved over to her desk. As a man, her colleagues rose; Charles, Edgar and Paul approached the door. Lucas hesitated; 'Marcia, I hope you –'

'I said the meeting is closed! Don't you understand plain English?'

Lucas scuttled out.

She sank back in her executive chair and closed her eyes. A faint headache was coming on. Damn, damn, damn. She didn't feel like settling to paperwork, let alone thinking about restructuring. Perhaps she was wrong to have cancelled the PL's meeting: in her present mood a bit of brusque chairmanship would have been cathartic.

The phone buzzed.

'Marcia, I have Derek Surman on the line. He says he'd like a quick word with you.'

'Put him through.'

'Principal? It's Derek Surman. Look, I thought I ought to forewarn you. I've balloted my members about the pay claim. Well, not all the papers are in yet, but it looks though they're going to reject the Exec's advice, and - '

'What? I thought the moderates were supposed to be in the majority.'

'Yes, well, I'm afraid your memorandum didn't go down too well amongst the staff; it gave the malcontents a chance to stir things up, and - '

'Never mind that. I don't have time to discuss it now. I'll see you this afternoon after Carter's hearing. I'm assuming you'll be representing him.'

She put down the receiver. Her headache had worsened. The day that had promised so well was turning into a disaster. The phone buzzed again.

'Yes?'

'Marcia, I have Rhodri Evans on the line. He'd like to make an appointment to see you; when shall I say?'

Evans. Surely his case was something that could be dispatched quickly and to her satisfaction? The need for action was overwhelming.

'Tell him to come and see me now, Sylvia. If he's teaching next session, tell him to cancel his class. Phone Adrian Havers and ask him to make the cover arrangements – oh, and while you've got him, tell him his presence is required at the Carter interview this afternoon. He doesn't know about it yet. Then phone Edgar Hickman and tell him I won't be needing him at that interview. Got that?'

She fished in her briefcase for a codeine.

* * *

'You're getting to be a frequent visitor up here,' said Sylvia as Rhodri entered, 'Still in your trendy gear, I see, and new shoes now! Whatever trouble you're in I can't see that 21st Century Casual will win her over; she's after the full Monty, mate. Better get a suit.'

'What sort of mood is she in?'

'Hard to judge. She was sunny enough earlier on, but something rattled her cage in the SMT meeting; I heard her shrieking, then all the boys made a quick exit. Harper looked like he was on the verge of tears.'

She buzzed through to the inner office and announced Rhodri's arrival.

'Go in. She still sounds a bit icy. Careful, Rhod, one false move and I reckon you'll be in for a handbagging.'

'Sit down, Mr Evans.' Marcia indicated the upright chair in front of her desk. She'd debated whether to sit with him at the boardroom table, but had decided that this would have hinted at negotiation. Let him squirm in the minion's seat, the one reserved for carpeting. Still wearing his new outfit, she observed, and were those brand new suede shoes?

'What is it you wish to speak to me about?'

307

'I'm grateful for your seeing me so soon after my request. You must be a busy woman.'

Soft-soaping, is he? Be on your guard, Marcia.

'I'm seeing you because I'm assuming you've decided to admit to scrawling insults over my memorandum. I wish to resolve this matter immediately; I have more important things to do with my time than to waste it on you.'

'No. I'm here to ask you what the chances are for early retirement.'

My God, is the man looking for an easy escape route? This must be a tacit admission of guilt. The impertinence of the fellow.

'Mr Evans, the chances of anyone being granted early retirement in today's financial climate are minimal, and I can assure you that you would be the last person to benefit from such a provision. In any case, you're not old enough.'

Mistake! I've left him an opening for debate.

'Oh, I'm not looking for an enhanced pension, if that's what you're thinking. No, I just think I've made my contribution to –'

'That's enough! I wish to ask you one simple question to which there can only be a yes or no answer. We're you, or were you not, responsible for the insubordinate comments on my memorandum?'

For the first time his gaze left her face. *One point to me!* For a moment he glanced down. *Another point!* There was then a momentary appraisal of her breasts before he looked her in the eye again.

308

'For what it's worth, I agree with some of the assertions you make in your memo. I don't care for how they'd affect me personally: I'm too old to change. But if that's the way things have to be to secure the college's future, then I'll take your word for it. I don't want to embarrass you by my scruffy boozing presence, so that's why I wondered about early retirement, see.'

'If you agree with the points in my memo, why did you deface it? Do you seriously expect me to believe what you've just said?' She fought to control her voice.

'I haven't said that I *did* deface it. You're very attractive when you're angry, did you know that?'

Marcia floundered. In all her years of management she'd never had to deal with a member of staff such as this. He seemed totally unawed by her position and status, spoke as though he were debating with an equal, and had the gall to make sexist comments. What a seedy little man. Leastways, he was seedy before the haircut and the new clothes. That bloody Welsh lilt. What should she do? To dismiss him from her office at this point would be an admission that he'd bettered her. *Keep cool, keep plugging away at the point at issue.*

'Mr Evans, I've asked you a straight question. I'm waiting for a straight answer.'

'Isn't there a danger that by doing so I would put us in a situation where both of us would be the losers? If I were to deny it, there's nothing you could do except possibly make the remainder of my time here a misery. If I were to admit it, you'd be forced to take some sort of action which would serve only to highlight the problems you have with written communication.'

'How dare you –'

'Oh, don't get me wrong, I'm not disparaging you. As I said before, why *should* be expected to be an expert on everything? What would be so wrong in using the services of an English specialist to free you up to deal with more important matters? He could help others in management as well – yes, how about a new appointment, a College Communications Consultant? It could be a nice little part-time post for someone.'

He was smiling at her, but his accompanying body language identified it as not an insolent grin but an open friendly gesture. If he bought some up-to-date glasses he could really be quite presentable. Was he in fact right? Would she be the loser by continuing to pursue the matter of the defacement? Was it really worth it, especially as he seemed to be trying to offer some sort of olive branch? The whole matter was beginning to bore her. A thought struck her.

'Whoever it was scrawled over the memorandum – and don't for one minute think that you're out of my sights – whoever it was, do you think he's shown his handiwork to anyone else in the college?'

'Oh, you can rest assured about that. He, or she, would be very discreet, I would imagine. Let's say of all my colleagues who might have done this, none would have told anyone else. Any more than I'd reveal to anyone the nature of this conversation.' This time his smile was conspiratorial.

She found herself relaxing. If he *had* done it, and she was pretty sure that he had, then only Sylvia was party to the evidence. And he was obviously regretting it; hadn't he already shown this by his attempts to smarten up? But if he'd gone to those lengths to conform, why his request for early retirement? Was there more here than was apparent?

'Why, may I ask, are you seeking early retirement?'

'Simple. Although I like teaching, I can't abide the mountain of admin. And I'm getting older; can't relate to my younger colleagues, they talk a foreign language. What I'd like, see, is to retire from full-time work but to come back on a part-time basis, just to teach for a few hours a week. Then I could get on with the novel I've been trying to write for the past two years.'

'You wouldn't get your pension until you were 60. Far be it from me to guess your personal circumstances, but I think you'd find it hard to survive on hourly paid work.'

'Ah, but there are other things I could do, perhaps as a sort of outreach worker.'

'Outreach worker? I'm not sure I follow you.'

'Oh, something like being a Communications Consultant.'

This time his grin was accompanied by a chuckle. An infectious chuckle. Marcia found herself smiling at his effrontery, then, to her amazement, throwing back her head and guffawing. He continued chuckling.

Recovering, she stood up.

'I think we'll say the matter is closed, Mr Evans. Count yourself a lucky man.'

He rose. 'And the other matter?' he said.'Early retirement?'

'Don't push your luck, boyo,' and as she said it she found herself grinning once again.

***

'Mr Surman and Mr Carter are here,' Sylvia announced over the telephone.

'Ask them to wait for just a few minutes until Adrian Havers arrives. Let me know when he does.'

Right. This time all the aces were in her hand. There was nothing that could possibly go wrong, nothing could be said to divert her from her chosen course. This was a formal hearing, so it had better be conducted across the boardroom table, herself and Havers on one side, Carter and Surman on the other. Even as she arranged the furniture she found herself smiling inwardly at the memory of her encounter with Evans. She ought to be feeling diminished, affronted, angry, but instead there was a strange sense of relief coupled with the glow that lingers after unexpected rapport has been established with an assumed opponent. She hadn't won, of course, but then neither had he. It was an honourable draw. Now for victory over Carter.

'Mr Havers is here.'

'Tell him to come in, please.'

'What's all this about?' said Adrian as he entered. 'Why's Carter here with his union rep? What do you want me for?'

'Sorry for the short notice, Adrian. This won't take up much of your time. This is a disciplinary hearing and all I need you for is to be a witness. I won't call on you to say anything.'

'But surely that's Edgar Hickman's role, isn't it, as HR director? And why wasn't I given advance warning?'

'Mr Hickman has other things to do. You didn't need advance warning: I told you, you're just here as a witness. Carter's in your Programme Area, so I thought it appropriate you should attend.'

She registered Havers' pursed lips. Tough, mate, but there's no way I was going to forewarn you of what is about to transpire. Wouldn't put it past you to tip Carter the wink.

'What's Mike Carter done?'

'You'll find out. Sit here.' She buzzed Sylvia. 'Tell them to come in now.'

She took her seat beside Adrian, facing the door, ready to eyeball Carter as soon as he entered. When he did, she was taken aback.

My God, what's he done to himself? Looks though he's been in a fight. Just the sort of thing that would happen to someone like him. Probably some outraged husband.

'Sit down, please. I assume, Mr Carter, that Mr Surman is here to represent you?'

'No, Principal.' Derek interjected before Carter could answer. 'My role as NATFHE representative

313

is simply to ensure that the correct procedures are complied with.'

She glanced at Carter, expecting at the very least an expression of surprise. There was none. His eyes were cast down, he looked almost hangdog.

'Very well. Mr Carter, this is a disciplinary hearing. I wish first to establish whether your position is still that you refuse to comply with the code of conduct outlined in my memorandum.'

He looked at her briefly, then down at the table. 'My position hasn't changed.'

'You're certain about that?'

'Yes.'

'That constitutes a refusal to comply with a reasonable management instruction, and can be construed as gross misconduct. I am therefore suspending you with immediate effect pending a dismissal hearing with the Chair of the Corporation.'

Carter jerked to an erect posture. 'What? Suspension? You cannot be serious! It's not gross misconduct, and it's a first offence. You can only give a first written warning – that's the procedure, isn't it Derek?'

'I haven't finished, Mr Carter.' Marcia was on a roll; she felt the adrenaline rush of executive power; this was what made the job worthwhile. 'This isn't your first offence, as well you know. You were given a written warning back in 1978 for what I would describe as gross moral turpitude. If that offence were to take place in a few months time you could be facing a gaol sentence for abusing your position of trust with a student under the age of 19.'

The moment had been worth waiting for. Carter was rigid apart from his eyes, which, after a momentary horrified stare into hers began to flicker, unfocussed, around the room. His head then began to move, jerkily, half-turning to look with mute appeal towards Surman, and then – yes – a backward glance towards the door leading to Sylvia's office.

'Well, do you have anything to say?'

Silence.

'You seem surprised, Mr Carter. Perhaps Mr Sparrow didn't reveal what was placed on your file? Here.' She extracted a single sheet from the folder in front of her and pushed it across the table.

Carter didn't even bother to examine it. His hands, she noted with satisfaction, had begun to shake. Derek Surman pulled the sheet towards him, glanced at it, then pushed it back.

'So, Mr Carter. If you have nothing to say in your defence, I am suspending you on full pay with immediate effect. You will be informed in due course about the dismissal hearing in front of the Chair of the Corporation. You are to clear your desk and leave the college immediately. Mr Havers will accompany you back to your workroom and then escort you from the premises. That will be all.'

Carter stumbled to his feet and, followed by Havers, made an erratic course, head bowed, towards the door. Havers had to grab his arm to support him.

Marcia addressed Derek, sitting silently across the table. 'All procedures followed to the letter, I assume, Mr Surman?'

'Yes. I can assure you, Principal, that NATFHE will not be supporting his case.'

'Good. Now, about this ballot.'

If Sylvia had been shocked by Carter's appearance when he entered fifteen minutes earlier, she was horrified by the sight that emerged from Marcia's office. Adrian was practically having to hold him up.

He stared at her wildly. 'You said you'd fixed it!' His voice was thick. 'She's got the file, the one you said you'd got rid of! I thought I could trust you!'

'Mike. Come on, out of here. You know what you've got to do.' Adrian hauled him through the door.

Sylvia found herself continuing to tap at the keyboard for several seconds before the enormity of what Carter had said overrode her automatic pilot. But she *had* destroyed that file extract, shredded it, how *could* Marcia have got hold of it? Mike must be mistaken, Marcia must have been bluffing. But how did she know what the minute contained? Had she seen it before all this blew up? She'd never asked for the file until last week. Had someone ratted on Mike? Who else would have known? Edgar Hickman knew, he'd been Mike's Head of Department at the time, but he was such a – no! not Edgar, it was Rhod! It *must* have been Rhod! He was party to all Mike's misdemeanours, and he'd been in Marcia's office twice in the past few days, and today he'd emerged looking pleased with himself. What was going on? Why would Rhod do such a thing? Was there some sort of trade-off? Was this why he'd smartened himself up?

Her head buzzed with unanswered questions, her heart thumped with anxiety; she stood up, sat down again, covered her eyes with her hands, wound her legs round the chair legs. Thoughts hurtled around in parallel, conjecture on what might have happened jostled with fear of what might happen next; then, overriding everything came the realisation that Mike was blaming her.

She reached for the phone; dialled Mike's workroom number. Barbara Deakin answered.

'Barbara, it's Sylvia; could I speak to Mike Carter please?'

There was the muffled silence that comes from a hand covering a telephone mouthpiece. Eventually – 'Hello, Sylvia; it's Adrian Havers. I'm afraid Mike can't speak to you at present.'

'But I must speak to him, it's urgent; can you ask him to call me back please?'

'Is this a message from the Principal?'

'No, it's personal, well, it's about College business but not from the Principal.' *God, my voice is trembling.*

A pause. 'Sylvia, you're obviously not yet party to what's just happened. Mike has to leave the premises immediately. I can't let you speak to him.'

'Is he there?'

'Well, yes, but - '

'*Please* Adrian, just one word.'

Another pause. 'OK, Sylvia, but no conversation. Just tell him what you have to. Then he must leave. Here he is.'

'Mike? Mike, it wasn't me; I *did* destroy the papers. Someone must have told her; Mike, I think it was Rhod - '

'Sylvia.' Derek Surman had emerged from Marcia's office and was standing beside her. 'The Principal says would you go in please?'

She stared at him with unseeing eyes, put down the phone, then, automaton-like, entered the inner office. Marcia was seated at her desk. She indicated the boardroom table; papers were scattered over it.

'Please put Mr Carter's personal file in order; the papers need to be in date sequence; no, don't take them out, do it in here, please.'

Sylvia knew, suddenly and instinctively that this was the end game. There was no alternative but to act out a charade of innocence. Her fingers fumbled over the papers: there weren't many; yes, this was the one, a photocopy of the original that she had destroyed, so long ago, it seemed; was it only last Thursday? She placed it in its correct sequence, closed the folder, and forced herself to look at Marcia. Her face was expressionless.

'There will be one more item to insert in Mr Carter's file, a brief note on this afternoon's meeting, but I think it would be best if I filed that, don't you, Sylvia? After all, we don't want any more important items to go missing, do we? It's fortunate that you have a boss who takes the trouble to tidy up your office when you've left it in disorder, isn't it?'

Sylvia did not even begin to make an attempt to answer. A condemned woman, she stood mutely awaiting the executioner's axe.

'We will be having a very brief conversation in the near future, Sylvia. In the meantime, I suggest you return to your office and - what's the phrase that's used? Ah yes, consider your position.'

***

Rhodri dried the supper dishes carefully and stacked them in the cupboard over the draining board, then brushed the crumbs from the kitchen table into a dustpan and emptied them into a newly-purchased rubbish container stored under the sink. He made himself a coffee and carried it into the living room. He sipped his coffee and mused on the events of the day.

There was obviously no forgiveness in Barbara's heart. The meeting with the Principal had gone well, though. Strange that the request for early retirement, made in jest and as a diversionary tactic, now seemed not an unattractive prospect. There were possibilities to be exploited there. And then there was the drama of Carter's departure from the College, the unexplained escort provided by Adrian Havers, the telephone call which had resulted in Carter turning to him as he was hustled out of the workroom shouting that he, Evans, was a duplicitous traitorous shit. When Adrian had returned several minutes later to announce to a silent workroom that Mike Carter had been suspended pending a dismissal hearing, the shock had resulted in no observable reaction from any of those present, except for a slight smile, instantly suppressed, from Elizabeth.

He rolled a cigarette. He really must try to cut down, give up, even. Megan would be pleased. There were essays to mark, but he was insufficiently settled. He was sad for the passing of the old order, but there was also a lurking excitement within him at the hint of not unwelcome changes in the air. The words 'green shoots of recovery' came to him, and he snorted out loud at the cliché, wondering which dire politician it had been who'd coined the phrase: Carter would know, of course.

The door bell rang; he started. Who the hell? Carter perhaps, to tell him what had happened and why he was being blamed? Or Barbara, wanting to talk things through? Oh Christ, not Christine; surely she'd been seen off for good?

He opened the door.

'Rhod.' said Fiona. 'Can I come in for a minute?'

'Of course. It's really good to see you, Fi.'

He meant it. She looked as she always did, but with perhaps just the hint of circles under her eyes.

'Golly, you're tidy,' she said as he ushered her into the living room.

'Ah, well, I've had Megan here, see. Coffee?'

'No thanks, I can't stay long. It's just there's something you need to know. About how I came to

320

find out about, well, about you and Mike and Barbara. You see –'

'No need to tell me. I've already sussed it. It was Christine Fitzroy, wasn't it?'

'Yes. Pathetic little bitch.'

'Fi, I'm sorry. I'd completely forgotten that she knew you. I was trying to shake her off, see, make her realise what a depraved character I am. Never thought through what I was doing.'

'Oh, don't apologise. You did me a favour, I reckon. But I'm still upset you all held out on me about Mike for so long. I thought we were all friends, well, not Stu and Lisa, but the rest of us.'

'Group solidarity and peer group pressure, bach. Truth to tell, none of us thought you and Carter would last as long as you did. Didn't think you'd be one to kow-tow to his innate chauvinism. Oh, sit down, won't you.'

She sprawled with her usual easy grace on the settee. It was the first time she'd been in his house, he realised. She had the effect of making the room shabby. He sat in the armchair opposite. She smiled at him, somewhat wearily.

'I'm surprised you're here,' he said after a moment's reflection. 'Now you know what you do about me you must find me as disgusting as you do Carter.'

'No, I don't, Rhod. It's not the orgies that upset me – my God, far worse things happen amongst the County set, believe me. No, it was Mike's lies and deceptions. OK, you're a dirty old bugger, but you've never claimed to be anything else. You're fundamentally honest, aren't you? And you're not manipulative, not like Mike. And you're not vain. You just like women, don't you?' She stretched her long jeaned legs, catlike, and yawned. 'Sorry. Not had much sleep for the past three nights.'

'Fi, could you do me a favour?'

'What?'

'It's not an easy one. Could you make contact with Barbara and explain what happened, that it wasn't deliberate malice on my part? She won't listen to me.'

'Do think she'll listen to me? After I called her a whore last Friday?'

'Oh, it probably didn't even register. Anyway, Barb's very forgiving of her sisters – there's a bit of 70s solidarity lurking there.'

'OK, I'll try. You'd better give me her phone number.'

'What about you, Fi? What are you going to do? Not stay with your mother, surely?'

'I've no alternative, have I? Before all this happened I was thinking seriously again about going to University.'

'What's to stop you? Go for it, Fi; you've got a lot of potential – sorry, didn't mean to sound patronising – I mean you're wasted hanging around the sticks; you're too intelligent.' As he spoke, a vision came of Fiona at university, flowering in her intellectual awakening, confident in her beauty and maturity amongst the gauche teenage freshers, pursued by postgraduates, lusted after by lecturers. She'd have a whale of a time.

'I'd have to take an Access course first, to get immediate entry, wouldn't I? And there's no way I can do that at the college, not with Mike around.'

'Ah. I've news for you. I don't think Carter will be there.'

She sat up, alert. 'Why, what's happened?'

As he gave a résumé of the afternoon's events. After he'd finished she remained silent.

'Go on, Fi. Join the Access course now. You could complete it by next year, be at University by 2002. Anyway, it's not just for your benefit – it would be good to see you around the place. Wouldn't like to lose contact with you.'

She looked at him evenly. 'And I don't want to lose contact with you, Rhodri, You're a kind old sod, aren't you? Did you know there've been times when I was tempted by your offers of a cuddle?'

He laughed. 'Now she tells me! Too late now, bach, things are too complex. Time I sorted my own life out. Things have fallen apart; the days of the *Woodman* are over; that era's ended. No more chasing after young women, they're too much effort. Think I might buy a pipe; I've got a few years to turn myself into Mr Chips. And I've got my novel to finish.'

'Novel? Are you writing a novel? You never said. How long have you been doing that? What's it about?'

'Oh, it's complex; boring, probably. You don't want to hear about it.'

'Oh yes I do. And I think I will have a coffee, if you don't mind.'

PART TWO - TWO DAYS IN MAY 2002

Saturday

Geoff found Julie sitting alone in the bedroom.

'What are you doing up here, love'? Are you all right?'

She sniffed and nodded.

'Hey, you're not crying, are you? I thought only the bride's mother was supposed to do that.' He sat down and put his arm round her.

She turned and pecked him on the cheek.

'I know, I'm being silly. But the house'll seem empty without Jimmy.'

'But Jules, he's hardly ever been here ever since the time he went to University.'

'I know. But his room's always been there, his bed made up ready for when he wanted to spend a few days with us. Now he's got his own home with Emma.'

'Aye, but he's not far away. We're lucky he got a job in town and married a Streetbridge lass; happen we'll see more of them than most parents do when their kids get wed.' He got up and took off his jacket. 'Bloody hell, I'm sweating cobs in this gear.'

'But it really suits you, morning dress: helps disguise your beer paunch for one thing. You'll put it on again when you go back down, won't you?'

'What d'you mean, beer paunch?' He sucked in his stomach. 'It's a warm day; I reckon most of the lads'll be pleased if I keep it off; they're dying to get out of theirs, I bet.'

'You don't think we went over the top, with this wedding, do you?'

'How d'you mean?'

'Well, for a start having the reception here instead of at the bride's house or at a hotel. Are you sure Emma's dad wasn't offended? You don't think he might have felt, well, patronised?'

Geoff laughed. 'Old Tony? No. The old bugger was pleased to be spared the expense. Anyway, we compromised by having a buffet rather than a sit down job, didn't we? We've had all this out before, babe.'

'Yes, but all the guests. Were we right to invite so many people? Some of them hardly know Jimmy and Emma. I mean, it's their day, not ours.'

He stood in front of her and pulled her to her feet. 'You're mythering again, Jules. It was a grand excuse for a party; get old friends together, give some of 'em a chance to make amends. Anyway, I thought it'd be fun to see how the line-dancing crowd get on with the lot from the Chamber of Commerce. Don't worry about the youngsters, they'll do their own thing this evening without us old 'uns being in the way. Much better arrangement than this modern fashion of having a disco in the evening with all age-groups invited. No-one enjoys them.'

He pulled her across to the window with its view over the rear garden. A canvas gazebo had been erected over the patio. 'Look out there, it's a grand day,' he said.

Julie was still in a reflective mood. 'We've not really been to many weddings, have we? Not many of our crowd have had kids to get married, only a few of my school friends, and none of your old college gang except Rhod, and the Chamber people had 'em years ago. I suppose we're very conventional, aren't we? Old fashioned, even.'

'*Now* what are you on about?'

'Look at us. Nice house, comfortably off, kid well-educated, married to a nice girl, traditional church wedding, top hats and tails: it all sums us up, really.'

'Hey, come on, we had our moments, didn't we? You were a student, I was a lecturer, remember? I could be gaoled for that these days.'

She turned to face him. 'No you wouldn't. You didn't do the business till the day after I left college; had you forgotten?'

'It's something I'll never forget.' They embraced.

'Funny,' she said, 'considering how important the college was to us, and how we kept up with a lot of them after you left; funny that it's ended up with so few of them to invite here.'

'Aye, well, only Barbara and Rhod still work there, and Rhod's part-time now. I never thought Barbara's new bloke would come with her, he's never socialised with us. What's his name again?'

'Giles. How many more times? Hey, I'm glad we invited Megan though; she's always a restraining influence on her dad.'

'Not much need for that these days. When did you last see Rhod misbehave? Not that he gets much opportunity in the *Falconer*. And we haven't seen so much of him in there recently. Wonder where he gets to?'

'Goes to visit Megan perhaps? He talks about her quite a lot. Quite the proud father. And talking of misbehaving, are you sure Lisa's on the wagon? I still don't know why you invited those two.'

'She was still sober when I last ran into Stu, three weeks ago that was. And you know why I invited them. I think it's time for a bit of a reconciliation. We're none of us getting - '

'Don't say it! That's what my dad says!'

Laughter filtered up to the window through the gazebo roof, and the first guests to emerge into view in the garden were Jimmy and Emma's friends, manipulating plates and wine glasses with ease, chattering exuberantly, tossing heads of glossy hair, loose-limbed in their movements, glorying in the joy of their young adulthood.

Geoff and Julie peered down at them and smiled indulgently. 'There'll be a bit of malarkey amongst that lot tonight,' said Geoff. 'It always happens after weddings when you're that age. Must be those references to sex in the marriage service – you know, with my body I thee worship, and all that.'

'Course, it's not just Rhod and Barbara here from the college,' said Julie. 'There's the Principal, whatd'yacall'er, Marcia.'

'I don't think of her as being from the college,' said Geoff, 'she's one of me Chamber of

Commerce friends. She's quite a lady – look, there she is.' He indicated her emerging from the gazebo. 'Hey up, old Chowdery's latched onto her already. He's always trying to chat her up. I don't fancy your chances there, mate.'

'D'you still not know if she's got a fella? She's a good looking woman.'

'No. She plays her cards close to her chest – and a bloody nice chest it is too.'

'Old ram.' Julie tappped his cheek lightly. 'And there's someone else here from the college, have you forgotten?'

'Who?'

'A student. Fiona.'

'She's not a student, not any longer. The Access course finished last week, so Rhod told me. She'll be off to university in September.'

'I'm still amazed she went back to Simon, after –' she stopped, seeing in time where the conversational route-map might lead.

The danger had presented itself to Geoff at the same time. He took her hand. 'Come on, we're supposed to be the hosts. Better get down there and mingle. Oh, and for what it's worth, Marcia's tits aren't a patch on yours.'

***

Rhodri, standing at the edge of the lawn waiting for Megan to emerge from the house, surveyed the scene with an aspiring novelist's eye. White-coated waiters and black-skirted waitresses wandered respectfully amongst the assembly, replenishing glasses. Many of the older men were formally dressed, sweating under their stiff collars and waistcoats, their ample wives in flowery dresses and large hats, thickening ankles crammed into tight shoes The younger people's eclectic styles reflected many of the trends that had come, gone, and come again since the birth of youth culture, though the sartorial and tonsorial excesses of the 1970s were mercifully absent. It was the quintessential English wedding party, held on a warm sunny day when spring starts to merge imperceptibly into early summer.

He was acutely aware of the distinguishing features of an early 21st century gathering. The scene sparkled with the tinsel of the electronic and digital age, the mobile phones and cameras seemingly worn as fashion accessories by all save the very oldest. He wondered how many of the text messages would be remembered, how many of the downloaded images would make hard-copies, let alone be lovingly inserted into an album. The professional wedding photographer's survival rested on the tendency for instant visual gratification to be succeeded almost immediately by the need to dispose of the outdated.

It was the young people who defined the era, of course. Rhodri thought of Megan as a child, rampaging like these kids round the legs of their elders. But back then Megan and her friends were incontrovertibly children: today the dress of the young girls spoke of a precocious puberty begun at the age of eight. Those in their late teens and early twenties, peer-group fellows of the bride and groom, seemed at first glance to be the same as affluent, attractive young people had been for decades. They were self-conscious in their self-assurance, desperate to impress by a studied indifference, wise to the ways of their limited experience, confident in their disparagement of the mores of their elders, each playing the role that his or her carefully cultivated image required – joker, flirt, wit, wise-arse, thinker, life-and-soul, coquette, soul-brother. But they too were of their time, these born in the early Thatcher years; more assertive, acquisitive and declamatory than their predecessors. Yet their abrasive edges were softened by affectionate body language; they kissed and embraced each other casually, unselfconsciously, with no hint of sexuality. They seemed entirely comfortable in their own skin. They spoke of iPods and downloads, of chilling after getting well hammered at awesome raves, their statements delivered with a faint south London twang and with the rising inflection derived from childhood exposure to Australian soaps.

Rhodri turned to watch the school friends of the bride's mother. They were giggling and chattering, while their husbands, acquaintances but not friends, stood awkwardly, groping for conversation. Some of the wives, blessed with genetic good fortune, still managed to wear skirts above the knee, though most had surrendered to thickening thighs. All, however, had seized gratefully on the current vogue for cleavage. Why not, thought Rhodri? If a girl's still got it, why not flaunt it? He was all for it.

Across the lawn from them was another group, a few years younger, rather more boisterous. Geoff had sheepishly told Rhodri that they were members of a Line-Dancing club to which he and Julie had once belonged. Rhodri studied them: no doubt their defining memories were those of the era of disco. Twenty-five years later and no longer constrained by child-rearing, they'd probably found that their youth could be partially recaptured through a medium which permitted the maximum of rhythmic expression with the minimum of the gymnastics so problematic for those with stiffening joints. They seemed not entirely comfortable in the social situation in which they found themselves; they huddled in a tight circle, their raucous laughter defensively defiant in the face of the disapproving looks cast in their direction by the members of the Chamber of Commerce. Geoff had been thoughtful enough to provide lager to augment the champagne and wine, and the first of the empty cans had already been dropped. The bling-covered females had Pauline Prescott coiffures, their slap was far from discreetly applied, their dresses were one size too small, their heels an inch too high. The males showed a preference for closely cropped hair and stubbly chins; a few had removed their jackets and rolled up their shirtsleeves, revealing tattoos on their muscular upper arms. Rhodri thought it wouldn't take many more lagers for a disapproving glance to be met with the question 'Who you lookin' at, mate?'

He turned to study the members of the Chamber of Commerce, still gathered round the buffet tables under the gazebo. He knew some of them by sight from his visits to the *Falconer.* They were an eclectic bunch. All that served to distinguish them as a group was the expense of their attire; otherwise, the members were heterogeneous in age, background, dialect and style. The senior ones, exclusively male, grey of hair and florid of complexion, were the dying remnants of the old Streetbridge bourgeoisie; shopkeepers, independent hoteliers and publicans, solicitors' partners, antique dealers, jewellers. Their conversation was being conducted in trumpeted staccato bellowings, largely ignored by their stout, tightly corseted wives. There was a larger tranche of younger ones, women among them, representatives no doubt of the new wave of entrepreneurs unleashed on the country in recent years – restaurateurs and wine-bar owners, beauticians and hairdressers, luxury car-dealers, executives of IT companies, tourist operators, marketing consultants. Rhodri imagined what Carter would have said about this lot, had he been there - all they have in common is the pursuit of wealth; they're resigned to Blair but cannot forgive him for having been elected.

Where the hell had Megan got to? He walked through the gazebo and back into the house. In the spacious living room he entered another age, inhabited by guests who sat in easy chairs, plates

333

on laps, gratefully accepting the longed-for offer of cups of tea. This is the forgotten generation, he thought, ignored by the nostalgia industry, too old ever to have been young. The sounds of their adolescence were air-raid warnings, ITMA, Workers' Playtime. Their young adulthood slipped away in the grey world of prefabs, rationing and utility furniture, and when they later emerged into the sunlit uplands of the affluent society they discovered they were prematurely middle aged, and that the fruits of their sacrifices seemed designed mainly for the delectation of their children. Remembering his mother, Rhodri knew that they weren't bitter; they were delighted that things had turned out so well for their offspring. They were content to sit and watch all their tomorrows and occasionally to reminisce of times past. And these new digital hearing aids were wonderful, weren't they?

Megan must still be titivating herself in one of Geoff's bathrooms. Rhodri walked back out in the garden. What has happened, he wondered, to the members of *my* generation, we whose music was supposed to have changed the world, we who were supposed to have stayed forever young? Now we're approaching sixty: is it *our* turn to accept the cool waters around us have grown; is it *our* old road that's rapidly ageing? He gazed round the garden. We are under-represented at this gathering, he thought, no more than half a dozen of us, and we don't form a cohesive group. Indeed, we're avoiding each other.

'Indeed, Ms Martell, things have not turned out so badly as we might have expected.' Mr Chowdery was in full flow. 'At least they no longer seem to be at the beck and call of the Unions; inflation is under control, is it not? And people have money to spend. My turnover is very satisfactory, very satisfactory indeed.'

Marcia was listening with only half an ear. Mr Chowdery, despite his wealth and influence, still had the over-effusive eagerness to please characteristic of the first wave of immigrants from the Indian sub-continent. But at least he was prepared to listen to her with respect, to treat her as a fully-fledged member of the Chamber of Commerce. She'd been disappointed by the reception she'd received when she'd first joined, and after fourteen months of membership was still angered by the attitudes that seemed to prevail at meetings. She was patronised, not on account of her sex but for the fact that she was a public sector employee, and it was the younger members who were the most dismissive. She'd found herself growing to dislike some of her contemporaries in the Chamber: the occasional unthinking sexist remark from the old boys such as Fred and Mr Chowdery were benign in comparison to the studied rudeness that came from those whom she'd begun to characterise as barrow-boys, and girls. Her hopes that she might find opportunities for social contact had been dashed; the thought of an evening spent alone in the company of one of these louts made her cringe.

'Oooh hello, Marcia, hello Mr Chowdery; nice spread, isn't it?'

She was grateful for the intervention of Gordon Williams, one who also suffered disapprobation at the Chamber, but for different reasons.

'Hello, Gordon. Yes, Geoffrey's done us proud. Are you enjoying yourself?'

'Oh yes, nice to get out and see new faces; quite a mixture here, isn't it? Quite a few of my clients here, of course, like Geoffrey's wife and her mates, and oooh, look, there's Rhodri! He's one of yours, isn't he? He's quite a regular of mine now. I'm sure that sexy mare he's talking to is the one who was with him when he first came to the salon. I'm going over to chat to them – embarrass Rhodri: he's a sweetie really, but he can be *so* grumpy! Byeee!'

Marcia had been studiously avoiding making eye-contact with Rhodri Evans. It had taken a few months for Geoffrey Baines, whom she'd assumed to be a Streetbridge retailer of long standing, to reveal that he'd once taught at the college and was acquainted with several of her staff, and she'd been disturbed to learn that these included Evans and Carter. She had known that the former would be a guest at the wedding, and her discomfort at his presence was alleviated only by her thankfulness for the latter's absence. She watched Gordon's prancing progress towards Evans and his young female companion and observed the interaction between them. Something about the couple's body language pointed to their relationship being affectionate but decidedly

336

asexual. Wondering about this, she was deaf to Mr Chowdrey's observation that people like Gordon brought shame on the Chamber of Commerce and that in any case hairdressing wasn't a proper commercial enterprise. Evans chose that moment to look towards her: they exchanged courteous nods.

Barbara dropped her cigarette end onto the lawn and surreptitiously ground her sole on it. She and Giles were standing on the fringes of the commercial group. Giles, an IT specialist in a Levington insurance company had found something in common with one of its younger members. He'd taken a lot of persuading to come to the wedding. Despite her abandoning the Friday *Woodman* sessions over a year ago he still nursed deep suspicions about her colleagues, and it was only repeated assurances that Carter would definitely be absent and that Evans would be accompanied by his daughter that finally broke his resistance. Privately, Barbara was as relieved as he. There had been a rapprochement with Rhod after Fiona's shuttle diplomacy, but their relationship was polite and guarded; the old casual friendship based on the memory of shared excesses gone forever. Not that she saw much of him now he was part-time. She saw even less of Geoff and Julie, sometimes coming across the former when she called in at the shop, once or twice bumping into the latter in Sainsbury's. She'd been surprised to be invited to the wedding; she hardly knew Jimmy, but Julie's scrawled plea at the back of the

337

invitation to come and renew old friendships had touched her.

Now she was here, she wasn't certain why she'd come. She'd seen Fiona at a distance, but she was locked into a braying circle of businessmen and thus far they'd exchanged only waves. Rhod seemed to be concentrating all his conversational efforts on his daughter: with a jolt she realised that Megan was now well into her thirties. Geoff and Julie were circulating furiously. The sight of Marcia disoriented her: what the fuck was the Principal doing here? She received a tight smile, which did nothing to answer her unspoken question. She watched her boss for a while, curious to see if she had a consort, but she was being monopolised by that little old Asian guy whom she recognised as having served her curry on a regular basis, years and years ago. The only others present whom she knew were Stu and Lisa, and she'd need a few more drinks to be able to cope with them. She'd not spoken to them since the night of the debacle in the *Woodman.*

There was a tap on her shoulder. 'Hi Barb, long time no see.'

It *was* Stu, Lisa by his side.

'Well, hi Stu; hello Lisa.' She managed to inject the appropriate amount of enthusiasm into her voice.

'How're things, Barbara?' asked Lisa.

'Oh, OK; pissed off with work, of course. How about you two?'

'Oh, we're fine, aren't we Stu?'

'Yeah.' To Barbara's surprise, his affirmation was accompanied by the placing of an affectionate arm around his wife's waist. She looked at them anew; they did, indeed, look well. Stu had lost weight, Lisa was clear-eyed, her hair shone, her make-up was discreetly applied.

'What's been going on at the college, then?' said Stu, 'We've lost touch since – well, since we don't see you or Rhod any more.'

Barbara seized gratefully on the neutral conversational opening. 'It's all bloody change, as usual. There's a big re-organisation under way. According to Derek, Martell got in some sort of external consultant to plan it for her. A lot of people are leaving – the nice ones, of course. Only the bastards seem to survive, like that creep Harper. Old Edgar Hickman's retiring, and Charles Jay; rumour has it they're going under some sort of cloud. Arthur's going as well.'

'Arthur Giddings? The Head of Languages? Thought you'd be pleased about that; thought he drove you mad.'

'He did, but his replacement's going to be even worse. It's Elizabeth Selby, and she's an uptight, po-faced bitch. And about 30 years younger than me, the cow. God knows how she got promotion.'

'Wasn't she one of those two girls who were in the *Woodman* that night that ...' Lisa's question tailed away.

'That's the one; the redhead. The other one, Heidi, she's leaving. Got some sort of translating job in Germany. Anyway, what about you, Stu? Still social-working?'

339

'Yes, still at it, but not round here for much longer, I hope.'

'Oh? Why's that?'

Lisa answered. 'Stu's on the look out for jobs in Derby. Not promotion or anything, any job so we can move to be near my old friends.'

A waiter approached and asked them if they wanted another drink.

Barbara opted for a white wine, noticing as she made her request that both Stu and Lisa were drinking from tumblers.

'I'll go and get ours,' said Lisa, and made her way to the drinks table.

There was an awkward silence, broken eventually by Stu. 'In case you're wondering, Lisa's given up the booze. She's joined AA. I keep her company by drinking mineral water as well. She's doing all right. My part of the bargain was to try and move to Derby; least I could do really. Streetbridge has given us nothing but grief.'

Barbara groped for a response. Stu seemed to have lost his old embittered, sarcastic mode of exchange, and she wasn't sure how to respond to the new man. Eventually she opted to say, lamely, that she was very pleased for them both. She wondered whether to follow this by saying that she'd miss them, but decided against the delivery of insincere social niceties. Christ, she'd be air-kissing them next.

'Dad, don't your colleagues talk to you now that you're part-time?' Megan and her father were standing alone at the far end of the garden.

340

'There's only Barbara who's my colleague now,' Rhodri drained his wineglass and looked longingly at the cans of lager being downed, increasingly raucously, by the line-dancers. 'And as for the others, well, now I drink in the *Falconer* the only ones I see are Geoff and Julie, and not much of them.'

'Well, look, they're free now.' Megan indicated the couple standing together at the edge of the patio. 'Let's go and chat to them before they're grabbed by anyone else. I haven't spoken to Julie for years.'

The two women embraced with joyful exclamation. Rhodri and Geoff exchanged grins. Guffaws and squeals suddenly burst from the lager drinkers, invoking looks of disapproval from the bride's friends.

'T'was ever thus,' observed Rhodri. 'The young always find the misbehaviour of their elders disgusting, don't they bach?'

Megan stuck her tongue out at him, momentarily her daddy's little girl again.

'Hi, Rhod,' Lisa had walked over and joined them. 'Hi Megan, I haven't seen you for years.' She turned to her hosts. 'Thanks for inviting us. It's really nice to see you all again.'

Geoff, surrendering to the sentiment of the occasion, leaned forward and kissed her. Lisa looked abashed, then smiled broadly and said, 'Oh, let's have kisses all round,' and embraced first Rhodri, then Megan. She hesitated a moment before offering her cheek to Julie, who pecked at it, then suddenly flung her arms round her. Geoff was right; this was a time for reconciliation.

Lisa beamed at her old friends, then turned to look for Stu. He was standing alone, uncertainty writ large.

'Stu!' she shouted, 'Come over here! They'd all like to talk to you!'

Fiona had managed to exchange only a few waves and words with her old friends outside the church, and now, at the buffet, she was trapped amongst Simon's acquaintances from the Chamber of Commerce whose business interest extended to Levington. Simon hadn't known why he'd been included in the invitation, having met neither the betrothed nor their parents, but Fiona had explained that Geoff and Julie were climbing steadily up the ladder of Streetbridge society and would as a matter of courtesy include the names of spouses in formal invitations. She'd added that in any case it would be his last chance to meet her English Literature tutor who had been so helpful in guiding her through her Access course. He'd muttered that he'd have nothing in common with some scruffy lefty intellectual, but, faithful to his resolution to support her in her academic endeavours, he'd come along.

Fiona had at first been pleased that he'd found people whom she knew, but found she was slipping into the role of dutiful partner that she'd abandoned years before, and it had taken only a few minutes to remember how much she hated it. She was also feeling uncomfortable in her short skirt and high heels after a year of dressing in jeans: Simon's acquaintances made no attempt to disguise their leering glances at her legs, and their wives were frosty as a consequence. Once the conversation turned to the dire effects of Gordon Brown's last budget on company profits, her attention and patience began to waver.

Glancing around, she noticed the gradual coalescence of her former friends into a single group gathered around the Geoff and Julie. When the group was finally joined by Barbara and her partner (who's he, she wondered?) she turned to Simon, and interrupting his analysis of the economic situation, said that they really must go and talk to their hosts.

Simon allowed himself to be dragged away, and spent a few minutes standing in awkward isolation while Fiona was greeted effusively by Geoff, Julie, Rhodri and Barbara, less enthusiastically by Stu and Lisa. She introduced Simon to each in turn, and it was Rhodri who began to engage him in conversation. To her surprise, they seemed to have something to say to each other, and she registered the look of pride on Simon's face when Rhodri praised her academic ability. Relieved that social disaster did not seem to be imminent, she turned to Barbara, who for the moment was not included in the banter that had begun amongst the group.

'Never thought we'd all be together again, Barbara. The *Woodman* days seem like another lifetime.'

'Another country,' said Barbara, 'I restrict my social life to Levington now; far simpler, and Giles is happier.'

'Is that your fella?' asked Fiona, nodding towards the balding man talking to Rhodri and Simon. 'He looks nice; why did you never bring him over Streetbridge in the evenings?'

'Oh, come on, Fi,' Barbara lowered her voice. 'With Rhod and Mike around? Giles met them once; they were pissed of course, full of innuendos. Giles hated them from that moment on.'

There was a pause. Both were aware that Barbara had broken the unspoken convention that Mike and Rhod's names were best not linked in the same sentence. But Fiona seized the opportunity that had been presented.

'What's happened to Mike, Barbara?' she muttered. 'Have you seen him recently?

'You're not still –'

'No, no, of course not. Just interested. I know he got a job at the DHSS just after he was sacked, but I've never seen him around town. Rhod refuses to even mention him.'

'He seems to spend a lot of time away; his house has been locked up since the New Year. His car's not there. No-one knows where he is. The best for all of us, I reckon.'

'Yes,' said Fiona, 'Probably.'

A further brief silence was interrupted by the intervention of Stu. 'Well, Fiona, I hear we have to congratulate you.'

'Why?' There was still a distinct edge between them.

'University, of course. All change for you again. I bet Warwick won't know what's hit it when you get there. Oh, I suppose you'll be commuting every day from Benton, though. You'll miss out on the social life.'

'Warwick?' Fiona's voice became uncharacteristically shrill. 'What makes you think I'm going to Warwick? I'm going to Leeds. It's time I spread my wings: I've lived round here all my life.'

The stricken look on Simon's face as this news was broadcast was observed only by Barbara.

The bride and groom had left and had been followed shortly thereafter by their contemporaries. The line-dancers were staggering away in loutish disgruntlement following Geoff's insistence that his CD player was out of bounds and that in any case he'd disposed of all his C&W discs at Jimmy's insistence. Julie's friends were collapsed in the lounge alongside the grannies and granddads. Those members of the Chamber of Commerce remaining were dispersed into small separate interest groups. Geoff and Julie were in the terminal stages of exhaustion.

Stu, Lisa, Fiona and Barbara were saying their respective farewells and assuring each other that they shouldn't leave it so long until they next met up. Rhodri had already gone through that protracted ritual and was waiting by the door to the lounge for Megan, who was evidently having some difficulty in escaping from the outpourings from a miserable-looking Simon. Marcia, on her way into the lounge, glanced at him.

'Hello, Mr Evans,' she said, hesitating briefly on her way. 'Would I be right in thinking the young lady with you today is your daughter?'

Rhodri confirmed that this was the case.

Marcia nodded, bade him goodbye, and entered the house. Rhodri rescued Megan from Simon, gave a final valedictory wave to his hosts, and hustled his daughter through the house and out through the front door.

'What's the hurry, dad?' she asked as they reached her car.

'I'm aching for a cup of tea and a kip, bach. Not as young as I was, see.'

Sunday

He took his mug up to the spare bedroom and placed it on the desk beside the keyboard. The screensaver was performing its kaleidoscopic dance. He took a swig of coffee, nudged the mouse and the last page of the manuscript swam into view. He'd had no inspiration whilst downstairs boiling the kettle. It wasn't really writer's block, was it? No, just indecision as to how to write the inner monologues that would indicate the thoughts of his hero, or rather his anti-hero. It had been easy enough in the first half of the book which dealt with the hero's childhood, adolescence and time at university: that was pure imagination. But now, in the second half, the contemporary chapters, what had in fact become semi-factual was bloody hard to write as fiction.

He scrolled up to the start of the chapter, read it through again. Bugger. The present tense just didn't work. He'd wanted to give a sense of immediacy, of dramatic tension, something to contrast with the slow unfolding of the story in the previous chapters, but the result verged on the Mills and Boon. He'd had problems with bloody tenses before - introduced flashbacks even into the retrospective chapters and had often found himself grappling with the usage of the past simple and the past perfect, sometimes within a single paragraph. He knew the grammatical rules, for God's sake, but slavish adherence to them seemed to result in a style so stilted that it could have been written by a committee whose remit was to restore the teaching of grammar to the school curriculum.

Better stick with the simple past and make it a straightforward linear narrative. But he was still left with the problem with how present it. He was getting weary of it. It had started as a process of catharsis: now it all seemed so unimportant. Still, there might be some literary merit lurking amongst the purple passages. He might as well try his luck with a publisher, though he knew the chances of success were a thousand to one.

He wished he still smoked. He reached for his chewing gum. But mastication didn't really help. He remembered old Hazel from his University days, also wrestling with her first novel, saying that sometimes she found herself cleaning the oven, scrubbing the toilet, washing down the paintwork, anything to put off the dreaded task of having to commit words to paper.

Come on, you prat. Think. You knew the anti-hero well enough, what was he thinking in those situations?

Oh for Christ's sake, this is a novel, at least, partly. The anti-hero can think whatever the writer wants him to. It needn't be Carter, just someone modelled on the front that Carter presented to the world. After all, he'd used Carter's name just to keep the essence of the man alive in his imagination. But that was when he was manufacturing a past for him, his past before he joined the college, the past that he had never divulged.

But then the present had intervened. It was all down to Megan, of course, and what she'd told him about Carter, that had made him think about introducing contemporary episodes. And Carter's nemesis during those eight January days last year had been the clincher: that was when fact began to supersede fiction; when writing became an act of gleeful revenge. Strange how the very act of writing had made him realise that Carter had sometimes been the victim of his own charisma. He'd even begun to feel a bit guilty about his part in Carter's downfall.

Down in the living room the telephone rang. Salvation. He ran down the stairs, picked up the receiver.

'Hello?'

'Rhodri? It's Marcia. Is your daughter still with you?'

'No, she left this morning.'

'How are things? You left the wedding hurriedly.'

'Yes, well, things to do, see.'

'I hope one of those things was looking at the draft of my report to the Governors. I need to put it to the SMT this week.'

'Yes. Finished. Your grammar and syntax are improving, bach. Reckon you'll soon be able to dispense with my services.'

'Not all of them, Rhodri.'

'Glad to hear it. Shall I bring the report round tonight?'

'I was assuming you would. Just one thing, though. Make it a bit later than last time. The nights are drawing out. Neighbours, you know.'

'You know I'm the soul of discretion. But it's the same in the morning; light by five. Are you expecting me to leave before dawn?'

'Not this time. But I think I'm going to have to teach you to overcome your aversion to hotels. See you about nine, Rhodri. 'Bye.'

He found he was smiling as he replaced the receiver, and was still grinning as he mounted the stairs. *Good old Marcia.* While talking to her, the answer to his literary dilemma came to him in a flash. Yes, he'd re-write the contemporary chapters from her point of view, and those of the others. Marcia had already told him a great deal, and she'd also let slip much of what had happened in the Management Team. Fiona had revealed everything that happened to her, bless her. And Edgar Hickman was wonderfully indiscreet that time Rhodri came across him, rather the worse for wear, in the *Swan*. And Heidi, of course – she'd been all too eager to tell the entire workroom about her involvement. Perhaps Geoff would give his perspective – and Sylvia hers: *she owes me, after all*. Stu probably wouldn't play ball. His part in it would have to be left to the imagination. As would Elizabeth's. And bloody Christine – it would be great to assassinate her character. All the names might have to be changed of course.

No, he had no need to feel guilty about Carter. It had taken a lot of pillow talk to get Marcia to relent and let the old bastard have his pension immediately. Almost as much as it had taken to persuade her to reinstate Sylvia.

It would be a very long book. Best perhaps to ditch the first half? Or save it perhaps for a separate story – yes, maybe a prequel.

He started again from the new beginning -

The alarm clock jangled her awake. She groaned and turned over, her blonde hair tousled on the pillow. A smooth-skinned, firm-fleshed leg ...

CPSIA information can be obtained at www.ICGtesting.com
Printed in the USA
LVOW041750280912

300768LV00001B/8/P